Deadly Trust

Ellen Rogers

A Lanie Montgomery Mystery

LYSTRA BOOKS
& Literary Services

Deadly Trust
© 2014 Ellen Rogers

Published by Lystra Books & Literary Services, 391 Lystra Estates Drive,
Chapel Hill, NC 27517.

ISBN printed book 978-0-9911502-0-5

ISBN ebook 978-0-9911502-1-2

Library of Congress PCN 2014934983

Fiction; mystery

Book design by Kelly Prelipp Lojk

Cover photo by Laura Cullen

LYSTRA BOOKS
&z Literary Services

WWW.LYSTRABOOKS.COM

For Tom
with all my love

In memory of Reinmeister
by Pennant out of Reinglanz
May 22, 1992–September 10, 2001
and in gratitude to his extended family:
Jennifer Eastmon, Joy Beaston, and Dr. Terri Arledge

acknowledgments

This book would not have been possible without the support and assistance of many friends and supporters. My eternal gratitude to Pat Walker for her sharp editorial eye and her even sharper wit. Thanks, also, to Jackie White, Anne DeKeyser, Jo Ann Williams, Mary Jo Tull, Julie Iaquinta, and Jennifer Eatmon for their willingness to slog through the drafts and revisions and give me their valuable feedback.

I would be remiss not to acknowledge the influence of the many four-footed companions for whom I have had the honor of being selected as a keeper: Rommel, who epitomized St. Francis de Sales's observation that "nothing is so strong as gentleness, nothing so gentle as true strength"; Snert, that most joyful, and artful, of Australian shepherds; Dagmara; Rudy; Sauce and Spirit (Spear); Taenzer; and all the others who have graced my life over the years.

A big "thank you" to those friends who have graciously allowed me to use their names for various characters in the book; I hope it makes you smile!

one

He inched forward to peer through the massive French doors, being careful not to lean into the diffuse light from the library that filtered through the thin silk draperies and pooled on the flagstone terrace. He could just see the top of her head above the back of the wing-back chair, haloed by the single lamp that burned in the large high-ceilinged room. "Cleopatra on a Brunschwig & Fils throne," he muttered.

He couldn't count the times he'd stood in front of that chair and suffered the sting of her adder's tongue, endured the litany of his faults that spewed in a venomous stream from her tiny bow mouth, its lipstick red as the carnations in the perennial beds that bordered the long pond. He still dreamed of that mouth, stretched in a malevolent smile, every feature of her face fading like the Cheshire cat's into the thin air of his dreams.

Rage flooded through his body, the adrenaline making him feverish and icy cold in turn. He shivered and pulled his head back into the neck of his heavy coat, a tortoise retreating into its shell. He willed himself to be patient.

Earlier, as he'd crept along the back of the house, careful to stay in the sheltering shadows of the camellias, he'd heard voices. Not the voices that echoed in his head, but real ones, raised in anger. He'd considered aborting his mission, but he'd waited too long for this moment, dreamed of it, planned it. Now he was going to exact his revenge.

He shuffled his feet softly on the flagstones to keep the blood moving and looked up at the sky. The wind had picked up, buffeting the long-leaf pines that swayed and moaned above his head. Soon it would blow away the clouds covering the full moon. He needed to be gone before its bright light stripped away the darkness that gave him shelter. He chanced another look in the window. There'd been no voices since he'd taken up his post on the terrace. She was alone in the soft pool of light. He reached for the knob and silently eased the door open. Slowly he parted the curtains and slipped through, closing the door behind him.

The broodmares picked their heads up sharply as the French doors leading to the rear terrace slammed open and banged against the wall of the house. A figure stumbled out, sprawled on the stone flagging, then rolled down the stairs and, scrambling to his feet, sprinted toward their pasture, breath whistling in panic. The broodmares' curiosity turned to wariness, but they stood their ground, their leggy foals crowded close to their flanks. The runner slammed into the rough board fence and, hugging the post, pulled in ragged, heaving breaths. The smell of fear and coppery blood flooded the horses' nostrils and they shifted uneasily in place, ready to bolt.

He turned around and slid partway down the fence post, bloody hands propped on his shaking knees.

The alpha mare cautiously approached him, her long, elegant neck outstretched. He cried out in terror as he felt warm breath on the back of his neck and leapt to his feet, catching a glimpse of dark, liquid eye before the sound of hoof beats pounded away from him across the pasture. Clouds drifted away from the full moon setting over the top of the barn, briefly bathing the pasture in cool, cleansing light before covering it once more, allowing the crisp silhouettes of the mares and foals to merge with the sudden darkness. The racing hoof beats stopped. The mares whirled around to stare, heads high in alarm, unshod feet stamping the frost-rimed ground. The smoke-gray plumes of their anxious breaths rose in the cool air.

The minutes ticked by as he waited for his heart and breathing to calm and the wind to dry the tears streaking his face. The clouds reluctantly gave way to the insistent wind and moved on, leaving the pasture, once again, bathed in moonlight. He slowly lifted two halters from the gatepost, ducked between the fence boards, and stood quietly until the mares approached and allowed halters to be slipped over their heads. Only the horses noticed as a shadow separated from the barn wall and watched, silently, as the first two horses were led through the gate and down the dirt lane.

Luisa glanced up as the horses approached her in the semi-darkness. They were headed to the barn for their morning feeding, their human escort sandwiched between them, head buried in a thick, hooded coat against the cool air. The metal snaps and rings on the halters jangled like halyards in time to the swaying bodies. The smell of spring earth rose with each lazy step of their unshod feet. The spindly-legged foals, tripping along behind their mothers, usually brought a smile to her face, but today she was oblivious to their antics. She buried her head further into her thin sweater and hurried on to the house.

Today, when she could least afford to be late, everything that could go wrong had. She knew her employer would have no tolerance of the needs of feverish babies, or the vagaries of used-up vehicles. She fingered the crucifix hanging on the cheap metal chain around her neck and said a prayer of thanks for her friend Maria, who'd sworn to make the kitchen sparkle as she shoved Luisa out the door after last night's party with instructions to go home to her sick baby and leave the cleaning up to her.

She unlocked the back door, stepped into the laundry room, and exchanged her sweater for a clean, crisply starched apron. The heels of her worn, flat shoes echoed on the stone floor as she entered the vast, silent kitchen and flipped a bank of switches, flooding the room with bright florescent light. The white cabinets and gleaming stainless steel appliances stood in stark contrast to the gray light of emerging morning she could see through the wall of floor-to-ceiling windows. Copper pots shone softly from the rack above the granite-topped workstation.

Her gaze dropped to the floor and she clapped her hands over her mouth, stifling a soft moan of dismay behind work-roughened fingers. Muddy patches and paw prints, dried to a crusty brown, covered the floor and led through the open door to the dining room where they were lost in the darkness of the wood floors and oriental carpets. She dropped her hands to her sides and clenched the thin stuff of her cheap uniform.

Rommel, the cause of her distress, trotted in from the dining room, thick, black nails clicking on the stone tiles. He whined and shoved his dinner-plate-sized head under her apron. She shoved him away roughly. "Get away from me," she spat, careful to keep her voice down. "Look at this floor!"

He sat down in front of her and cocked his head, the round, mahogany spots over his eyes raised. Then he tilted his broad, short muzzle to the ceiling and howled, the sound rising from some deep, primitive place in his belly and echoing off the walls and ceiling. The silky, black hairs on her arms and back of her neck stood up.

"Shut up!" she hissed at him. Bending over, she grabbed him by the muzzle and squeezed until the howl dwindled and died in his throat. "Do you want to get me fired? If you wake Mrs. Cameron or her guests we'll both be dead!" She glanced nervously at the ceiling overhead and released him.

He licked his lips uncertainly, then gently took her arm into his mouth and tugged. "Stop it!" she said, snatching her arm away and wiping it on her apron. "I don't have time for your games this morning." He stood up and padded to the entry to the dining room, pausing to see if Luisa was following. She wasn't. He padded back, sat in front of her and whined, lifting his paw, brushing it gently down her apron.

"Oh, all right!" she said impatiently. "But I better not find a stinking, dead squirrel like the last time."

She followed him out of the kitchen. His big pads scuffing the tile floors reminded her of her old father shuffling along in bedroom slippers. The dog slipped through a partially opened door from the dining room into the foyer, then vanished into the parlor. Luisa stopped in the central hallway. Morning light leaked in through the fan light over the massive front door revealing muddy paw prints so numerous that no pattern was discernible on the black-veined white marble, as if he'd paced all night, stacking print upon print, like an angry child's finger painting.

Luisa shoved the parlor door wide and followed him in, her hand groping along the right-hand wall for the light switch. She slipped on the polished wood, scrambling to catch herself as she hit the floor. Rising to her knees, she wiped wet, sticky hands on her apron. She felt the dog's warm breath on the side of her face, smelled the rankness of it. Digging her fingers into his broad neck, she used his solid body to leverage herself to her feet and groped again for the light switch. Soft lamplight chased the darkness into the corners of the high ceilings as the dog sniffed at the blood congealing in his mistress's lap and pooling on the floor around her chair. Luisa screamed and screamed, the sound echoing through the room and rising to the upper floors of the house.

After a moment, the dog joined his voice with hers in a mournful requiem for the dead.

anie Montgomery pulled up to the red brick building across the street from the Southern Pines train depot, and let Snert out of the back seat of her rusty 1990 pickup truck. The former general store was coming up on its fifth anniversary as her feed and tack shop. It didn't seem possible that so much time had passed since she'd given up her lucrative estate planning practice in New York to return to her hometown. Broad Street was dark and quiet around her, the Amtrak Silver Star still somewhere between Camden, South Carolina, and the little town of Hamlet, south and west of Southern Pines. She loved seeing it pull into the station each morning at 7:06, brakes squealing, to pick up the few passengers headed to Raleigh and points north.

To her left she could see the lights were on next door at the Cosmos Bakery, where Jennifer Abbott would be getting ready for a busy breakfast business. Jennifer, too, had given up a job, and also a marriage, and moved to Southern Pines from Atlanta. The bakery she'd started with the proceeds of her divorce settlement was an enormous hit. She catered all the big events in town: weddings, graduation parties, birthdays, anything that warranted good food and drink.

Inside the store, Lanie turned on the lights and checked the online orders while Snert sniffed from one end of the store to the other in case anything had changed since they'd closed up at eight o'clock the night before. As she threw her purse into her desk drawer, she heard the rumble of a diesel engine from the back of the store that signaled the arrival of Dave Branch with her Wednesday morning feed delivery. She rolled up the metal door of the loading dock and waved as he backed carefully into the narrow slot. "Good thing I showed up early!" she called to him.

He smiled and cut off the engine. "It's a big order so I figured you'd need a little extra time to get it sorted." He began tossing the sacks of feed and supplements onto the dock while Lanie started loading them on a hand cart. A sharp pain in her back, a reminder of an old riding injury, caused her to stand upright with a gasp.

"Hey! Don't do that!" Dave protested. "You don't need any more steel rods in that back of yours."

"If I'm going to get this stuff priced I've got to get moving. It flies out the door as soon as word spreads it's here," she replied. "I'll be fine once it loosens up."

"Well, let me do it. It won't take me five minutes."

When he'd unloaded her order from the truck, Dave shifted the remaining bags to her storage area, then hopped in his truck, waving as he drove off.

The sweet smell of horse feed filled the back storage room and Lanie took in a deep breath. One of the things she loved most about her shop was the odors: new leather, molasses, the aroma of cinnamon buns from the bakery next door, the smell of the dried herbs she used to concoct her specialty supplements. She got busy sorting the feed and supplements according to the orders she'd received so that she and her assistant, Rhonda Lewis, could find them easily when customers stopped in to pick them up.

Today, her best friend, Betsy Anderson, won the prize for the largest order. Betsy owned an equine practice and boarding kennel out on Young's Road that specialized in rehabbing injured sport horses. While in residence they received only the best in feed, hay, and supplements, not to mention acupuncture, massage, and a host of other modalities. She was also the reason Lanie had Snert, a neurotic Australian Shepherd who had been turned in to the Moore County Animal Shelter by his exasperated owner. Betsy cruised the shelter on a regular basis, depositing rescued dogs with friends and clients wherever she perceived a canine, or human, need.

Second prize went to her ex-boyfriend, Chopper Crisafulli. She slammed the bags of feed down harder than was strictly necessary as she got his order together. Over the last year and a half, Chop's early promises of making their committed relationship permanent had devolved into arguments followed by resentful silences. She straightened up and brushed a loose strand of blond hair from her face, feeling her throat tighten. The final straw had been logging onto their shared computer to find an e-mail Chop had carelessly forgotten to delete. What she'd read explained the furtive, whispered phone calls that abruptly ended the moment she walked into the room. Faced with the evidence of his betrayal, she'd told him to pack his bags and leave. Chopper, who was a large-animal vet, knew every horsewoman in three counties, all of whom were vying to take her place. The fact that Chopper wasn't being shy about taking advantage of the opportunities fueled Lanie's indignation. "Nature hates a vacuum, girl," Betsy had pointed out. Lanie got it, but that didn't mean she had to like it.

She unlocked the front door and moments later her first customer of the day, Doug Erikson, strolled in on the heels of Lanie's assistant, Rhonda, as the chimes on the mantle clock struck six-thirty. They were preceded by Doug's fierce-looking pit bull, Baby, another of Betsy's rescues.

"Hey Lanie!" called Erikson, closing the door behind him.

"Hey yourself," she replied.

A retired investment banker, Doug was hot tempered and impatient and litigious, known for barking at friend and foe alike, though Lanie was convinced the bark was worse than the bite. He had a trophy wife and two trophy kids, none of whom were enamored of the bucolic life offered up in Southern Pines. Doug's two refuges were his horses and the local fox hunting club, which he enthusiastically supported. Baby, whose disposition was as sweet as the icing on Jennifer's cinnamon buns, was neither hot tempered nor impatient, and accompanied Doug wherever he went.

"Your order's almost ready, Doug," said Lanie. "I'll be right back with the damages."

She walked to the store room adjacent to the loading dock. Outside, Jo Ann Williams and Hugh Jennings, both members of Lanie's hunt club, were backed up to the dock, chatting while Rhonda completed their orders. Jo Ann waved goodbye and hopped in her truck as Hugh walked up the wooden steps to join Lanie in the storage room.

"Mornin'," he drawled in his soft North Carolina accent. "Here I thought I'd be the first customer of the day, but Jo Ann beat me again."

"You're not even close," Lanie said with a laugh. "We usually leave Jo Ann's order on the dock so she can pick it up before she heads to Chapel Hill." She pulled Doug's order ticket off the top feed bag, and she and Hugh walked toward the front of the shop.

Hugh shook his head. "I wouldn't want that commute."

"Me either."

"Morning, Doug," Hugh said as he they approached the counter. "How was your weekend?"

"Great," he growled, "except for the running back and forth

to Raleigh so Giselle could shop at a 'real' mall, and to Durham for some damn symphony."

Lanie smiled in sympathy and patted his arm as she went to ring up his order. "It'll get better."

"Right," he said brusquely. "I'm in a hurry this morning, Lanie. Got a meeting with my attorney, and I want to get this stuff unloaded before I leave for Charlotte." He walked into the adjoining room and began flipping through a rack of saddle pads.

Hugh leaned close to Lanie. "I see he's his usual bright and sunny self," he whispered. "Wonder who he's suing now?"

Lanie winked and handed Hugh his receipt. He straightened up. "Better go help Rhonda finish up. I need to be on my way."

Doug walked to the counter and laid a dressage pad down. "Add a container of your hoof dressing," he said to Lanie. "I'm going to step next door for some coffee while you load me up."

He paid his bill, and Lanie headed to the storage room for the dressing. She heard the sleigh bells on the back of the door chime and looked around to see Christian Cameron walk through the door. As Chris approached the counter, Doug stepped in front of him, blocking his way. He and Chris exchanged angry words. Lanie, searching the shelves for the hoof dressing, was too far away to hear what they were arguing about, but the tone was obviously hostile. When Chris moved to go around him, Doug shoved him backward. Chris fell heavily to the worn, heart pine floor, then scrambled to his feet, his handsome face suffused with anger. Baby, sitting nervously at Doug's heels, shot Lanie a concerned look.

"You're an asshole, Erikson," Chris shouted. Lanie heard that loud and clear.

Doug smirked and brushed past him, knocking him aside with his shoulder as he walked casually toward the door. Chris grabbed him by the back of his shirt and spun him around. "Listen, you jerk," he snarled.

Lanie grabbed the container of dressing off the shelf, and strode to the front of the store. "That's enough guys! Break it up before somebody gets hurt."

They ignored her.

"Get your hands off me," Doug snarled. He pushed Chris back, then punched him in the face, knocking him into a rack of bits, sending Chris and the display crashing to the floor. Without a backward glance, he strode purposefully to the door, down the steps, and turned toward the bakery. Blood streamed from Chris's nose, splattered the front of his white shirt, and dripped onto the floor. His right eye was already swelling shut. Baby gave him a sympathetic look as she trotted after Doug, her tail tucked tightly between her legs.

Lanie ran to the bathroom, grabbed a roll of paper towels, and rushed back to the front of the store where Chris still sat on the floor, his back propped against the counter. Blood covered his hands.

"Oh, my gosh! Chris, are you okay?" She knelt beside him, tore several sheets from the roll, and handed them to him. "Let me go next door and get some ice to put on that eye."

"That's okay, Lanie," came his muffled reply. "Everything's fine. Really." He lowered the towels and gave her a lopsided grin. "Everything except my pride, that is."

"What in the world was that all about?" she asked as she stood, grasped his hand, and helped him to his feet.

"He accused me of buying Rocket Man out from under him. In case you hadn't noticed, Doug doesn't like to lose."

"He's been awfully touchy lately, don't you think? Any little thing seems to set him off."

"Oh, you know Doug. He'll be over it in a day or two." He checked his nose in the standing mirror, gingerly exploring it with his fingers. "I'd planned to pick up some shipping boots, but I think I'll send Rick for them later." He flashed a bright smile at Lanie, and looked around at the display rack and bits littering the floor. "Let me help you clean this up."

"Don't worry about it," Lanie said, "Rhonda and I will get it."

She walked him out to his car, and handed him some fresh paper towels.

"Thanks, Ms. Nightingale. I owe you one," he said, opening the Jaguar's door and sliding behind the wheel.

Lanie laughed. "You can buy me a drink next time you see me."

"Done." He roared off down Broad Street with a wave.

She returned to the store to find Bryan Dawson in front of the counter ruffling Snert's ears. A handsome man, tall and broad shouldered, with thick reddish eyebrows and a shaved head, he always had a quick smile and a kind word for everyone. He was an equine dentist who based his practice in Southern Pines, but spent much of his time on the road, traveling the racing circuit, farms, and horse shows. He had a gentle manner with both animals and people.

"Hey old man," he said to Snert, "how's life treating you?" He straightened up. "What's up, Lanie?" He flashed a smile.

"Oh, the usual. Other than Doug Erikson and Chris Cameron getting into a fist-fight in my store first thing this morning." Lanie picked the rack up from the floor, and she and Bryan began gathering up the scattered bits.

Rhonda appeared from the storage room and caught the tail end of their conversation.

"Chris and Doug got in a fight?' she asked. "You mean like punching each other?"

"Well, Doug was doing most of the punching, but essentially, yes." Lanie couldn't stop the giggle that bubbled up. "You should have seen Chris fly backward when Doug shoved him."

"What were they fighting about?" Bryan asked.

"I don't know, I couldn't hear them. Chris said Doug was upset because he bought a horse out from under him."

"Doesn't sound like anything to get that upset over." Bryan shrugged. "Then again, Doug's been a little out of sorts the last few weeks."

"I've thought the same thing. I wonder what's got a burr under his saddle?"

"Hard to say," Bryan replied. He smiled at Lanie and Rhonda, then gave Snert a final pat. "I'm going to head next door to the Cosmos for a cup of Jennifer's excellent coffee. Can I bring you ladies anything?"

They shook their heads, and he left with a wave and a promise to be right back.

Shortly after seven, the bell over the front door rang, and Joy Alexander walked in, followed by Bryan with a steaming cup of coffee and a savory scone.

"I guess you heard the news," Joy said, her face downcast.

"What news?" Lanie asked.

"Marge Cameron and I got into it at the party last night."

"Over what?"

"Marge is replacing me as Reinmeister's rider."

Lanie was momentarily speechless. "You're kidding me! Reinmeister would be occupying a can of Alpo if it weren't for you!"

Tears welled in Joy's eyes and threatened to spill over. "I know. It wasn't very smart of me to get into it with her in public, but I just couldn't *believe* it," she wailed softly. "It still hasn't really sunk in."

Joy was a local girl who, through talent and a lot of hard work, had clawed her way up to the top levels of the eventing world. To meet expenses she taught riding lessons, cleaned stalls, broke young horses, anything to fund her dream of riding for the Olympic eventing team. Two years ago, she'd prevailed on Marge Cameron to let her try her hand with Reinmeister, a young Trakehner that Marge had, in frustration, given up on.

Marge had paid thousands of dollars for him as a three-year-old because of his obvious talent as a dressage prospect. Unfortunately, although he had the ability, he didn't have the desire to be a dressage horse. He rebelled against the discipline, and her nephew, Chris, tried to force the issue. Reinmeister, known familiarly as Bubba, responded by lying down in the barn aisle and refusing to get up. He stoically endured beatings and resisted all efforts to make him stand up, including the use of a front-end loader. In his unhappiness, he became unpredictable and dangerous. Marge couldn't, in good conscience, sell him to an unsuspecting rider, and had decided to recoup at least a small portion of her investment by selling him by the pound at the Siler City livestock auction. That was when Joy begged for a chance to try to rehabilitate him. In exchange for managing the Cameron Farms show barn, she asked for nothing more than a place to live, an offer the ever-parsimonious Marge couldn't refuse.

Horse people say that Trakehners are like Siamese cats; they're one-person animals. And so it proved for Joy and Reinmeister, though not without an epic battle of wills along the way. With patience, she eventually earned his trust and introduced him to eventing, which he took to with enthusiasm. They were now poised to compete at the Olympic selection trials in Lexington, Kentucky, in a few short weeks. If they placed well enough, they could be on their way to a slot on the team.

"I wish there was something we could do to help," said Lanie, "but I'm sure Marge will come to her senses and reconsider."

"I hope so," Joy said. "I've been driving around all night wondering what to do. I decided to give her some time to cool off and try to reason with her later." She took a shaky breath. "I love that horse. I don't know what I'll do if I can't ride him anymore."

"Who's she proposing to take your place?"

"Her talented nephew, of course."

Lanie groaned and turned to Bryan. "Can't you do something about this?"

"Me?" he sputtered.

"Yes! You and Marge are close." She wasn't sure what the polite terminology was for a relationship between a younger man and an older woman, much older in the case of Marge, but "close" seemed politic enough.

"I'm just the guy she calls on whenever she needs an escort to one of her social engagements," he protested. "That doesn't mean I have any influence with her." He smiled ruefully at Joy. "If I did have any influence, I'd certainly speak up for you, but I'm afraid Marge wouldn't listen to me any more than she'd listen to you. You know how she is. Once her mind's made up, that's the end of the discussion."

Down the street, the sound of sirens grew as emergency vehicles barreled up Pennsylvania Avenue and crossed Broad Street. Lanie and Joy, followed by Rhonda and Bryan, stepped outside to see what was going on. An ambulance and two fire trucks, followed by two Southern Pines police cars, roared over the railroad tracks, lights flashing. Moments later they were followed by a convoy of highway patrol cars. Lanie could hear Snert howling inside the store, protesting the assault on his ears.

"Whatever it is, it must be serious," said Rhonda. "That's a lot of rolling machinery!"

"No kidding," said Lanie as the sirens died in the distance.

"See you, ladies!" said Bryan. "I got back in town last night and wanted to stop in and say hello. I'll catch you later."

"I need to go myself," said Joy. "I've got lessons to teach over at Braeside."

"Hang in there," said Lanie, patting her on the shoulder. "Things will work out."

Joy smiled ruefully, and walked slowly to her truck.

Lanie and Rhonda returned to their work, loading trucks and helping customers with bits, boots, gloves, and other equine necessities.

Just before noon, Betsy Anderson blew through the door like a nor'easter. She'd come directly from an early morning foaling, and her straight, brown hair was tied back in an untidy ponytail secured with hay string. Her clothes, wrinkled and mismatched, ended at the dirtiest pair of Wellington boots Lanie had ever seen. A big grin split her broad face, and her piercing blue eyes sparkled as she entered the shop. Snert leapt in excitement as she pulled two grubby dog biscuits out of the pocket of her jacket and handed them over.

"Time for lunch!" Betsy said. "I've spent all morning birthing a baby over at Broad Creek Farm and I'm starving! Where we going?"

Lanie eyed her friend's attire. "Maybe we should stick to someplace with an outdoor seating area."

"Suits me. How about the Tavern?"

"Their outdoor seating area isn't open yet."

"They won't care if we sit at the bar. Come on. I'll drive."

Lanie hesitated. She was all too familiar with the condition of Betsy's dual cab truck, which was generally knee deep in fast food bags, hamburger wrappers, and yellowed copies of client invoices, ultrasound machines, and dirty leg wraps. Except on special occasions, a metal stock trailer was, as now, hitched to the bumper at all times.

"It's a nice day. Why don't we walk instead," Lanie suggested.

On the way to lunch Lanie filled Betsy in on the morning's happenings.

"Sounds like your day's off to a good start," Betsy said.

"I feel bad for Joy. She looked like she'd been poll axed."

"Marge will come around. Chris and Bubba don't have the best of histories."

At the Tavern they found two seats at the bar and ordered lunch, a salad for Lanie and a cheeseburger for Betsy, loaded with bacon and sautéed mushrooms. Lanie added a glass of Sauvignon Blanc. When their order was delivered, Betsy dunked a French fry in the pool of ketchup on her plate and popped it in her mouth. "So what's going on with Chop?"

"I'm trying to be civil, but all we seem to do is argue. He insists he doesn't understand why I threw him out. He thought everything was perfect."

"So quit trying to make him understand," Betsy said, a ketchup-laden fry suspended between plate and mouth. "You're trying to convince him of the righteousness of your position." She swallowed and wiped her fingers on a paper napkin. "Which, I might add, is like trying to teach a pig to sing. It's a waste of your time and an annoyance to the pig."

Lanie slammed her fist down on the bar top. "What really ticks me off is that he's going around acting like a martyr! Everybody in town feels sorry for him because I threw him out. Inviting him over for dinner, making sure he's not lonely. Nobody gives a damn if *I'm* lonely." Her voice had risen along with her indignation, and several people dining in the bar were eyeing them curiously.

Betsy popped another fry into her mouth and chewed

thoughtfully. "Am I missing something here?" When Lanie didn't answer, she picked up her hamburger and continued. "You know, you don't have to defend your decision to me. Or to anyone else for that matter. You weren't happy. You did something about it in an adult manner. Stop second guessing yourself." She put the hamburger on the plate and, leaning over, peered closely into Lanie's face. "You *are* sure this is what you want to do, right?"

Lanie sighed and twirled her wineglass in circles on the polished bar top, not looking at Betsy.

"You still don't want to tell me who he was seeing?"

"I don't want to say." Lanie turned her gaze to the brightly colored array of liquor bottles behind the bar.

Betsy pushed her half-eaten burger away. "Do you know where he's staying?"

Lanie shook her head. "He still owes me half the expenses for the last three months he was there, but he keeps dodging me about it. He's claiming poverty." She snorted and took a gulp of her wine. "I have half a mind to put his stuff on craigslist. At least I'd get something out of him."

"I understand the feeling, but taking the high road will pay off in the end. You're going to have to see him at the hunts, out at restaurants, in your store. Southern Pines is a small place."

"Okay, okay! You're right!"

Betsy grinned. "Nice him to death and shame him into doing the right thing."

She paid the tab while Lanie polished off her wine, and they stepped out into the bright sunlight. As they reached the corner of Pennsylvania Avenue, they met Jennifer Abbott, the owner of the Cosmos Bakery next to Lanie's store. Her arms were loaded with plastic storage tubs filled with sweet-smelling baked goods. "Hi guys!" she said cheerily. "I've got one more delivery and then back to the grind." She turned her face up to the sun. "Wish I could stay out here and enjoy this weather, but you know what they say—no rest for the wicked!"

"You got that right," Lanie replied, as Jennifer continued down the street.

"I still say she's got a secret lover hidden away somewhere in that bakery," Betsy said.

Lanie frowned. "You could be right, but as small as this town is I'm sure we'd have heard about it long before now if she did."

"Tell me the one person, man or woman, you've ever seen her out with. All she does is work!"

"I haven't actually seen her out with anyone, but I did see Doug Erikson strolling down the alley toward New Hampshire a few nights ago."

"Really?" Betsy said with interest as she watched Jennifer disappear down the street. "Doesn't necessarily mean he was at Jennifer's."

"True, but he sure wasn't at the feed store, and there isn't much else down that alley that's open at that hour."

They crossed the railroad tracks and turned right on Broad Street heading back to the feed store. Angela Cameron drove past them, blew the horn and waved. The top was down on her Mercedes, and her mane of blond hair billowed in the breeze as she headed toward Connecticut Avenue and, presumably, home. Lanie's mouth tightened as she watched her go. She and Angela had grown up together, and had been best friends until high school, when Angela had decided Lanie's blond good looks and bright, warm personality were too much competition. They remained friendly, but not friends. Angela married Chris Cameron right after graduation and moved into the big house his aunt, Marjorie Pierce Cameron, built for them on a portion of the Cameron Farms property. Angela spent her time, and Marge's money, in New York, Palm Beach, and Los Angeles, while Chris competed with Marge's prize-winning jumpers. Lanie had left Southern Pines for the University of Virginia, favorite horses in tow, determined to earn a spot on the eventing team.

"Must be nice to look like a movie star and drive around in fancy cars," Betsy said.

"I wouldn't know."

Betsy gave her an appraising look. "Don't be bitter. You had all that, but you opted to chuck it and move back here and open up a feed store." Betsy laughed. "You traded thirty-five-hundred dollars a day in billable hours for less than that a month."

Lanie laughed with her. "You're right. And I'm not sorry I did either."

"Speaking of the Camerons, are you going to the hunt club meeting tonight?"

Lanie shook her head. "I don't feel like having to answer a zillion questions, and I don't want to run into Chop."

"You know, you can't avoid every social situation where you might see him for the rest of your life," Betsy said. "Come on, getting out would do you good."

"Maybe next time."

Betsy let it drop, and they parted at the store.

Later that afternoon, as she sat at her desk checking orders, Lanie heard the faint sound of Rhonda's cell phone coming from the front of the store. Moments later Rhonda rushed into her office, her normally rosy face as white as parchment.

"You're not going to believe this," she said breathlessly.

"What's wrong?" Lanie jumped up and rushed around the desk. She gently pushed Rhonda into a chair and sat down beside her. "Is John okay?" John was Rhonda's boyfriend, who served as a volunteer EMT with the fire department when he wasn't working at the chicken processing plant in Candor.

"That *was* John!" Rhonda gripped the chair seat tightly with both hands, as though it was the pitching deck of a boat and she was in danger of falling overboard. She took a deep breath and started over. "That was John on the phone. He said Marge Cameron was murdered. That's what all the commotion was about this morning."

Stunned, Lanie slowly lowered herself into the chair next to Rhonda. "Are they sure?"

Rhonda nodded. "John says she was beaten so badly you couldn't recognize her." She gripped Lanie's arm, her eyes round and bright with horror, and more than a touch of excitement. "He said the State Bureau of Investigation's involved and Drew's hopping mad about it."

Drew Parker was the Moore County sheriff, a brusque, capable man with years of experience. Though as Lanie reflected on Marge Cameron, she could see why the decision had been made to bring in the big investigative guns. Marge was the granddaughter of a North Carolina governor, and daughter of a United States senator. Her deceased husband, Richard, had been ambassador to some small island country, Lanie couldn't recall where, before being called home when war broke out. She was a legendary beauty in her day, and rich as Croesus.

"Who would want to kill Marge Cameron?" Lanie asked.

"I'd think that line would stretch from here to Candor," said Rhonda, "but to be beaten to death!"

The bell over the door tinkled as a customer came in. Rhonda jumped up and headed out of the office, eager to spread the grisly news. Now that the initial shock was over, Lanie thought, Rhonda was taking a certain enjoyment from being the bearer of bad tidings.

She sat quietly for a moment, trying to assimilate the news. Finally, she reached across the desk and picked up her cell phone. She punched in Betsy's number and waited impatiently for her to pick up.

"Yo! Didn't I just leave you?" Betsy asked with a chuckle.

"Betsy! Marge Cameron is dead. She's been murdered!"

three

Drew Parker finished his conversation with the dispatcher and got out of his patrol car. It was one of a dozen Southern Pines, Moore County sheriff, highway patrol, and unmarked police cars scattered on the semi-circular driveway in front of the main house at Cameron Farms, their light bars flashing and rotating in a kaleidoscope of blue and red. It had been a long, grueling morning. One that, he knew, would stretch into a long, grueling day. He was already exhausted.

His gaze turned to the Greek Revival house, which stood in splendid testament to the grandeur that was Pinehurst and Southern Pines in the late nineteenth century. The peaceful exterior was in stark contrast to the grisly scene he'd found in the parlor early this morning. His tired eyes followed the four massive, round columns soaring upward from the raised porch as he reflected that privilege and wealth didn't provide immunity against a violent death.

To his right, a single-story wing sprawled toward fenced pastures. Late morning sunlight filtered softly through eighty-foot-tall long leaf pines, dappling the emerald zoysia lawn and setting the white clapboard siding aglow in its warmth. On the opposite side, the medical examiner's van idled under the porte cochere. Its driver leaned against the door, smoking a cigarette. The smell of it drifted across the lawn, and, for the first time in over a decade, Drew felt an urge for a cigarette. He sighed, jammed his hat on his head, and, shifting his heavy gun belt to a more comfortable position, walked slowly back up the drive to the house.

He admitted to himself that this case was way more complicated than the usual Saturday night bar fights, stabbings, domestic disputes, and mangled wrecks on Highway 1 that were the meat and potatoes of a county sheriff's life, but it still smarted that the SBI would be "assisting" him. The way he saw it, he didn't need, and certainly hadn't requested, any assistance from the State Bureau of Investigation. He didn't like it, but it looked like he was going to have to accept it. The "suggestion" had come straight from the governor's office in Raleigh. He acknowledged to himself that, so far, the lead SBI investigator, Michael Donovan, was sticking to the agreement, but he'd surely be looking over Drew's shoulder. He shrewdly balanced that with the ability of the SBI to provide the complex and comprehensive forensic expertise this case would require, but he had no illusions that results would have to be fast. And he knew it wouldn't be an easy case. A bludgeoned body, its face completely obliterated, wasn't your everyday murder. It smacked of a very personal motive. All he had to do was figure out who held such a grudge against Marge Cameron.

Inside, the marble-floored foyer was laid with brown wrapping paper to delineate the walking areas. The sweet scent of beeswax candles and the cloying smell of the lilies in the floral arrangements fought for dominance, and gave it the smell and feel of a funeral parlor. Every highly polished mahogany surface was clouded with a greasy five o'clock shadow of gray fingerprint powder, as were the door handles, surfaces, and moldings. At the far end, a staircase, lined with ancestral portraits, spiraled gracefully upward before being lost in the silent upper stories of the house.

As he stepped into the parlor he was relieved to see the attendants from the medical examiner's office in Chapel Hill were finally wheeling a loaded gurney to the door leading to the porte cochere and down the steps, where they lifted it into the back of their van, securing it tightly before closing the door and driving slowly away. He was glad to see it go. The SBI and county crime scene teams were packing up lights and cameras in preparation for departure to another part of the house. One of the technicians looked up briefly, and then returned to his work.

"Where's Donovan?" Drew asked.

"He's around someplace," the tech replied without looking up. "Probably in the dining room."

Drew crossed the hall and tapped lightly on the door with his knuckles before pushing it open. A man stood at the far side of the room, in front of the floor to ceiling windows, cell phone jammed to his ear. The windows were framed in rich draperies that pooled in an excess of silk on the floor. Drew's wife called it "puddling." He called it a monumental waste of money and fabric. Donovan looked up at the sheriff, and waved him in, a scowl on his handsome face. In his mid-forties, he was blessed with a combination of brown eyes and sun-streaked, blond hair. The wrinkles radiating from the corners of his tired eyes evidenced a disregard for sunscreen or sunglasses. Despite the stuffiness of the room, his starched white shirt, French cuffs restrained with gold cuff links, retained its crisp finish, and his black wool pants their creases. Dainty feet, for a man well over six feet tall, were encased in soft Italian leather. He grunted, slammed the phone shut, and set it on the dining room table. He crossed his arms, and leaned against the mahogany server at his back, his steady gaze on Drew.

"How's the media circus going?" he asked.

Drew shrugged. "About what you'd expect. They're six deep in front of the gate and blocking the road with their cables and satellite vans. I've posted additional staff at the intersection to detour traffic. Bunch of damn vultures, if you ask me."

Donovan nodded. "That they are." He straightened up and looked out the window to the pasture where mares and foals grazed quietly, oblivious to the activity around them.

Drew removed his hat and rubbed his bald head tiredly. "Body's finally headed to the medical examiner, and we've completed all the interviews with the house guests. None of them heard anything. The help, Luisa, is still under sedation, so we won't be able to talk to her until we get the go-ahead from the docs."

Donovan nodded and turned away from the window. "The nephew is waiting in the library to talk with you," he said. "Did Mrs. Cameron have any other family?"

Drew shook his head. "Her only son was killed in an automobile accident about forty years ago." Like most long-time residents of Southern Pines, Drew was familiar with the story. "Happened on the Fourth of July. He ran his Porsche off the road into a bridge abutment. Fire was so hot there wasn't anything left of him or the car." He twirled his hat brim in both hands. "They buried him the next day." He shrugged at Donovan's surprised look. "Things were different back then, and the Camerons carried a big stick. Still do."

When Donovan didn't respond, he cleared his throat. "If there's nothing else, I'll get on with it." He shifted his gun belt and went in search of Christian Cameron.

He found him in the library, sitting rigidly in an upholstered winged-back chair by the cold fireplace, which on this damp spring morning smelled sharply of wood smoke. Chris stood up as Drew glanced at the Southern Pines police officer standing watch, dismissing him with a nod. Chris didn't offer to shake Drew's hand.

"I want to see my aunt," demanded Chris.

"I really don't think you want to do that," Drew said tiredly. He placed his hat on the vast mahogany desk that dominated the room before gesturing Chris back to his seat. He sat in the matching chair on the other side of the fireplace, adjusting his gun belt to a more comfortable position. "We'll let you know just as soon as the medical examiner releases the body. I'm sure they'll give the autopsy top priority." He studied Chris appraisingly. "What happened to your face?"

Chris absently fingered his swollen, blackened eye. "Doug Erikson and I had a little disagreement."

"When was that?"

"This morning."

"Over what?"

"Over a horse."

Drew let it drop for the moment. "Do you have any idea who might have wanted your aunt dead?" he asked bluntly.

"No, I don't."

"She have any enemies? Anything unusual going on that she might have shared with you?"

Chris's eyes shifted to the window, then back to Drew before he responded. "She and Joy Alexander had a run-in over that damn horse at the party last night."

Drew already knew this because his wife, Darlene, had worked the party at Cameron Farms. Her part-time job at the Cosmos Bakery gave her access to most of the big functions in town, and she delighted in sharing with her husband the gossip she gleaned as she served plates and filled wine glasses. Personally, Drew didn't think Joy would kill Marge over a ride on a horse, but it wasn't out of the realm of possibility. Not probable, but certainly possible. He listened patiently while Chris relayed the story. When he fell silent, Drew nodded. "Any financial or business problems?" he persisted.

"My aunt was a very wealthy woman. The only financial problem she had was how to spend her money."

Darlene had also told Drew that Marge had announced she was planning to leave Cameron Farms to the U.S. Eventing Team, along with a very sizable endowment, to provide them with a year-round training facility in Southern Pines. With her only son dead, Chris would more than likely benefit from her estate. He made a mental note to contact Marge Cameron's attorney. And her trust officer, Henry Banner. "Anything else you think might be significant?"

Chris paused and looked down at his hands, clasped tightly in his lap. He looked up at Drew, his expression reluctant. "I walked over to the barn late last night," he said slowly, "to check on a sick horse." He took a deep breath before continuing. "I saw Joy coming back from the house. She went right past me without seeing me, and upstairs to her apartment."

"What time was this?"

"I didn't note the time, but if I had to guess I'd say it was around two in the morning."

"Can Angela back you up on that?"

Chris looked at him steadily. "We sleep in separate bedrooms," he finally replied. "I doubt she heard me go out, but feel free to ask her."

"I'll do that."

Drew rose heavily from the chair and walked over to the desk to retrieve his hat. A faded photograph in a silver frame held pride of place on the right hand side. He picked it up and peered closely at the blond young man dressed in riding boots and breeches. He stood with an arm around Marge's shoulders, a broad smile on his handsome face, a blue ribbon in his free hand. Her son Richard, taken not long before he died, from the look of it. He set the photo gently back on the desk. A few papers were stacked neatly next to a pile of leather-bound ledgers. A Mont Blanc pen with a malachite barrel sat atop a picture of a jumper sailing effortlessly over an enormous oxer, a young Chris looking intently toward the next jump. Drew picked up the photo and turned it over. *In Flight, Palm Beach Grand Prix* was stamped on the back along with the photographer's name and business address. Drew turned the photo so Chris could see it. "Handsome animal," he remarked.

"That's In Flight," Chris said. "He was a very talented Grand Prix horse." He walked over and took the photo from Drew's hand, studying it. "He died from colic not long after this picture was taken." He handed the photo back.

"A shame," Drew said, shaking his head. He set the photo down and looked at Chris. "Anything else you can think of that would help us find who killed your aunt?"

Chris shook his head.

"If something comes to mind, let me know."

Chris nodded and left the room.

four

Snert leapt into the back seat of the extended cab truck and Lanie, armed with two large travel mugs of coffee, wended her way through the back roads to Connecticut Avenue on the short trip to the store. She passed Cameron Farms, peaceful and still in the early morning quiet, though a contingent of determined news crews were still parked outside the front gates.

The farm was comprised of five-hundred acres secluded behind ornate, wrought iron gates, home to Chris and Angela, and to Marjorie, Chris's curmudgeon of an aunt. The pastures bordering Connecticut Avenue were dotted with foals and sleek brood mares. Dogwood and crepe myrtle, buds still tightly furled, lined the board fencing, their trunks obscured by a riotous growth of azaleas and rhododendrons. Unknowingly, Lanie had the same thought Drew Parker had had the morning before—the serenity of the setting belied the brutal happenings of the last twenty-four hours. She shivered, then resolutely put it out of her mind for the moment. When she reached May Street she turned left, deciding on the spur of the moment to take the long way to the store.

She rolled through the streets of her hometown, asleep and silent in the early morning darkness. As she crossed intersecting streets, all named for northern states, she could see Broad Street to her right, and, occasionally, the gleam of the railroad tracks that divided it in half.

She rolled down the window, and let the scent of the pines, whose healing properties spawned the sanitariums that sprang up in the early 1900s, and gave the town its name, wash over her. Snert stood up in the back seat, and squeezed his nose past her shoulder, sniffing the rushing air. She smiled and scratched the bridge of his quivering nose.

"They're all gone now, Snertie, those sanitariums. Along with most of the old resorts and hotels." He gave her a swift lick on her cheek to acknowledge her words.

She turned right on Illinois and right again onto Broad Street, heading back in the direction of the store. As she passed the coffee houses, upscale dress shops, and restaurants, she thought about how much the town had grown and thrived, boasting a vitality that Pinehurst, just next door, had yet to develop. It was odd, she thought, how two towns that lay cheek by jowl could be so different.

Southern Pines was populated by locals and regular folk, lured by its laid-back style, and a contingent of wealthy residents who maintained full-time or seasonal horse farms, linked by the fraternity of expensive horseflesh. Hunters, jumpers, harness racers, three-day event horses, dressage and combined driving horses, even the once plebeian cutting and reining horses, all populated a community where inclusion was largely determined by the size of your investment portfolio and the quality of your equine stock.

Pinehurst seemed devoted to luring affluent retirees who could no longer stand the cold of their native climes, but weren't desperate enough to move to Florida. It was also a Mecca for golfers. The crown jewel of its courses, Pinehurst Number Two, was the site of two U. S. Opens in recent years, and two more coming up in a few short months.

As she rolled along, she sipped her coffee and reflected. She had no regrets about leaving the crowded, dirty streets and constant noise of New York, though, if pressed, she might admit that she missed seeing a Broadway show staged by someone less amateurish than the local theater company provided. But, in general, she was content. Her divorce had left her with two retired event horses, a two-horse gooseneck trailer that had seen a lot of horse shows up and down the East Coast, and a pickup truck that of late wheezed alarmingly whenever it met a grade steeper than the average eighty-year-old could walk. Her house was cozy, if small, as was her four-stall barn. She had all she needed.

Feeling her spirits lift with the rising sun, she sang along to Stevie Ray Vaughn on the radio, pounding the steering wheel in time to the driving beat. Snert pricked his ears and looked at her intently. She hadn't sung in a long time. Lanie glanced at him in the rearview mirror and laughed out loud at his expression. She pulled up to the store with a grin on her face.

Dave was sitting on the sidewalk in front of the store atop several bags of oats, his truck idling at the curb. Snert bounded from the truck, racing to greet him as he stood up.

"He loves seeing you," said Lanie, grabbing the exuberant dog by the collar. "Do you need me to go open the overhead door?"

"Nope. Just got a small order of feed and a couple of packages that were propped against your front door. I didn't see any need to risk the paint on my truck by going around back to the loading dock."

"Consider it a test of your driving skills to squeeze in there." She peered at the packages from England. "Doug's stuff finally arrived from Beval Saddlery. That man spares no expense when it comes to his riding apparel. He'll be thrilled to know it's finally here."

"Probably a defense against all that money Giselle spends on designer shoes."

"He doesn't stand a chance of winning that contest," she said as she unlocked the door. "Come on Dave, show us your muscles and tote those bags on in here."

He grinned and hefted one bag to his shoulder, carrying the other in his spare hand.

"Isn't that something about Marge Cameron?" he asked as he waited for Lanie to open the door to the store room.

"It's the biggest news in town. You can't walk down the sidewalk without a reporter sticking a microphone in your face. Betsy and I tried to go to dinner in Southern Pines last night, but we gave up." She shook her head. "What a horrible way to go, too. You'd think once you'd made it to that age you'd be safe from a fate like that."

"No kidding."

After Dave left, Lanie called Doug and left a message that his order was in, then spent the rest of the morning catching up on bills. When she emerged from her office, Bryan was sitting on the loveseat, reading the paper. Snert was curled up beside him, head on his lap.

"Hey, Lanie, what's cooking?"

She sniffed the air. "Smells like lemon poppy seed muffins with sugar icing at the Cosmos Bakery this morning."

A few moments later Chopper and Rhonda walked in together. Lanie turned her back, and pretended to study an invoice from the feed mill, ignoring Chopper.

"I'll get your order," Rhonda said to Chop as she headed to the back of the store. Chop stuck out his hand to Bryan. "Hey, buddy! When did you blow back into town?" he asked.

"Night before last."

"Just in time for the gruesome news about Marge."

Bryan shook his head. "A terrible thing."

"Hey! I have a client who's in need of your services." Chopper was a veterinarian, but artificial insemination was his special-ty, not filing teeth, so he was happy to pass that work along to Bryan.

"Send 'em on. I'll be around for a couple of weeks."

"Great! Maybe we can get together for a round of golf. I just got a new set of clubs and a new driver."

Lanie's lips tightened as she turned to face him. Against her better judgment she spoke up. "If you've got money for golf clubs then it shouldn't be any problem for you to pay me the rent and expenses you owe me."

Chopper's swarthy face turned red with anger and embar-rassment. He turned and stalked toward the door.

"Damn it, Chop, I'm tired of you jerking me around!" she shouted after him. "You better pay me or I'm putting your crap out for the garbage men!" The door slammed shut behind him.

Bryan, gentleman that he was, buried his face in *The Pilot* and pretended he hadn't heard Lanie shrieking like a fishwife. Rhonda busied herself with straightening the items in the dis-play case.

Betsy walked in and shut the door. "What the hell's the mat-ter with Chop? He just about knocked me down! And he didn't even speak!"

"Oh, nothing," said Lanie with disgust. "It seems Chopper has plenty of money for new golf clubs, but can't manage to scrounge up money to pay me what he owes me."

"Ah…"

"So I told him to pay up or I was throwing his stuff out. And good riddance, I might add!"

"I see." Betsy leaned her arms on the display case and waited until Lanie met her gaze. 'You know, I had hoped that you and Chopper could see your way clear to treating each other with re-spect during a process that's painful for both of you, even though it was for the best." Lanie dropped her gaze. "This isn't about money, Lanie. Chopper makes plenty of money. It's about his vanity. He's hurt at being tossed out," Betsy continued, "and I agree he's doing his passive-aggressive best to make your life a misery for it, but you're not going to score any points by pouring salt on his wounds. You've got to find a way to get past this, and stop letting him get under your skin."

Lanie looked up, and Bryan gave her a sympathetic smile from behind his newspaper. Before she could respond to Betsy, the door opened and Rick, the groom at Cameron Farms, stepped in, looking around cautiously. He walked to the counter and quietly asked for Chris's shipping boots. Lanie thought he might be thirty or fifty. He was painfully shy, and when he'd been in the store before, he didn't even look her in the eye.

He was tall and awkward looking, his shoulders stooped and rounded. The knees of his jeans were torn and his flannel shirt lacked several buttons. An old woolen ski cap, minus its pom-pom, was jammed down on his head, his graying blond hair protruding out from under it.

Lanie had seen him working around the horses at Cameron Farms, and she knew that was where his natural gifts shone. His quiet voice and manner were a restful counterpoint to Chris's brusque, heavy-handed ways. She had seen how the horses responded to Rick, and that was good enough for her.

"Good to see you Rick," Lanie said. "Chris said you'd be stopping by." She slipped into the back room and returned with the shipping boots, laying them on the counter. "How are things at the farm?"

He ducked his head and picked up the boots, hugging them tightly to his chest. "Busy," he muttered, before turning and scurrying out the door.

"That's an understatement," Betsy said as she watched him walk away.

"He's creepy," Rhonda said with a shiver. "He never has anything to say. He just stands there staring at you."

"He may not be the most social person you'll ever meet," Betsy agreed, "but he sure knows how to take care of horses. In fact, I've tried to steal him away from Marge a couple of times, but he's not interested."

"I don't think he's unfriendly," said Lanie, "he's just got no social skills. At least he doesn't go around giving people unsolicited advice." She gathered up a sheaf of papers, and walked toward her office. "Thanks for the support," she said over her shoulder to Betsy. She walked in her office and slammed the door.

Betsy sighed. "Looks like it's going to be a long summer," she said to Rhonda and Bryan. She walked to the front door, and paused. "Tell her I'll pick her up at six."

Betsy pulled up to the valet parking stand outside Chris and Angela's house on Thursday evening, sans the stock trailer. She put the gear shift in park and looked at Lanie, slouched in the passenger seat. Lanie had spent the balance of the day filling online orders while Rhonda took care of the steady stream of customers that came to buy, or to sit on the loveseat and speculate about the murder of Marge Cameron. She didn't like calling hours, or funerals, and wasn't looking forward to more of the same conversation that had swirled around the store all day.

"I didn't mean to make you mad," Betsy finally said.

Lanie sighed. "You didn't make me mad. You were right, and I'm sorry I snapped at you."

"It's not too late to change your mind," Betsy said. "I'll be glad to take you back home."

"You know I can't do that." Lanie pulled on the door handle. "I can't not show my face tonight." She stepped out onto the driveway, looking around for Chopper's truck. Not seeing it didn't mean he wasn't there, though she was hoping he'd come and gone, or would stop by after she'd left. As they approached the house with food trays in their arms, Bryan stepped onto the side porch and waved them down.

"It's about time you showed up," he said, fists on his hips. "There's an obscene amount of fried chicken in there!" he exclaimed, pointing to the kitchen behind him. Lanie and Betsy exchanged an amused look at Bryan's frazzled manner. "Jennifer put the maid to work helping her and Darlene serve and told me to organize the kitchen," he said in response to their unasked question.

Glad of something to occupy her time, Lanie followed him to the kitchen. The table and countertops were laden with food: pecan and chess pies; casseroles of all kinds, squash, tuna, broccoli; cookies and cakes; and, of course, an obscene amount of fried chicken.

Despite Betsy's urging to accompany her to the living room Lanie put on an apron and set to work helping Bryan consolidate the chicken onto one enormous platter. When they'd finished, it was stacked almost a foot high and she and Bryan shared a laugh at the sight of it. "You weren't kidding!" said Lanie. "That's incredible!"

They continued working in companionable silence, washing and drying the seemingly endless stream of plates, utensils, and empty casserole dishes Darlene, Sheriff Parker's wife, deposited, lining them neatly on the counter so their owner's could claim them at a later time. Having brought order to the kitchen, Lanie knew she couldn't avoid the inevitable any longer.

In the living room, Angela was ensconced in a high-backed chair next to the window with Chris and Chopper standing watch on either side of her. Chris looked over when Lanie entered and smiled.

"Thanks for coming, Lanie," Chris said, stepping forward to take her hand and give her a kiss on the cheek. His eyes were black and blue, and the swelling had spread to the rest of his face. Chopper ignored her as he engaged Angela in conversation. Lanie felt like retreating back to the kitchen, but she refused to give Chop the satisfaction.

"I'm sorry for your loss, Chris. I don't know what else to say," said Lanie, giving him a hug.

"Aunt Marge would have been glad to know you came, Lanie. She liked you a lot."

Lanie stepped back, blinking in surprise. In her experience, Marge Cameron didn't like anybody much, but she knew grief made people say strange things sometimes. She walked over and spoke to Angela, ignoring Chopper back, and made her way to the bar. She ordered a vodka on the rocks from Darlene and joined Jennifer, who stood with Doug and Giselle Erikson.

"Isn't this the most awful thing?" Giselle said, taking a gulp of her wine, her eyes over bright with an excess of alcohol. She clung to Doug's arm, weaving slightly on her four-inch Christian Laboutins. Lanie thought she might be enjoying the evening a bit too much. She saw Jennifer wince, obviously entertaining the same thought. Doug looked as though he'd rather be anywhere but sharing space with his wife.

"Yes, it is. It's a horrible situation for Chris and Angela."

"Oh, I think they'll be right as rain as soon as the funeral's over and the will gets read," Giselle chirped. "Don't you?" She took another swig of her wine, smiling maliciously at Jennifer and Doug.

"That's enough, Giselle!" Doug said, and steered her away to the buffet table.

"That woman is just awful, isn't she?" said Jennifer as she and Lanie made their way over to an empty window seat and sat. "I don't know how Doug stands her!"

"Love does make for some strange bed fellows," Lanie said as she flagged down a passing waiter and ordered another vodka. "Just a lot of pretty words if you ask me. You think you have a perfect relationship until you wake up one morning and find you don't. You're just like everybody else, going through the motions."

"Whoa!" Jennifer laughed. "How many of those have you had?" she asked, pointing at Lanie's glass with her own. She looked at Doug and Giselle arguing quietly in the corner. "I don't think there's much love in that relationship. The only two things Giselle loves are Doug's money and herself."

Lanie looked at Chopper, still standing by Angela's chair talking with Chris. "Men aren't very smart about women are they?"

Jennifer choked on her wine, her eyes sparkling with amusement. "Speaking of which, how *are* things with Chopper?"

"I don't know. I thought I was doing the right thing." She sighed. "But if that's the case why am I so angry?"

"You go through the same stages at the death of a relationship that you do with the death of a loved one, Lanie. Shock, anger, grief. It's a process, and you'll come out the other side of it eventually. Relationships change, like everything else in life. Despite all that "til death do us part' crap, nothing lasts forever."

She sipped her wine. "You should have given up on Chopper a long time ago."

"You sound like Betsy."

Jennifer patted her on the knee. "Take my word for it. If you give yourself enough time and distance, you'll realize you made the right decision."

Bryan walked in from the kitchen and smiled at them from across the room.

"Things could be a lot worse. You could be Bryan, struggling with a child that won't have anything to do with you. Now that's a tragedy," Jennifer said emphatically.

Lanie looked at her in surprise. "I didn't know Bryan had any children."

Jennifer nodded. "A daughter."

"How tragic! Why won't she have anything to do with him?"

"Oh, the usual. Mommy and daddy split up. Daddy's the bad guy, blah, blah, blah."

"How do you know all this?"

"I guess it's that truth serum I bake into my applesauce muffins," she said, eyes sparkling.

Later that evening, Doug Erikson walked through Chris and Angela's deserted kitchen to the back door. Looking around, he made sure no one was watching before he slipped out onto the porch and quietly pulled the door closed behind him. After a moment, Jennifer emerged from the shadows and placed her hand on his arm.

"What do you think?" Jennifer whispered.

"I think we shouldn't be seen together," he replied, looking around nervously. "I don't think anyone suspects anything, but we need to keep it that way."

"You're right, of course. I'm sorry. Do you think anyone suspects?"

He glanced over his shoulder toward the kitchen, ignoring her question. "This is dangerous, I need to get back before someone comes looking for me."

He slipped back into the kitchen, leaving Jennifer alone in the dark.

Betsy dropped Lanie off at her farm off of Old Mail Road. Lanie always felt good coming back to her piece of land, carved off of an old estate that was split up when the family matriarch passed away. She brought the horses in and fed and blanketed them before skipping their stalls. As she walked from the barn to the house, Snert following closely behind, the moon was rising over the trees, bathing everything in its path with light. She closed the door and locked it behind her. She washed up the few dishes from her evening meal, filled Snert's water bowl, and walked to her bedroom at the back of the house. Stripping off her clothes, she fell into bed, exhausted.

Snert kept watch over her through the night from his place at the side of her bed, ears pricked in vain for the sound of Chopper's truck.

five

On the Monday morning of Marjorie Pierce Cameron's funeral, The Good Shepherd Episcopal Church was packed with both mourners and the simply curious. Sheriff's deputies held the television crews and newspaper reporters at bay on the other side of the street as friends and family made their way into the sanctuary.

Betsy and Lanie took a seat in one of the back pews. Chopper sat at the front, a respectful two rows behind the pew reserved for family, and across the aisle from Doug and Giselle, who were seated behind Jennifer and Bryan. Betsy leaned over and whispered, "Where do you suppose Joy is?"

Lanie shook her head.

The governor, surrounded by SBI agents, headsets discreetly hidden under their suit collars and weapons out of sight, and half a dozen state legislators took their seats on the right hand side of the church. Sheriff Parker and Agent Donovan stood just inside the door to the sanctuary, silently observing the crowd.

"Maybe Jennifer and Bryan have something going," whispered Lanie. "It would explain why he spends so much time at the bakery."

Betsy hid a smile behind her program. "I *told* you she had a secret lover," she whispered back.

"She told me last night that Bryan had a troubled relationship with his daughter. Did you know he *had* a daughter?"

Betsy shook her head. "I don't know much about him at all, except that he's a great dentist."

The church quieted as Chris and Angela walked down the aisle and seated themselves on the front pew. Angela was dressed in black Vera Wang, her face obscured behind a large hat and veil. She sobbed quietly into a handkerchief. Chris stared vacantly toward the elaborately embroidered altar cloth, ignoring the flower-laden, mahogany casket in front of the altar steps.

Reverend Tomick delivered a mercifully brief eulogy and they were soon filing out, in reverse order of the way they'd come in. As a major contributor to the hunt club, Marge would be buried in the Aiken Foundation cemetery—an honor reserved for a select few. A horse-drawn hearse, its black velvet curtains drawn, waited in front of the church. Two black-as-coal Friesians waited impassively, the black ostrich plumes affixed to their bridles bobbing in the slight breeze, as the coffin was lifted into the back of the hearse. The driver shook the reins gently, and they made their slow way down Ridge Street and turned left for the long trip to the cemetery.

six

After returning from the cemetery, Lanie flipped the sign on the door to Closed. After sending Rhonda home for the day and changing into her jeans in the small bathroom adjacent to the store room, she sat in her office, Snert curled up at her feet. She tried to focus on getting her billing in order, but her thoughts kept returning to the brutal murder of Marge Cameron. When Snert flew out of the office, barking furiously, it was a relief to have an excuse to get up from her desk and abandon her efforts.

She unlocked the front door to find Joy Alexander standing on the steps, her hair unwashed, her face streaked with tears. Lanie pulled her in, shut and locked the door behind them, and led her to the loveseat. "What's wrong?" she asked, picking up her hand.

"Chris and I had a huge fight Saturday night. He threw me out. Told me to get my stuff and leave." She wiped her running eyes and nose on the sleeve of her sweatshirt, and took a shaky breath. "I've been sleeping on the floor of the old ice house."

"I thought Marge tore that down years ago!"

Joy shook her head. "It's still there. It's just so overgrown with kudzu you can hardly see it anymore. I had to struggle to get the door open enough to squeeze through."

"Why didn't you call me? You could have stayed at my place until things get straightened out."

"I wasn't thinking. I just threw some stuff in my pillowcases and left." Her voice trailed off. "I drove around for a while trying to figure out what to do, and then I remembered the ice house. So I parked my truck at the old McAllister place, behind the barn, and walked through the woods to Cameron Farms." She looked at Lanie, her red-rimmed eyes worried. "When I got to the edge of the woods I could see the police swarming all over the barn, and there were lights on in my apartment." She began to sob.

Lanie walked to the counter and got a box of tissues, then returned to the loveseat, handing them to Joy. "How can I help?"

"Would you go to the farm and get my stuff and my day planner from the ice house? And check on Bubba? I'm afraid to leave him there alone!"

"Are you saying you think Chris will hurt him?"

Joy nodded.

"I can't imagine Chris would deliberately injure a valuable horse like Bubba, but if it will make you feel better, I'll certainly check on him. And get your things."

She walked back to her office, retrieved her purse from the desk drawer, and walked back to the front of the store. "You stay here with Snert. I'll be back as soon as I can."

They were interrupted by a banging on the front door. Finding Betsy standing outside, Lanie grabbed her by the arm and pulled her in. "Perfect," she said, "you're just in time to go out to Cameron Farms with me."

"Why? And why are you closed in the middle of the day?" She stopped when she saw Joy. "Hey," she said. She took in Joy's tear-streaked face and looked at Lanie expectantly. "What's up?"

"I just didn't feel like working after the funeral. I gave Rhonda the rest of the day off and hung a sign on the door saying we were closed until tomorrow morning." She looked at Joy. "Chris threw her out."

"Can he do that?" Betsy asked.

"That's a good question," Lanie responded, "but without knowing what the provisions of Marge's will say I can't answer it." She looked at Joy, slouched on the couch. "In any case, she needs some clothing and her day planner."

"Sure. You drive."

Lanie and Betsy left Joy in Snert's care and headed down Broad Street, turning left on New Hampshire and then left again onto May Street. They decided to use the back entrance off Young's Road to avoid the ever-present reporters at the front gate on Connecticut. On the way, Lanie filled her in on her conversation with Joy.

When they passed Fox Ridge Farm, Lanie turned right onto a dirt road and crept along until she spotted the lane, little more than a track through the heavy scrub, that denoted the little used back entrance to Cameron Farms. Turning, they bumped along the rutted track until they reached a dilapidated wooden gate. Putting the truck in park she waited while Betsy got out and shoved it open.

She pulled through, and waited for Betsy to get in before continuing. She topped a slight rise and slammed on her brakes as a horse galloped down the fence line on their left. Spinning on his haunches, he raced toward them and lifted himself effortlessly over the roof of her truck. Dirt from his hooves clattered on the hood and windshield as he sprinted away. Lanie could clearly see the cross-country studs in the bottoms of his shoes. "Loose horse!" screamed a knot of people chasing him, frantically waving their arms.

"No shit," muttered Lanie as she threw the gearshift into park.

"Holy crap!" said Betsy. "That's Bubba!" She leapt out of the truck and joined the chase, shouting at Lanie to shut the gate as she raced to join the pursuers. Bubba was running joyfully in large circles, tail flagged, head high in the air, whinnying with what Lanie was certain was derision. *Catch me if you can!* Every time they got close enough to put a hand on him he was off again, sand and clods of grass stinging their faces. She jumped out of the truck, sprinted to the gate and dragged it shut, then joined the chase.

Thirty minutes later, and tired of the game, the bay allowed himself to be cornered, and Betsy was able to grab him by his halter.

"He looked like he was enjoying that," Lanie said, joining the winded, tired chasers grouped in front of the horse.

"It's just like him," Betsy panted. "He's a genuine, dyed-in-the-wool butthead, this one."

Lanie bent over, hands on her knees, and tried to catch her breath. Looking up at the horse, she was, as always, struck by his beauty: small black-tipped ears that almost met in the middle; a deeply dished, dry-boned face, and large expressive eyes that were the finishing touches to a compact, muscled body and high arching neck. A sheen of sweat on his dark mahogany chest and flanks was already drying in the light breeze. His black mane, pulled short, flopped haphazardly on either side of his neck, giving him the appearance of a super-sized Welsh pony. He snorted softly, blowing warm air in her face, and nuzzled her arm.

"Watch him," Betsy said as she pulled a dirty glove off with her teeth and stuffed it in her coat pocket. Rick, the groom, handed her a lead rope and she attached it, giving it a yank to get his attention. "He looks harmless enough, but he's got the temperament of a pony. Mean as a snake." The harshness of her words was belied by the loving pat she gave his sweaty neck.

"He's too smart by half," said Lanie, straightening up. "I swear he's part Arab."

Betsy blew her sweaty bangs off her forehead and smiled. "He's pure sneaky Trakehner. Though they actually have a good bit of Thoroughbred and Arabian blood." She gave Bubba a final pat and led him away. "See you down at the main barn," she called over her shoulder.

The chase team piled into the bed of Lanie's truck, and she drove them to the barn. While waiting for Betsy and Bubba to make their way down from the pasture, she got out and wandered over to the whitewashed fence bordering the cross-country schooling field. From her far right a horse and rider galloped over the top of the hill, racing for the final ditch and wall and the finish flags. As they passed through the flags the rider brought the horse down to a canter, making a large looping circle in front of Lanie.

When horse and rider came to a halt, Lanie waved them over. The small gray mare approached at a ground-covering walk, closing the distance rapidly. They stopped at the fence in front of Lanie, and the rider pulled off her safety helmet, shaking out her long coppery hair. "Is there something I can help you with?" she asked. "If you're looking for Chris I think he's in the dressage arena."

"Sorry, I should have introduced myself. I'm Lanie Montgomery." She extended her hand, which the young woman shook cautiously.

"I recognize the name," she said. "You used to be a big time amateur eventer."

"Used to be," Lanie said.

"I'm Elisabeth, and this is Lucy. " She stroked the mare's neck. "Am I in trouble for using the cross-country field? We're supposed to be doing trot sets, but she has such a big jump I couldn't resist taking a few fences."

Lanie laughed. "Your secret's safe with me." She reached

over the fence and rubbed the mare's velvety nose. "She's lovely. What's her breeding?"

Elisabeth smiled. "Irish Sport Horse. She does really well on the dressage, too.

"Always a bonus," Lanie agreed. She admired Elisabeth's creamy, alabaster skin and brilliant hair. "I always wanted to be a redhead," she said.

"That's because you aren't one. I fry like an egg in the sun, and freckle like crazy. My mom was a brunette. I got my hair from my dad."

"Luck of the genetic draw, I guess. Your mom must have had a red gene as well or you'd have had better luck."

Elisabeth grinned. "Yeah, genetics is a funny thing." She looked at Lanie appraisingly. "Why don't you compete anymore?"

"I gave it up years ago. Law school and work got in the way," Lanie hedged.

"That's too bad. It's a great sport." She tucked her helmet under her arm. "I used to ride jumpers, but I got tired of it and switched to eventing."

"Well, it looks like you have a great horse for it."

Elisabeth sighed. "I wish she *were* mine. My horse died a few years ago and I can't afford to replace him." Her blue eyes met Lanie's. "My mom and dad split up, and when my horse died my dad kept the insurance money." She kicked her feet out of the stirrups, swinging them back and forth. "I got caught in the crossfire. My dad said my mom would just drink up the money." She shrugged. "So for now I'm just a lowly working student, riding other people's horses."

"Stick with it, you'll get there."

"I plan to. "

Lanie heard the sound of hooves behind her and turned to see Betsy and Bubba strolling down the driveway toward the barn. She turned back to Elisabeth. "It was nice to meet you and Lucy. Good luck with the eventing."

"Thanks." Elisabeth replaced her helmet and turned the mare away.

Lanie met Betsy and Bubba at the pasture gate and followed them into the barn.

"Who was that?" Betsy asked, watching Elisabeth and Lucy trot away.

Lanie shrugged. "Never seen her before."

While Betsy put Bubba in the wash stall and scrubbed off the sweat and dirt, Lanie strolled down the aisle toward the field behind the barn. There were twenty spacious stalls, a tack room, and a feed room. A short, broad hall to the left led to an indoor arena, where Rick was raking the footing with a small tractor, a cloud of dust thickening the air in his wake. The stall occupants munched their mid-afternoon hay, knee-deep in fragrant cedar shavings. The rubberized brick floor in the main aisle was spotless. Water buckets brimmed with fresh water. Feed buckets were scrubbed clean and turned upside down in an empty wash stall. *Even in the midst of tragedy, horses and barns have to be tended to*, Lanie thought.

She walked across the field, angling toward the back of Marge's house, keeping an eye out for Chris. She didn't want to have to explain to him why she was here if she could avoid it. Kudzu blanketed the tangle of scrubby trees that lined the fence, and enveloped the icehouse completely. Joy was right, she realized, if you didn't know it was there you'd never notice it. It had been a favorite place to play when she, Chris, and Angela were children.

She turned sideways and squeezed through the narrow entrance, stepping down carefully into the darkness of the cool, stone-lined room. Dug deep into the ground in the days before refrigerators were even thought of, its thick stone walls and floors had kept ice from melting in the hot Sandhills summers. Light from narrow slits high in the walls dimly illuminated delicate draperies of cobwebs.

Joy had spread a jacket on the dirt floor and used one of the stuffed pillowcases to rest her head. A day planner rested on top of the jacket. Suddenly anxious to be gone, Lanie grabbed the planner and the pillowcases and headed back the way she'd come.

When she returned to the barn, Bubba hung his head over his half-door, hay trailing from his mouth, watching her with soft, brown eyes.

"Find what you needed?" asked Betsy.

"I think so." Lanie walked over to Bubba's stall and dropped the pillowcases in the aisle, placing the planner on top. She unlatched the stall door, stepped in, and ran her hand down his clean, damp neck, her hand stopping halfway down. She pushed his mane back to get a better look. "He has a Prophet's Thumbprint!"

Betsy snorted. "You don't believe that old tale do you?"

"It's the mark of a courageous horse, one descended from the Arabian broodmares so prized by the Prophet Mohammed that he marked them with his thumbprint."

"Yeah, well, in his case I call it the *Devil's* Thumbprint," said Betsy. "He can be a complete little shit when he wants to be, which is a lot of the time."

"My first eventer had one, too," Lanie said softly. She tousled Bubba's pony-like forelock and stepped out of the stall, dusting hay off her clothes.

"You ever miss it?" asked Betsy.

Lanie picked up Joy's planner and flipped through the pages, ignoring the question. "Hey, there's a completed entry form for the selection trial in here," she said, "and Joy's listed as the rider."

Betsy looked over her shoulder. "That might be good news for Joy."

"Could be, but it's more likely Marge mailed in a different entry form substituting Chris."

"What are you two doing here?"

Startled, they spun around to find Chris standing in the barn entryway holding a lathered horse by the reins. The smile on his face didn't reach his blue eyes, which coldly took in the two of them frozen in the barn aisle. He slapped a dressage whip against his tall boots, causing the horse to snort and pull back in alarm. The rumble of the tractor died abruptly, and Rick appeared from the arena and took the horse from Chris, stroking its neck and murmuring softly, whether to the horse or himself, Lanie couldn't tell. He led the horse down the aisle to the wash stall.

"Hey Chris!" said Lanie. "You startled us."

"I wasn't expecting to see you."

Lanie motioned to the two pillowcases resting on the aisle floor. "Joy came by the store a little while ago. She asked me to come get some things for her.

Chris shifted his long legs, clad in spotless white riding breeches, and crossed his arms. "I know you two are friends of Joy's, but she'd taken Reinmeister as far as her abilities allowed. I finally convinced Marge of that, and she chose me to take him on to an Olympic medal." He shrugged. "No hard feelings. Just a business decision."

Lanie glanced around at the horses. All of them had pinned their ears and moved to the backs of their stalls. Only Bubba stood his ground at his stall door, ears flat, head bobbing up and down in agitation. She looked at the entry form in her hand, then up at Chris.

"Really? This designates Joy as the rider. It's signed by your aunt and dated the day before she died."

"Let me see that!" He strode toward her, snatching at the papers and knocking the planner out of her hands. Papers scattered over the brick floor. Betsy bent, scooped them up quickly, and handed them back to Lanie.

"Those are the old ones. I was there when Aunt Marge filled out the new ones!" He stepped toward Lanie with his hand outstretched. "Give them to me right now!"

"If they're the old entries, it won't matter if Joy has them," said Betsy in an attempt to placate him. "She's already lost the ride on Bubba. You can afford to be generous here, surely."

"Maybe I could, but I'm not going to be."

His contemptuous tone got Lanie's back up. "I'm afraid I can't give them to you Chris," she said. "This stuff belongs to Joy. She asked me to come get some of her clothes and her day planner and that's all I'm doing." She tried a smile. "Besides, if your aunt signed new entry forms then, like Betsy said, you've got no use for these. I'm going to suggest to Joy that she turn them over to Henry Banner. If they're not germane to the settlement of Marge's estate, he can decide what to do with them."

She shuffled through the papers. "Besides, there's nothing here that looks important. Other than the old forms, there's just a handwritten list of horses and some telephone numbers." She scanned the list. "Passing Through, In Flight, Episodic." She looked at Chris. "Any of those ring a bell?" When he didn't answer she shrugged and stuffed the paper in the pocket of her jeans.

Anger blotched his face. His fingers clenched and unclenched the whip. "Who the hell do you think you are?" he asked softly. He glared at them for a moment, then abruptly waved his hand, dismissing them. "You're trespassing on my property. Get the hell out of here before I call the police!"

Behind them, Bubba kicked viciously at the wall of his stall.

"What's going on here?"

Betsy and Lanie turned to see Bryan standing by the wash stall, his equipment bag in his hand. Lanie wondered how long he'd been there and how much of the exchange he'd heard.

"What's it to you?" Chris responded.

Bryan shrugged. "I wouldn't think you'd want any more trouble right now."

"No one gives a damn what you think. It's you who needs to worry about being in trouble. Not me." He locked eyes with the dentist, then turned to Lanie and pointed the whip at her face. "Take that stuff and get out of here." He threw the whip on a tack trunk and strode out of the barn, brushing Bryan aside with his shoulder as he went.

"That was scary!" Betsy said with a shaky laugh.

Bryan turned to watch Chris as he headed toward his house, then turned back to them. "What's his problem?"

"Damned if I know," said Betsy. She related the exchange with Chris.

"That's a side of him I've never seen," said Lanie. "I thought he was going to hit me."

"Some people don't handle stress very well," said Bryan. "I'm sure he's got a lot on his mind, with everything that's going on."

"Given his history with Bubba, I can't believe Marge would even consider putting him on that horse," Betsy said thoughtfully.

Bryan sighed. "Marge only cared about the results, and Chris certainly delivers on that front, albeit sometimes at the expense of the animal." His gaze traveled between the two women. "Come on ladies, I'll walk you to your truck."

As they walked out, Betsy said, "The only name on that list I recognized was Episodic."

"What list?" Bryan asked sharply.

"Lanie found a piece of paper in Joy's day planner with a list of horses and some telephone numbers. I recognized Episodic. About ten years ago he won some major Grade 1 stakes races and then died of colic a few weeks before the Kentucky Derby. He was heavily favored to win it."

"I guess I missed that part of the conversation," said Bryan as they got to the truck. He opened the door for Lanie, pushed it shut, then leaned on the open driver's side window. "If you ladies are no longer in need of my services, I'll be going about my day." He stood up and tapped the window frame lightly. "Happy trails!"

"Thanks for rescuing us, Bryan," said Lanie. "Stop by the store when you get a chance." She was anxious to get away. She started to drive off, then stopped abruptly and pounded the steering wheel with her fist. "Damn it!"

"What?"

"I got the day planner, but I forgot the clothes. She put the truck in park, jumped out, and ran back to the barn. Bryan was nowhere in sight. The pillowcases were at the door to Bubba's stall where she'd dropped them. She grabbed them and turned to go back to the truck. As she reached the barn door, a car pulled up in front of her, and a man stepped out, blocking her exit.

"May I ask what you're doing?"

She stopped, the pillowcases in one hand, the other shading her eyes. The sun, bright behind him, haloed his blond hair.

"I'm a friend of Joy's," Lanie finally replied.

"The trainer."

She nodded.

"What's in the pillowcases?"

"Clothes. She asked me to stop by and get them for her." Lanie dropped them in the aisle.

"Why would she need you to do that?"

"Why do you want to know?" Lanie asked, irritated by his questions. "And who are you, anyway?"

"Michael Donovan," he replied, walking toward her as he pulled his identification from the inside pocket of his jacket and handed it to her. "State Bureau of Investigation." He walked over to the pillowcases and prodded them with the toe of his shoe. "Mind if I take a look?"

She examined his credentials carefully before giving them back to him. She bent over and picked up a pillowcase and turned it upside down, shaking the contents onto the floor in a jumble of blue jeans, sweaters, sweatshirts, underwear and socks, deodorant, toothbrush, and a tube of toothpaste.

"Help yourself," she said, stepping back.

A smile touched the corner of his mouth fleetingly, then disappeared. "And the other one?"

Silently, Lanie picked it up and upended it. Paddock boots, sneakers, and a pair of fuzzy, pink bedroom slippers, complete with rabbit whiskers, hit the floor with a clatter.

Lanie stood silently and observed him as he squatted and picked through the clothing and shoes, separating them with a pen. He was good looking, she'd give him that, though a trifle *too* good looking for her taste. He straightened up and looked at her. "Do you have a name, other than 'friend of Joy's'?"

"Lanie Montgomery."

"You're rather closemouthed, Ms. Montgomery. Why is that?" he asked, surveying the array of clothing scattered in the aisle.

"My father taught me that you don't volunteer information, and that just because someone asks you a question doesn't mean you have to answer it."

His eyebrows met in a scowl. "Is that so? I guess your father didn't have much experience with murder investigations, then."

"Actually, he was a defense attorney before becoming dean of the law school at Beckham."

He held her gaze fixedly. "Where did you find this stuff, Ms. Montgomery? I hope you weren't foolish enough to remove it from Ms. Alexander's apartment, since it's been sealed as part of a crime scene."

Lanie shifted uncomfortably. "It was in the ice house," she finally replied.

"What ice house?"

"There's an abandoned ice house behind the main residence, along the fence line. We used to play there when we were kids."

He pulled his phone from the inside pocket of his jacket and punched in a series of numbers.

"Did you check the ice house?" he quietly asked whoever answered. He listened for a moment. "Do it now!" he said, and ended the call. He returned his attention to Lanie.

"Why would Ms. Alexander's things be in the ice house?"

Lanie gazed at him steadily. "She's been staying there since Chris threw her out of her apartment. And her job."

"Where is she now?"

Lanie hesitated for a moment before she replied. "At my store."

"I'm afraid you'll have to leave this with me," he said, indicating the clothes. "And leave your contact information. We'll need to get a statement from you."

Lanie gave him her address and cell phone number and stalked back to the truck. She jumped in and slammed the door, grinding the starter in anger.

"I thought you went back for Joy's stuff," said Betsy.

"I did," Lanie retorted, jerking the gearshift into drive and punching the accelerator. The back of the truck slewed in the bluestone gravel before straightening out. "I ran into an SBI agent. He confiscated it." She glared at Betsy. "I suppose I should count my blessings he didn't arrest me."

"So now what?"

"I guess Joy's just going to have to go shopping and wait until they release her stuff." She waited while Betsy opened and closed the back gate and returned to the truck. They rattled down the track and back to Young's Road in silence. When they arrived at the store, Betsy got in her truck and left for an appointment.

Lanie went in and broke the news to Joy about her apartment being sealed and having to leave the clothing with the SBI. She handed Joy the day planner, and then showed her the entry forms. "I found these in your planner," she said, "but I'm going to have to turn them over to Henry Banner, assuming his firm will be serving as executor of Marge's estate. It'll be up to him to decide what to do with them."

Joy looked at the forms. "These are the originals. Marge was supposed to mail them, but I guess she was already planning to pull me."

"There was also a list of horses and some telephone numbers in there. Do you know anything about those?" She pulled the paper out of her pocket and handed it to Joy.

Joy looked the list over, shrugged, and handed it back, a puzzled frown on her face. "I don't know what that is. Marge gave me the planner back a few days before she died and I haven't looked at it since. It's definitely her handwriting, though. Maybe she put it in my planner by mistake."

"Probably so." Lanie put the list back in her pocket. "Do you need somewhere to stay?"

"Thanks for the offer, but you've done enough already. I'll figure something out."

"No worries," Lanie said walking her to the door. "Keep your chin up. It'll all sort itself out." She handed her the day planner.

"When do you think they'll release my apartment?"

"I have no idea, but I'm sure they'll want to talk to you. You can ask them then."

"I can't wait," Joy said as she walked toward the door.

"Where are you going to go?"

Joy paused with her hand on the door knob. "I guess I might as well go by the farm and get my interview with the police over with."

"Stay in touch!"

Lanie spent the remainder of Monday afternoon mulling over the incident at Cameron Farms, pings from her inbox reminding her of the orders stacking up. Chris's behavior bothered her, and she kept returning to it like a tongue probing a sore tooth. At four o'clock, her cell phone rang, jarring her from her reverie.

"Hey Lanie, I need a favor." Betsy was calling from the kennel, shouting over the cacophony of dogs barking and howling in the background. "It's been a zoo in here this afternoon. The girl who cleans cages didn't show back up after lunch, and I've been busier than a one-armed paper hanger." She paused. "I need a place to park a dog for a few days. Can you help me out?"

"No!" said Lanie. "The last time I did that I ended up with a neurotic Australian shepherd. Absolutely not!"

"C'mon Lanie. The kennel's booked solid. Everybody's gone to the steeplechase in Aiken. I couldn't pound a teacup poodle in here with a sledgehammer. I really need a temporary place for this dog."

"Betsy Anderson, you are such a con artist," said Lanie.

Betsy laughed. "Chris called and left a message for me to pick up Marge's Rottweiler. It seems Angela doesn't want him in her house and the security people don't want him underfoot in the main house." Betsy's voice faded in and out as she shifted the phone.

"Did he apologize for being such a jerk?"

"Nope. I picked the dog up from Rick. And, I met Agent Donovan. That is one good-looking man!"

Lanie snorted. "I didn't notice."

"Maybe he needs a good girlfriend."

"Mind your own business." Lanie sighed. "I'll help you out with the dog for a couple of days, but I can't keep him indefinitely, understand?"

The noise from the kennel dampened as Betsy took the phone into her office. "Great! Thanks Lanie! Rommel's a sweetheart. He shouldn't be any trouble. I'll be able to take him off your hands after the weekend."

"Right. Why don't you stop by the house tonight and drop him off. I'll scrounge up something for dinner."

"I knew you'd come through," Betsy said. "Hey! By the way, he's deaf."

"Who's deaf?"

"Did you think I meant Donovan?" Betsy laughed. "Rommel, ditz. Marge's Rottweiler. He's been profoundly deaf since birth. But don't worry, he's really good with hand signals. See you tonight." Lanie was left with a dial tone as Betsy slammed down the phone before she could change her mind.

As darkness fell, Lanie pulled into her driveway and walked over to the pasture fence, whistling for the horses. After the long day she was ready for dinner with Betsy and a vodka and water, not necessarily in that order. The horses galloped across the pasture and slid to a stop at the gate, jockeying for position, each wanting to be the first to come in. She was irked to find their halters weren't hanging in the usual place on the gate, though she didn't remember returning them to their hooks beside their stalls inside the barn. She sighed. In her haste to get to the store this morning she'd probably just forgotten. At the barn door she kicked off her sneakers, exchanging them for her Wellies. Striding down the aisle, she checked the hooks on the stalls. No halters.

She pushed open the door to the tack room and stepped across the concrete floor, her hand feeling for the familiar leather. As she closed her fingers around them, a blow to the back of her head slammed her face into the wall. She slid to the floor, tangled in halters and lead ropes, as her vision faded to black.

seven

She awoke to the accompaniment of a crackling police radio and an excruciating pain in her head. Rotating red and blue lights flashed on the concrete floor of the stable aisle and leaked into the tack room, causing her to squint. Betsy's bright blue eyes, gazing into hers with concern, came into focus.

"Hey, girlie," Betsy said softly. "Are you okay?"

"What happened?"

"Don't know. I pulled up just in time to see somebody take a swing at your truck window. They took off when they saw my headlights. Sorry bastards!" she swore softly as she gently turned Lanie's head and examined the damage. "Unfortunately, it was too dark to see much more than shadows, and they had a head start on me." She gently probed Lanie's face, feeling for broken bones. "Good thing you went face first into the halters or you'd have had a broken nose to go along with the rest of it."

Lanie slowly stretched her arm out. "Help me sit up."

"Judging by that lump on the back of your head, I'm thinking you need to reconsider that idea."

"Just help me up, okay?"

Betsy shrugged. "It's your funeral." She eased Lanie to a sitting position.

Lanie immediately regretted the decision as her stomach threatened to upend itself into her lap and a stabbing pain in her head caused her to rock back and forth. She gripped Betsy's arm to steady herself, determined not to throw up.

"I called 911 when I found you, so the EMTs should be getting here any moment, but they're slower than the second coming—" She was interrupted by the arrival of the EMTs and their paraphernalia. Once inside the tack room, they eased Lanie back down to the floor and began their inspection while Betsy got out of their way and stepped outside to speak with the Moore County sheriff's deputy.

Thirty minutes later, after refusing the EMT's strong suggestion that she be transported to Moore Regional Hospital for x-rays, and after recounting to the deputy what she remembered, which was nothing, Lanie sent them on their way.

Betsy brought the horses in and fed them while Lanie sat on a hay bale, wrapped in a horse blanket, resting against the barn wall, her head cushioned by a saddle pad. "This is my best dressage pad, Betsy," she complained. "What if the blood seeps through the bandages? I don't want it to get all bloody."

"Well it's not like you've been using it the last few years," Betsy retorted.

Lanie closed her eyes and listened to the familiar, comforting sounds of evening barn chores: the click of clasps as Betsy coated the horses with blankets against the night chill, the sweet smell of timothy alfalfa hay, the quiet snorting of the horses as they burrowed into their buckets, lips stirring as they searched for favored bits of molasses-coated corn.

When the horses were put to bed, Betsy wrapped an arm around her and they headed slowly for the house. Their progress was halted as headlights swept into the driveway. The car eased to a stop next to Betsy, the window sliding down smoothly.

"Evening, Ms. Montgomery, Dr. Anderson" Donovan said. "I was on my way back to Raleigh when I saw your lights on, so I thought I'd stop. I have a couple of questions for you."

"That's some trick, seeing my lights from Young's Road."

He leaned out the window, taking in Lanie's Wellington boots and horse blanket shawl. "I won't take much of your time," he said, ignoring the jibe.

Lanie groaned.

Donovan peered at her more closely, then got out of his car. "What happened?"

"Nothing to concern you," Lanie replied. "Come on, Betsy. I need to sit down."

"I'll help you get her inside," Donovan said to Betsy.

"We don't need your help," Lanie began.

"Yes, we do. I'm afraid you'll fall," said Betsy. "Not all of us are ruled by our pride." She smiled at Donovan. "I'd appreciate the help. If you'll just hold on to her while I get Rommel out of my truck."

Lanie glared at her, but was too tired to protest further.

Betsy left Lanie in Donovan's grasp as she walked to her truck and let the massive Rottweiler out onto the bluestone driveway. Returning to Lanie, she took her arm, and the four of them made their way, haltingly, to the kitchen. Once inside, Lanie collapsed into a chair at the kitchen table, while Snert and Rommel sniffed around each other cautiously for a few moments. Introductions over, they competed to fill her lap with their noses, brows wrinkled in concern. Once assured, they settled to the floor at her feet.

"Lanie, meet Rommel," Betsy said as she headed out the screen door. "I'll be right back."

She returned with a metal bucket full of hot water and her medical bag from the vet box on the back of her truck. After pulling off Lanie's boots, she poured hot water into a bowl and set it on the kitchen table. She began to rinse out the dried blood matted into Lanie's blond hair. Donovan turned one of the wooden kitchen chairs around and straddled it, arms crossed over the back. The only sounds in the kitchen were the anxious panting of the dogs and water swishing in the metal bowl as Betsy repeatedly rinsed the towel.

Donovan finally broke the silence. "What happened?"

Betsy put down the towel and picked up her scissors.

"Don't even think about cutting my hair Betsy Anderson," Lanie said firmly. She looked at Donovan. "According to the sheriff's deputy, I probably interrupted some kids looking for something to steal. I never saw them."

"This cut really needs a couple of stitches, Lanie, and soon, or it'll be too late to stitch it," Betsy said. "It won't take me but a minute to whip them in there."

"Isn't that practicing medicine without a license?" asked Donovan.

"Only if you don't consider a VMD from New Bolton a license to practice medicine," Betsy retorted, laying out needles and sutures. She glanced at Donovan. "You planning to turn me in?"

He grimaced. "Isn't that going to hurt?"

"Probably." Betsy grinned. "But, she's an old eventer. They're tough as nails. It won't be the first time I've sewn one up in the absence of an MD."

"What's an eventer?" Donovan asked, looking from Betsy to Lanie.

"They're adrenaline junkies who get their fix galloping horses cross country over big-assed jumps that don't fall down when you hit them. Crazy as shit house rats, if you ask me. Every damn one of them." She tied off a suture with a flourish. "Lanie was one of the best in the country, could've gone—"

"Agent Donovan," Lanie interrupted, "if you're going to hang around, could you at least make yourself useful and brew some coffee?" She pointed to a cabinet next to the kitchen sink.

"Beans and sweetener are up there above the brewer, cream's in the fridge. Since Betsy seems determined to mutilate my scalp, add some bourbon to mine. It's in the small mahogany chest in the dining room." She pointed again.

Donovan ground the beans, and soon the aroma of French roast filled the kitchen. By the time the coffee had finished brewing Betsy had completed her task. "I only had to shave a really small spot," she said, holding her fingers apart to demonstrate the size of the wound. "You should be able to hide it pretty easily. If that sort of thing's important to you." She shook a finger in Lanie's face. "But, in the morning you need to see a *real* doctor for some antibiotics." She shot a glance at Donovan. "And a tetanus shot if you haven't had one in a while." Metal instruments clanged into the bucket as Betsy cleaned up. "I'll take this stuff out to the truck."

"Thanks," Lanie said, tentatively touching the newly inserted stitches on the back of her head. Donovan handed her the cup.

"You know," he said, "alcohol consumption, in conjunction with a concussion, is contraindicated."

Lanie did her best to glare. "How alliterative of you. I don't have a concussion."

Donovan turned back to the counter and poured himself a cup of coffee. "Are you always this cranky when you get hit on the head?"

Lanie ignored him. "What did you want to talk to me about?" She sniffed the aromatic coffee and closed her eyes, fighting the urge to fall asleep. She opened them to find his steady gaze on her face. The slamming of the screen door heralded Betsy's return. She ruffled Snert's ears before pouring herself a cup of coffee and joining them at the table.

"You saw Joy Alexander today," Donovan said, taking a sip of his coffee, eyes fixed on Lanie's face.

"Yes. I told you she was at my store."

"And she asked you to go out to Cameron Farms and get some personal items for her?"

"You already know that, too. She asked me to pick up some clothes." She paused to take a sip of bourbon-laced coffee, blowing on the hot surface before bringing it to her mouth. She ignored Betsy's questioning look, praying she wouldn't mention the day planner. "While we were there, Chris Cameron made an appearance and acted like a complete ass."

Betsy choked on her coffee, then wiped her mouth on her shirtsleeve.

"Did you take anything out of the apartment?"

"No. I never even went upstairs. She told me she'd been staying in the ice house. I went straight there and gathered up her things."

"Did you remove anything, other than clothing, from the ice house?"

Lanie considered lying, weighing the consequences. Not knowing what information Donovan had, she opted for the truth. "Her day planner was there, too. I found some entry forms for the selection trial and a passport for Reinmeister in the planner, which Chris tried to take from me when he confronted us in the barn. I was afraid if I left them Chris would destroy them, so I decided I'd turn them over to Henry Banner."

"Did it occur to you that you should have turned them over to me, or Sheriff Parker? That the ice house might be a part of the crime scene?" Donovan watched her intently, alert as a cat at a mouse hole.

Lanie's face flushed crimson and she shifted in her chair, ignoring Betsy's questioning look. She met his gaze defiantly. "If you thought they were so important why didn't you take them yourself? Besides, Henry's firm will probably be settling Marge's estate. He'll know how to deal with those entry forms."

"We didn't know Ms. Alexander was hiding in the ice house."

"You didn't know, or the search team messed up and didn't search it?" Lanie shot back. "Its existence isn't exactly a secret." She gazed into her coffee cup. "And she wasn't *hiding*. She just wanted to be close to Bubba so she could keep an eye on him."

"Those papers may contain information helpful to the investigation, Ms. Montgomery. Not to mention that you could be charged with removing evidence from a crime scene. Which," he said with a smile, "I assume you know, since your father is a lawyer and you, yourself, have a law degree. Or didn't they cover that in law school?"

Lanie remained silent, feeling his intense gaze on her face.

"The crime was committed in the parlor!" she finally responded. *Good Lord,* she thought, *that sounded like something from Clue. Colonel Mustard, in the parlor, with a lead pipe.* "Chris said Marge had completed new forms listing him as the rider. I was trying to make sure he didn't destroy the prior entry forms! As executor, Henry will determine what happens with the horses." She knew she was on shaky ground. She'd had no business removing the documents or the planner.

"It looks like you were trying to protect Joy Alexander."

"I was just trying to make sure the playing field stayed level, and that Chris didn't stack things in his favor." She hesitated. "Joy also asked me to check on one of the horses, Bubba."

"Did she ask you to put anything *in* the ice house?"

"Like what?"

"Just answer the question."

"No."

"*Did* you put anything in the ice house?"

"No. Why would I do that?"

"Does Chris know you have these entry forms?"

"Yes. I told him I was going to turn them over to Henry."

"And what was his response to that."

"He was really starting to get ugly when Bryan Dawson showed up." She thought for a minute. "Are you implying *Chris* came here looking for them?" she asked. "That it was Chris who hit me over the head?"

He shrugged. "Or Ms. Alexander." He took a sip of his cooling coffee. "Why did Joy want you to check on Bubba?" he asked, changing the subject.

"She trained him and now he's the horse everyone's fighting over. He and Chris have a stormy relationship, and Joy's afraid Chris will be abusive to him. Chris's goal is to win the Rolex and he'll do whatever it takes to make that happen."

Betsy spoke up. "I've treated a few of the horses Chris has ridden. Some of them had obviously been pushed when an idiot could see they were dead on their feet. And he's known for excessive use of the whip when things don't go his way in warm up or on the course. He's gotten a few yellow cards in his career."

Donovan held up his free hand. "Slow down. What does a watch have to do with all this and what's a yellow card?"

Lanie smiled. "It's not *a* Rolex, it's *the* Rolex. It's a four-star-level event, which this year just happens to be serving as the selection trials for the Olympics. The entry forms I found in the day planner listed Joy as the rider. They were signed by Marge Cameron." She reached down and stroked Snert's ears. "Not knowing what Marge's estate plan entails, I thought there was a chance that the estate would end up owning the horses. Also, not knowing if Marge actually sent in a different entry form with Chris as the designated rider, I thought it made sense to turn it all over to Henry and let him sort it out."

"So," he said thoughtfully, "Christian said his aunt had completed new paperwork listing him as the rider, but the paperwork you found listed Ms. Alexander." His gaze traveled from

Lanie to Betsy and back again. "Any sign of the new entry forms?" They shook their heads.

"When Marge and Joy were going at it at the party the other night, Marge made it clear she was replacing her," said Betsy reluctantly, "but I can't believe Joy would deliberately destroy those entry forms, or hurt Marge to prevent her from replacing her as Bubba's rider."

"She'd have a lot to lose if Mrs. Cameron followed through, though. Right?"

"Riding for the Olympic three-day event team is a major deal," conceded Betsy. "It means owners bring you good quality horses to train and compete, students line up for lessons, and you can charge a ton to give clinics to eventing wannabes. It's not the NBA, but it can be a very comfortable living."

"In other words, Ms. Alexander had a strong financial motive to keep Mrs. Cameron from making that change. Or for destroying any evidence she had changed it," he said.

Betsy started to protest, but he waved her to silence. "We interviewed Chris Cameron yesterday afternoon. He said he saw someone leaving the house in the early hours on the morning of the murder. He identified that someone as Joy Alexander. When we talked with her this afternoon, she denied being anywhere near the house. Said she'd planned to go see Mrs. Cameron the next morning and try to reason with her."

"If you're saying Joy killed Marge, that dog won't hunt!" Betsy said heatedly.

Lanie sighed and pulled herself stiffly upright. "Agent Donovan, why don't you tell us the real purpose of this visit."

He set his coffee mug on the table. "We found the murder weapon in the ice house this afternoon."

Lanie, Betsy, and the dogs looked at him intently, waiting for him to continue. "Ms. Alexander is being held at the Moore

County jail. Charged with the murder of Marjorie Cameron. She'll be transferred to Women's Prison in Raleigh sometime in the next day or so."

He rose from his chair, walked to the sink, and poured the cold coffee down the drain. Setting the mug down quietly, he leaned against the counter, arms crossed, and gazed steadily at Lanie. "I suggest you give me whatever papers you have." He paused. "You might also want to consider getting yourself some legal counsel."

eight

On Tuesday morning Lanie woke to find Betsy snoring in the chair by her bed. Lanie had tossed and turned, unable to get comfortable, or to still the thoughts whirling through her head like constellations. Reaching out, she gently shook Betsy awake. "What are you doing here still?" she asked.

Betsy dug the heels of her hands into her eyes and yawned. "I thought it would be a good idea to keep an eye on you for a few hours, just in case you had a concussion. I must have fallen asleep in the chair last time I checked on you." She struggled out of the deep chair and shuffled toward the kitchen. Lanie heard the screen door slam as the dogs were let out, followed by the smell of coffee brewing. She groaned as she sat up and propped the pillows behind her.

"So what the hell are you going to do?" Betsy asked as she returned to the bedroom and handed Lanie a mug of coffee.

Lanie sighed. "I don't know. Joy's in jail and Donovan thinks I'm trying to cover up for her." She shifted in the bed. "Maybe I *should* consider getting some legal representation."

"You're lucky you didn't get arrested yourself. What the hell were you thinking? Not turning that planner over to Drew or the SBI could have bad consequences for you."

"Don't lecture me, Betsy! I didn't know they considered her the prime suspect in Marge's murder. I was just trying to help her out."

"Just goes to show that no good deed goes unpunished. Fat lot of good playing girl scout will do you if Donovan decides to charge you as an accessory." She took a sip of her coffee. "I don't believe for one minute that Joy had anything to do with Marge's murder. And it wouldn't surprise me if it *was* Chris who bashed you on the head last night."

Lanie looked at her in surprise. "What would he gain by that?"

"A ride in the Rolex."

"Oh come on, Betsy! Knocking me over the head and stealing the entry forms from my truck wouldn't change anything. If I didn't know better I'd think it was you that got hit over the head last night," she said, gingerly probing the stitches in the back of her head. They felt stiff beneath her fingers, the wound sore to the touch. "I didn't know you disliked Chris so much."

"I deal with him professionally because I have to, but I don't really trust him. Not that he's ever done anything in *particular* to make me distrust him. It's just that my gut tells me he's lower than a snake's ass in a wheel rut," Betsy muttered into her coffee cup.

Lanie laughed. "I haven't heard that expression since my dad died," she said. "If it weren't for the upstate New York accent I'd swear you were a Southerner."

Betsy brushed her hair back from her face and grinned. "I plan to be reincarnated as a North Carolinian, so I'm practicing my colloquialisms."

Lanie sipped her coffee and gazed out her bedroom window at the pasture. "Donovan seemed pretty confident they had their murderer."

"Lanie," Betsy said, resting her elbows on her knees and cradling her coffee cup in her hands, "Joy would never in a million years have killed Marge Cameron." Betsy cut a look at Lanie and then gazed into her cooling coffee. "She reminds me a lot of you."

"Why's that?" Lanie asked.

"She has a passion for eventing and the talent to back it up. No trust fund, no moneyed owner with a talented horse. Just the opposite in fact." She gazed out at the horses in the pasture, then turned to look at Lanie. "Do you remember that saddlebred she competed all the way to advanced level? Beat the socks off everybody." She laughed, and set the coffee cup on the nightstand, clasping her hands between her knees.

"You know how hard she's worked. Over the years she's done whatever it took to make money to compete. Skipped stalls, taught up-down classes to little kids, rode anything that needed riding." Betsy warmed to her subject.

"When her saddlebred pulled a rear suspensory ligament, and I had to put him on six months' stall rest. With little to no chance he'd come back from the injury," she added. "I ran into Joy at the horse trials out in Raeford one Saturday a few years ago. We were standing next to Marge at the dressage arena when Chris and Bubba came in. Bubba went into the dressage test, stood straight up on his hind legs after the salute, and then bolted straight at the judge." Betsy laughed. "I wish you could have seen the faces of the judge and her scribe. I swear I thought he was going to jump the car they were sitting in." Lanie smiled, remembering the dirt clods clattering on the hood of her truck. "Anyway, Marge was furious and said Bubba was going to the livestock auction at Siler City. That's when Joy talked her into letting her take him on as a project. I used to stop by her place every week to check on her horse and see how things were coming with Bubba. I got to tell you, for the first couple of months I was pretty sure one of them was going to die. He'd go along just fine for a few minutes and then he'd explode, bolting down the arena like the hounds of hell were after him, bucking like a rodeo horse." She smiled, remembering. "One time Joy was warming him up and he was cantering along on the lunge line nice as you please, then he turned toward the fence and cleared it. *In side reins,* Lanie! The crazy bastard jumped a four-and-a-half-foot fence in side reins from about four strides out." Betsy shook her head. "The good news was he actually had that much jump in him. The bad news was I had to stick around and put fifteen staples in his stifle." She sighed and rubbed her face. "I swear, Lanie, I hate that this has happened to her."

Lanie ran the edge of her thumb around the rim of her cup and watched her retired eventer, Simon, who was approaching his twenty-fifth birthday, haul his pasture mate around by the halter. She thought about Joy, and her own past struggles to make her mark on the eventing world. "I wish there was something I could do."

Betsy's reply was interrupted by Lanie's phone shrilling from the nightstand. Lanie answered, and at the end of the brief conversation she turned it off and dropped it in her lap.

"Who was that?" Betsy demanded.

"Joy."

"I thought she was in jail!"

"She is. They moved her to Southeast Raleigh Prison in the middle of the night. She wants me to come see her. She says she needs to talk to me."

Later that morning, Betsy drove Lanie to Raleigh, an hour north and east of Southern Pines, to Southeast Raleigh Prison. It was a dreary, red brick structure located just outside of downtown, islanded by a high fence and a deteriorating neighborhood, and housed a strictly female population.

They entered the drab building that housed the warden and the prison's administrative offices. It was crowded with families, most with children in tow, waiting to visit daughters, mothers, lovers, and friends. Lanie left Betsy in the waiting room and walked out the back door of the administration building to the guardhouse. She checked in, and submitted to having her purse searched for cell phones and other contraband, then signed that she was visiting Joy Alexander. After several minutes, an escort arrived and led her across the hard-packed dirt grounds to the prison proper, where she was shown into a small room and told to sit. And wait.

Thirty minutes later the door from the cellblock opened and Joy was led in, her ankles and wrists in shackles connected by a chain that ran between them. She shuffled in, head down, and awkwardly moved the plastic chair back from the table so she could sit across from Lanie. A clear plastic barrier ran down the center of the table and separated Joy from Lanie. The guard took a seat in a corner where she could keep watch over them. Through a thick window in the door to the cellblock Lanie could see a second guard stationed outside the door. She was shocked that Joy was in shackles, but kept her face neutral.

She leaned forward. "Are you okay?" she asked.

Joy nodded slowly, obviously dazed and disbelieving. She finally brought her gaze up to meet Lanie's. "I need your help, Lanie. I need some advice and I didn't know who else to turn to."

"Of course I'll help you anyway I can, but what you really need is a lawyer. They'll assign a public defender if you can't afford an attorney on your own."

"But you *are* a lawyer!" she wailed.

"Not a practicing one." She paused. "And even if I were, I couldn't represent you. My specialty is tax law and estate planning. You need a criminal lawyer." Lanie started to reach across the table for Joy's hands, but was stopped by the plastic barrier. She sat back in her chair.

"But I didn't *do* anything! Don't they understand that?" Joy began to cry. Great heaving sobs shook her body. Tears streamed down her face and ran off her chin onto her orange jumpsuit. She awkwardly wiped her running nose and eyes on her sleeve. "I didn't kill Marge Cameron! You have to believe me! I was angry with her, yes, but I wouldn't have hurt her! You have to believe me!" she repeated, rocking back and forth in her chair, her eyes red-rimmed and frightened.

Lanie shot a quick look at the guard and lowered her voice. "The SBI said they'd found the trophy that was used to bash Marge's head in in the ice house. Do you know how it got there?"

Joy shook her head. "I have no idea. My apartment is full of trophies, and I never had any reason to lock the door. There's nothing there to steal. Nothing anyone would want. Anyone could have taken a trophy, and they'd all have my fingerprints on them." She sniffed and wiped her nose on her sleeve. "Just because one of my trophies was used to kill Marge doesn't mean it was me who killed her."

"No, it doesn't."

"And why would I be so stupid as to keep it? Somebody else put the murder weapon in the ice house to point the finger at me."

"I believe you, Joy." Lanie said soothingly. She paused. "Chris also told the police he saw you leaving the house on the night she was killed."

The shackles clanked as Joy covered her face with her hands. "I did go up to the house that night, Lanie, but I swear I only wanted to talk to her, to beg her, if I had to, to reconsider. When I got to the terrace I could hear her talking to someone. She sounded angry." Joy lowered her hands to her lap. "The curtains were drawn so I couldn't see who she was talking to but she definitely sounded mad." She shrugged. "Anyway, I decided I would wait until morning to talk to her and I left." She looked beseechingly at Lanie. "But I *swear* to you she was alive when I walked off that terrace! Please say you'll help me, Lanie."

"I'll do what I can, Joy, I promise. In the meantime, you need to be careful who you share this information with. What you say to me isn't covered by attorney-client privilege. Do you understand? You need to get yourself an attorney and don't say anything to anyone else until you've talked to your lawyer."

"I wouldn't know where to start, and I couldn't afford one even if I did."

"I'll call Hugh Jennings and see if he can recommend a criminal attorney in Raleigh."

"Thank you," she said quietly. She looked up at Lanie. "And please keep an eye on Bubba. Don't let Chris treat him badly. I'm afraid something will happen!"

Lanie signaled to the guard that she was ready to leave. "I'll do whatever I can. You know I will," she repeated. Joy was delivered back into the custody of the guard as Lanie was escorted back to the guard house. She checked out and walked to the administration building where Betsy waited, impatient to learn what Joy had had to say. Lanie was grateful that Betsy curtailed asking any questions until they'd gotten in the truck.

"Well?" said Betsy as they drove out of the parking lot. "How was she? What'd she have to say?"

Lanie's head was splitting and she felt suddenly drained. "About what you'd expect. She's terrified. She wanted me to represent her, but I explained that she needed a *real* lawyer—and fast." She rubbed her temples wearily, trying to erase her headache.

"What did she say about Chris seeing her leave the house the night Marge was killed?"

"I told her not to talk to anyone about anything until she had an attorney," Lanie hedged.

"I don't care if he did see her. I don't believe she killed Marge. Regardless of what Agent Donovan says." Betsy pulled up to a red light and looked at Lanie. "The killer knew she was sleeping in the ice house and put the trophy in there to implicate her. That means the killer is someone close to home."

"I agree. The question is who? Beating someone to death smacks of some pretty strong emotions. If we could figure out who wanted Marge dead that badly, and why, Joy would be free and clear." She looked at Betsy, who was concentrating on merging into the heavy traffic on the outer beltline. "You in?" she asked.

"On what?" asked Betsy, surprised.

"On helping me find out who that someone is."

"You must have a concussion! We're not detectives!"

"We don't have to be. We just have to focus on the personal nature of the crime and ask the right questions."

"Like what? And of whom?"

"I don't know. We'll make a list. Believe me, Bets, this crime was committed by someone who hated Marge Cameron enough to obliterate her face. We'll ask questions of everybody we can think of and see if we get a reaction."

Betsy sighed. "You're not kidding are you?" She looked across at Lanie and grimaced. "If Donovan finds out you're messing around in his investigation he'll put you in the jail." When Lanie didn't respond, she sighed. "Why do I always let you talk me into this crazy shit?"

"Oh, quit whining! Are you in?" She turned and gazed intently at Betsy.

"I'm in."

"We'll start with Chris and Angela. You take Chris, I'll take Angela."

nine

Lanie had no appetite for going to the store after Betsy dropped her at the farm. She didn't want to answer questions, or listen to other people's speculations about the crime, and she didn't feel like focusing on billing or balancing the business checkbook. She loaded Rommel and Snert into the truck, and made a mental note to drop it off to get the window fixed. She smiled at their docked tails wagging double time in excitement, happy to be along for the ride, and headed for Shooting Club Road, site of the former gun club where Annie Oakley used to give shooting demonstrations in the early 1900s.

She pulled up to the gate at the Moore County Wildlife Club, punched in the code on the keypad, and waited while the heavy gate made its ponderous journey to the open position. She drove slowly down the winding gravel road as the gate swung shut behind her, careful to heed the "NO DUST BEYOND THIS POINT" signs, and parked in front of the number four skeet field. Late on a Tuesday afternoon she had the place to herself. She put two big screw fasteners into the ground under the maple tree and hooked Snert and Rommel each to one.

Opening the back door of the truck, she lifted out a heavy metal case and carried it to the picnic table under the maple tree. She dialed in the combination, thumbed open the latches, and lifted the lid to reveal a Krieghoff K-80 shotgun, the over-and-under barrel gleaming softly from its velvet-lined slot. She closed her eyes and ran her hand over the polished walnut stock and metal receiver, the roughness of the engraving like Braille under her fingertips. The gun—a bequest from her father—reminded her of cold mornings when she slogged through the fields side-by-side with him and behind the setter-pointer mixes he called "drops." Her small hands, stiff with cold, had clutched her father's old Browning Citori as she waited, alert for the explosion of wings as the tiny birds were flushed from the safety of cover and took to the air.

She picked up the stock and a hypodermic tube filled with lubricant, greased the ears on the receiver, attached the barrel, and snapped the fore-end into place. Walking to the gun rack she placed the shotgun gently in a slot and returned to her truck.

Muscles straining, she wrestled a five-gallon bucket onto the tailgate of the truck and began to toss handfuls of bright yellow twenty-gauge shotgun shells into a small pail. She glanced up at the sound of tires crunching on the bluestone drive. Snert leapt to his feet, barking wildly as a vehicle crested the hill. Rommel stood up slowly, wagging his tail uncertainly. Her heart sank as she recognized Chopper's truck. It hesitated, as if he, too, was unsure whether to brazen it out or turn around and leave. After a moment he continued toward the skeet field and pulled in beside her.

He unfolded from the cab, walked to the back of the truck, and lowered the tailgate. Unlocking the vet box that filled the bed he slid a gun case from a cabinet. He looked up at her and smiled tentatively. "Not the most orthodox of places to carry your shotgun, but it does have the advantage of a sturdy lock," he said. Laying the case on the tailgate he began deftly assembling his gun.

His thick, dark hair, going gray at the temples, was jammed under a baseball cap emblazoned with Udder Edema. Snert, excited to see him after a long absence, yipped and strained the bounds of his chain. Rommel sat, quietly assessing the new arrival and Snert's frenzy. Chopper walked over and knelt in front of Snert, burying his face in the warm black and white fur around his neck. He looked at Rommel and grinned.

"Isn't that Marge Cameron's Rottweiler?" he asked.

"Yes," said Lanie shortly.

Chopper laughed. "Betsy got you again, did she?"

"It's only temporary."

"Right!" He hesitated. "You getting ready to shoot?" he finally asked.

"Yes."

"Mind if I join you?"

"It's a free country." She was well aware it was a courtesy to allow others to shoot with you, but she wasn't feeling particularly courteous where Chopper was concerned.

Undeterred, he wiped his hands on a rag, put in ear protection, and slipped on shooting glasses and a glove. "I'll open up the high house if you get the low one."

"Sure," she said to his back as he strode off without waiting for a reply. She walked to the house, orange bits of shattered targets and ejected shotguns shells crunching under her feet. The metal door rattled noisily as it rolled up to reveal cases of targets stacked almost to the floor of the loft above her head. She removed the wooden cover from the window and peered out. "Clear!" she yelled, before flipping the switch to turn on the target machine. The trap flung a target, and Lanie marked its trajectory before it shattered on the ground sixty yards away.

For the next hour she and Chop worked their way through the eight stations of the number four field four times, alternating pulling targets and shooting. "Pull!" and the occasional "good shot" was the only conversation. When they finished, Lanie re-loaded the low house trap, locked the door, and tossed the empty target boxes into the dumpster. The sun was beginning to set over the long-leaf and loblolly pines that bordered the far edge of the fields. Her stomach grumbled and she glanced at her watch, reminded that she hadn't put anything in it today but coffee.

She walked back to the picnic table and began disassembling her shotgun. Chopper put his gun back in the truck and walked back to where she was standing. "Great shooting," she said as she wiped down the barrel.

"Thanks. You did really well yourself."

He sat down on top of the picnic table, feet on the bench. "What happened to your head?" he asked.

Lanie gently fingered the line of stitches on the back of her head, the sutures stiff under her fingers. "Guess I didn't do such a great job of hiding it," she said with a rueful smile.

He smiled back. "Actually you did, but I couldn't help noticing when the breeze lifted your hair. What happened?" he asked again.

"If you must know, someone broke into the tack room and tried to steal some saddles. I walked in on them and got knocked in the head."

His dark brows creased in concern. "I'm sorry to hear that. Any idea who it was?"

She shook her head. "It was already dark by the time I got home. Whoever it was had broken out the light bulb in the tack room. Probably just kids." She closed the lid on the gun case. "They also broke the window in my truck. Betsy interrupted them when she stopped by for dinner. They didn't get a chance to take anything from the truck either."

He nodded slowly. "Did she get a look at them?"

"By the time she realized what was going on they'd taken off through the pasture. She wasn't able to follow with the truck."

"Sounds like kids all right." He gave her a bright smile. "The important thing is you weren't seriously hurt. Broken windows can be replaced. You can't."

"Like you'd care."

"You know, Lanie, we *did* live together for five years. I care about what happens to you."

"Really? "

He gazed out over the skeet fields and took a deep breath. "Why are we doing this? I thought we had a good relationship, that we were happy. Next thing I know you're telling me to pack my shit and leave." It was apparent from his tone that his ego was still smarting.

"Oh, come on Chop! You were just as miserable as I was. Always snapping and snarling at me, coming in at all hours with no explanation of where you'd been. Cell phone ringing at all hours of the night."

"I'm a veterinarian, for Chrissakes! It's my job to get called out at all hours! You know that." He cut a look at her and took a deep breath. "I really thought everything was fine," he said in a calmer tone.

"I'm sure you did. As long as you got fed and got to watch your football, basketball, and golf, everything *was* fine. For you." She took a deep breath. "And let's not forget the sex. The only time you were ever nice to me was when you wanted sex." She lowered her voice, trying to get a grip on her emotions. Chopper held his tongue. "But the final straw was finding out you were seeing someone else," Lanie said.

"Who the hell told you that?"

"Are you denying it?"

Chopper sat there looking shamefaced, unwilling to meet her gaze.

"Chop," Lanie said more quietly, "you made it clear over a year ago that you didn't want anything permanent from this relationship. We don't want the same things anymore. You've found somebody else, so it's best we go our separate ways and be done with it."

"I have *not* found somebody else! Why do you keep saying that?"

"I'm not discussing this anymore, Chop." Lanie loaded the gun case in the truck, unhooked the dogs, and put them in the back seat. "Even if you won't admit it, you know relationships require nurturing. They require you to consider the other person's feelings…"

"Feelings," he snorted. "That's all women go on about. Men don't want to talk about feelings."

Angry now, Lanie stepped toward him. "You know what? I don't give a damn anymore, Chopper. The only thing I want to know is were you, or are you still, sleeping with Angela?"

"No!" he said. "She's married to my friend!" He gazed at her steadily.

"In name, at least."

She wasn't sure if she was referring to Angela's marital status or the status of Chopper's friendship with Chris.

ten

Lanie kicked her shoes off on the back porch and walked into the kitchen in her socks. She filled the dogs' bowls with kibble before pouring herself a Crater Lake vodka and a splash of water and sitting down at the kitchen table. She took a sip and thought about her confrontation with Chopper earlier. Rommel finished his kibble, padded over from his empty food bowl, and gently laid his big head in her lap, soulful eyes turned up to hers. She rubbed his silky ears between her fingers, and he closed his eyes and leaned into her. His pleasure in this simple act made her smile. "If only men were so simple, Rommel," she said. The shrilling of her cell phone on the kitchen counter interrupted her thoughts.

"Where are you?" asked Betsy. "If you don't hurry all the good appetizers will be gone."

"Damn!"

"You forgot, didn't you?"

Lanie had, in fact, forgotten about the Black and White Ball. She groaned.

"Don't even think about backing out on me, Lanie Montgomery," Betsy threatened. "I paid a lot of money for this table and I'm expecting you to show up."

"Give me thirty minutes, Bets, and I'll be there."

Snert and Rommel trotted after her as she ran to her bedroom, shedding jeans and flannel shirt as she went. She turned on the shower and grabbed the only ball gown she owned, a gold sequined dress with spaghetti straps, from the closet while the water got hot. Twenty-five minutes later she was speeding toward the Harness Track in Pinehurst, struggling into her heels at stoplights, cursing the cold breeze that flowed in the broken window and mussed her hair. She turned left into the track, crossed over the railroad tracks, and then turned right toward the Fair Barn. Leaving her truck with the valet, she gave her ticket to the giggling teenage volunteer at the door and entered.

She loved the building, which was built by the Tufts family in 1917. In winter and early spring she enjoyed getting up early to watch the trotters and pacers at their morning training sessions at the track before grabbing breakfast at The Track restaurant. She reveled in its restoration, glad to see its mission-style splendor preserved, and its place as an integral part of Tufts' original Pinehurst Village validated. These days, it served as a venue for everything from the Black and White Ball to quilt and antique shows.

Inside, the humane society staff had transformed its austere interior. Lanterns hung from the exposed roof trusses that soared more than two-and-a-half stories overhead and cast their soft glow on men in tuxedos and women in colorful ball gowns. Tables groaning with silent auction items donated by local businesses lined all four walls.

Lanie plucked a glass of wine from a passing waiter and smiled as a woman dressed in red satin strolled by accompanied by an elegant black Great Dane sporting a dog's tuxedo vest. Several Dalmatians and black Labs mingled through the crowd with their handlers. On the far wall were crates filled with cats and kittens, all either black, white, or some combination thereof. The walls were hung with over-sized black and white photographs of animals available for adoption from the local humane society. She looked around for Betsy. Not seeing her, she sipped her wine and strolled along reading the biographies and back-stories that accompanied each photograph. At the end of the row she turned and surveyed the crowd. Agent Donovan, she saw, was cornered by Giselle and looking like he wanted to be elsewhere. Bryan and Chopper had their heads together, deep in serious conversation. As if he felt her eyes on him, Bryan looked up and smiled. Chopper scowled at her. Across the floor she finally spotted Betsy, dressed in a severe black pantsuit and creamy silk blouse, talking animatedly with Fred Harris, an elderly gentleman dressed in a tartan evening jacket. She caught Lanie's eye, flashed a cheery grin, and waved her over.

Donovan intercepted her. "May I have a word, Ms. Montgomery?"

"What brings you here?" asked Lanie.

"Just keeping an eye on things," he replied. His eyes narrowed. "Care to tell me what you were doing at Southeast Raleigh Prison earlier today?"

"My! Word certainly does get around. What possible interest could you have in my visit to see Joy?"

"Everything about this case is my business."

Lanie feigned innocence. "I was there simply as a friend."

"Your acts of friendship may well result in unintended consequences."

"Agent Donovan, as I told you before, I was just helping a friend by collecting some personal items. Which, I might add, I turned over to you."

"After I asked you for them." He looked at her intently for a moment. "I'll be keeping an eye on you, Ms. Montgomery." He walked away.

She stuck her tongue out at his back.

"That was very adult," Betsy said, walking up behind her, followed by Fred Harris. "Glad you could finally make it." She smiled. "You remember Fred, don't you? He bred Tattered Colors."

"Of course I remember Fred," Lanie replied. "And Tattered Colors as well. He was quite a racehorse."

She offered her hand to Fred Harris who shook it gingerly, his fingers gnarled and swollen with arthritis. "It's a great pleasure to see you, Lanie," he said. He had piercing blue eyes set in a face full of wrinkles and a thatch of white hair shorn close to his round head.

"Lanie's in need of a good boyfriend, Fred. If you know anyone suitable let us know," said Betsy.

Lanie blushed with embarrassment. "Betsy!" she protested. She turned to the old man. "Please excuse her, Fred. She's obviously been over served." He laughed and leaned in, whispering loudly in Lanie's ear, blue eyes sparkling. "Pinehurst may be a small pond, my dear, but it's well stocked!" He winked. "Especially for someone as lovely as you."

"You're very kind."

"Come on, Lanie, I'm starved," said Betsy impatiently. Waving goodbye to Fred Harris, she dragged Lanie toward their table. Lanie looked back and smiled at Fred, raising her wine glass in a silent toast. He winked, and saluted her with his own.

Betsy wove her way through the mass of people with Lanie in tow, stopping to chat along the way. As they made their way toward their table they came face to face with Chopper. Standing next to Angela, handsome in his tuxedo, he was surrounded by a laughing crowd. It seemed to Lanie that they all had a smile and a good word for him. The men slapped him on the back and asked how his golf game was progressing. The women, especially Angela, flirted outrageously. Chris sat at the table, a scowl on his face, idly swirling the wine in his glass, conversing with no one.

"I'm surprised they're even here tonight," said Betsy, as she waved and smiled at the group. "It seems a little soon after

Marge's death to be whooping it up, don't you think?"

"You'd think so," said Lanie quietly, turning away from the sight of Chopper with his arm around Angela. "Let's go grab something to eat, Betsy. I haven't eaten all day."

When she and Betsy reached the buffet, they loaded their plates, re-filled their wine glasses and made their way to their table. Doug and Giselle were already seated, talking with a couple Lanie didn't recognize. Next to them were Jo Ann Williams and her husband, Joe Agresta. Jo Ann patted the empty chair beside her. "Come sit and tell me how you're doing. We need to catch up."

Lanie sank down beside Jo Ann, suddenly tired. The emotional toll of the day, both with Joy and Chopper, had finally caught up with her. "I'm hanging in there, Jo," she said. "This murder, and Joy's arrest, has really taken it out of me."

"Joy had nothing to do with Marge's death," said Jo Ann emphatically, "and the truth will come out. Mark my words." Like many people in town, Jo Ann had contributed to Joy's competitive aspirations by throwing her considerable influence behind her. In addition to her job as chief operating officer of an investment company, Jo Ann served on several local boards, and was active with the hunt club.

"I hope you're right. I went to Southeast Raleigh Prison this morning to see her. I felt terrible for her when I saw her in an orange prison jumpsuit. They had her hands and feet shackled."

"That's awful!" Jo Ann replied. "Well, let me know if there's anything I can do." As if she wanted to turn the conversation to something more pleasant, she said, "Was that Fred Harris you and Betsy were talking to earlier?"

Betsy chimed in. "Yep. It's good to see him out and about. He's an FFV, you know," she continued, popping a shrimp into her mouth and washing it down with a sip of wine.

"A what?" asked the woman sitting across from Betsy, her expression puzzled.

"First Family of Virginia." Betsy reached over to Lanie's plate and snagged a stuffed mushroom. She put it in her mouth and chewed thoughtfully. "He's rich as Croesus. Owns an equine insurance company that insures big-time race horses all over the world, and a famous stud farm in Upperville, Virginia. He's bred some really fine Thoroughbreds, including Tattered Colors. If that horse hadn't had a bad break from the gate, I really think he would have ended the Triple Crown drought."

"What's his connection to this area?" asked Jo Ann, a relative newcomer to Southern Pines.

"He spent a lot of time here when he was younger. You know, riding to hounds, dancing the night away at the Carolina with the likes of Marge Cameron. He married a local girl. She died about ten years ago, but he continues to spend a considerable amount of time here during the winter months." She looked around and gestured at the Fair Barn. "He's really big into historic preservation. Spends winters in Pinehurst, though he pretty much keeps to himself, and goes back to Upperville when the weather gets too oppressive here."

Lanie turned as a shout of laughter rose from the party at Chris and Angela's table. Chris stood up and fell on his face. Chopper tried to help him to his feet, but Chris shook him off and walked unsteadily toward the buffet. One of the servers filled a plate for him and helped him back to his table, where the plate sat untouched. Chris removed the cork from another bottle of wine and refilled his glass, glaring at Angela, seated across the table, engrossed in conversation with Chopper. Lanie turned back around and tried to concentrate on the gentleman to her right, a guest of Joe and Jo Ann's. Another shout of laughter arose from behind her, and Lanie and Jo Ann turned to find

Chopper striding in their direction, Chris on his heels. Chris had a bottle of red wine in one hand and a brimming wine glass in the other. He waved the glass at Chopper, slopping it on the floor in the process.

Betsy glanced up from her plate. "Uh oh."

"Hey Crisafulli," Chris said belligerently, "don't run off! I need to talk to you." His blue eyes were bloodshot, and he swayed on his feet.

Chopper kept walking toward the far exit, passing Betsy's table without a glance. "Some other time, Chris," he said.

"Don't walk away from me, Chopper!" Chris yelled. "I'm talking to you!"

People at nearby tables looked up and conversations fell silent as Chris followed Chopper, sipping at his wine. "You've avoided me long enough," he continued, his words slurring.

Chopper stopped and turned to face him. "Look Chris," he said calmly, "it's obvious you've had a little too much fun tonight and you're not in any condition to talk." He looked around at the curious crowd. "Besides, this isn't the place."

"Is that right?" Chris stared at Chopper for a moment. "What's *obvious* is that you've been paying a little too much attention my wife." He flung the contents of the glass in Chopper's face and swung the wine bottle at his head. Chopper ducked, throwing himself at Chris and tackling him. They fell onto Betsy's table, bringing it crashing to the floor and knocking Jo Ann from her chair. Screams rose as they rolled and punched at each other. Lanie could feel wine soak into the bodice of her gown and trickle through her scalp onto her neck.

"Someone stop them!" she cried as the two men wrestled on the floor, scattering guests and tables as they went.

As Lanie bent down to help Jo Ann to her feet she saw Donovan step from the crowd. He reached down, grabbed Chris by his jacket, and flung him into the arms of a group of men standing at the periphery of the fight. Then he pulled Chopper to his feet. Blood streamed from a gash over Chopper's right eye and mingled with the wine stains on his shirt. Lanie snatched a napkin from a nearby table and held it to his head, trying to stop the bleeding.

"Thank you for intervening," she said, glancing up at Donovan. "I don't know what the hell Chris was thinking!"

"My pleasure Ms. Montgomery." He smiled. "You certainly do manage to be at the center of things." He took in her wine-stained hair and gown before turning his attention to Chopper. "Do you want me to call the police?"

Chopper took the napkin from Lanie and re-applied it to his eye. "No thanks," he mumbled through lips already beginning to swell. "Chris is drunk out of his mind. I'm sure he'll call me tomorrow, apologizing all over himself." He gave Donovan a lop-sided grin. "Just make sure he doesn't try to drive home. He needs to sleep it off."

The crowd began to surge toward Chopper and excited conversation once again filled the room as Chris was led out the door. Chopper was soon lost to Lanie's view. She turned and watched Donovan move back through the crowd. He stopped and spoke to a tall, elegantly slim woman, dressed in silvery, floating chiffon. Her blond hair was swept back in a sleek chignon at her neck. Diamond earrings flashed as they both turned to look at her. His head bent solicitously to hear what she was saying, then he took her gently by the arm and they melted into the crowd.

Lanie felt heat rise and spread through her face and neck. *Damn him!* she thought, looking down at her ruined gown. But she didn't know if she meant Chopper or Donovan.

Lanie stormed into the kitchen and slammed the door behind her so hard that it sprang back open, still fuming from the incident at the Fair Barn. Snert and Rommel, in anticipation of her arrival, were sitting at attention, ears pricked and heads cocked, their faces a study of puzzlement at her demeanor as she strode to the kitchen table and threw down her beaded purse.

"I had a great time tonight, thank you for asking," she said, kicking off her heels. They flew through the air and bounced off the kitchen wall. Rommel slid down to the floor and whined. Though he couldn't hear her words, he had no trouble reading her body language. She peeled off her ruined dress and stepped out of it, leaving it in a crumpled heap on the floor.

"You two stay here," she said, walking toward the back of the house. "I don't need your help, and I'm in no mood to trip over you."

She returned twenty minutes later with a bottle of Crater Lake vodka in one hand and a glass in the other. Her hair was wet from the shower, face bare of makeup. She wore her favorite bathrobe, old and worn and soft, belted loosely around her waist. The stone kitchen floor felt cold and rough under her bare feet. She filled her glass with crushed ice and vodka. Taking a sip, she turned to find the dogs exactly where she'd left them.

"Here's to the end of a perfectly delightful evening," she said, raising her glass to them. Snert slid down alongside Rommel and wagged his stump of a tail uncertainly, showing his anxiety by yawning widely.

Lanie sighed. "I haven't even started to tell you what happened and you're already bored. I thought you were supposed to be man's best friend." She added another splash of vodka to her glass, then propped against the counter, looking at them. "Glad to know I can count on you for some sympathetic ears." She looked at Rommel. "Well, two ears anyway."

"Who are you talking to?"

Lanie screeched and spun around, clutching her bathrobe closed. The dogs leapt to their feet, snarling, the hair on their backs bristling. Donovan stepped through the partially open door and closed it gently behind him. "It's dangerous to leave your door wide open like that. Somebody could walk right in and you'd never know it."

Lanie's fright turned to anger. "What are you doing here?"

He shrugged. "I stopped by to make sure you were okay." His gaze took in the dress heaped on the floor. "Too bad about your dress."

Lanie topped up her glass again. She was feeling a little tipsy, but was beyond the point of caring. "I'm sure you and your date were quite entertained by the whole thing. Along with the rest of Pinehurst and Southern Pines."

"My date?"

"You know, the Ice Queen."

He looked momentarily puzzled before comprehension flitted briefly across his features. "Ah yes, the Ice Queen." He rubbed his jaw in an unsuccessful attempt to hide a smile. It didn't improve her mood that he was laughing at her.

"Let me guess," she said, "you've finally come to arrest me for removing sweat pants and tee shirts from the scene of a crime."

Ignoring the comment, he pointed to her glass. "Any chance there's another one of those available?"

She threw her hands in the air. "Sure! Why not serve a strange man a glass of vodka in my bathrobe in the middle of the night. It will be the perfect end to a really, really perfect day!" She stalked into the dining room and returned with a glass, which she set down on the counter. "Help yourself."

Donovan walked to the refrigerator, filled his glass with ice, then poured two fingers of vodka and took a sip. "This is really good," he said appreciatively. "What is it?"

"Crater Lake. It's from a very small distillery in Oregon."

"Tell me again who your friends are?" he asked, undoing his bowtie and the top button of his starched tuxedo shirt as Snert cautiously approached him.

"The Aussie is Snert. The Rottweiler is Rommel. The Rottie's only here until Betsy can find a permanent home for him."

Donovan held out his hand and whistled softly to Rommel.

"Don't bother," she said. "He's deaf."

"That must make life difficult for him."

"He doesn't know he's deaf. Snert serves as a hearing ear dog, for lack of a better term. And he knows hand signals." She signaled to Rommel, who got up and trotted over to her.

"Impressive." Donovan poured another splash into his glass and raised the bottle to Lanie. She shook her head. He leaned against the counter next to her and took another sip. "So what was the fight between Chris Cameron and Dr. Crisafulli about tonight?" he asked.

"Why do you ask?"

He smiled. "Do you always answer a question with a question?"

For the first time since she got home, Lanie smiled. "Chris started it. Apparently he thought Chopper was a little too chummy with Angela and wanted to make an issue of it. When Chop tried to walk away, Chris got even angrier, and threw his wine in Chop's face. Then he hit him with the wine bottle."

"Do you think the accusation about Angela was valid?"

Lanie hesitated. "I think Chris was drunk, is what I think. He and Chopper have been friends a long time."

"You didn't answer my question."

"Why are you asking me? Why don't you ask the parties involved?"

"I plan to." He took another sip of his vodka. "Joy Alexander's going to be arraigned tomorrow morning."

"She didn't kill Marge Cameron."

"The evidence says otherwise."

"Evidence can be misleading. You're wrong on this, Donovan. You need to spend your time looking for the real killer. There are lots of people who had better motives to kill her than Joy. Like whoever benefits from her estate, for a start."

He nodded. "I got a copy of her will and trust from Henry Banner today."

"So, where's the money go?"

"Her estate is worth close to a billion dollars. The trust provides that half of it, including the farm, goes to the U.S. Eventing Team. The other half goes to her lineal descendants."

"Like I said, that's a lot of motive for murder. Since her only son is dead, that makes Chris her closest lineal descendant." She thought for a moment. "Who gets the horses?"

"The horses were owned in her sole name."

Lanie knew that meant the horses would now be owned by the estate and Marge's executor, presumably Henry Banner, would control if, when, how, and where they competed. If she and Betsy could figure out who murdered Marge, Joy might have a chance of riding in the selection trial. She made a mental note to contact Henry Banner.

Donovan's voice interrupted her reverie. "Why do I get the

feeling you're not going to heed my advice to stay out of this?" he asked.

"No harm in asking a few questions," she responded.

"There could be a lot of harm in asking questions." His brown eyes gazed at her steadily. "For you."

"I thought you had your murderer locked up in Southeast Raleigh Prison."

eleven

Lanie stuffed the last bite of country ham biscuit into her mouth and licked the grease and mustard off her fingers. *The Pilot* was open on the glass-topped table in front of her, stained with the drippings from her breakfast. The murder of Marge Cameron and the progress, or lack thereof, of the investigation, along with fund-raising results from the Black and White Ball, an appeal from the police department to remain on the lookout for an escapee from Cherry Hospital, who'd now been on the loose from the state mental hospital for four months, and preparations for the 2014 U.S. Open, both men's and women's, vied for attention on the front page of the Pinehurst newspaper. It was only published twice a week, and as today was Thursday, the news wasn't technically new any more, but she'd been so busy she hadn't had time to read a paper.

Her view from the front porch of the Old Towne Deli took in the village green, and beyond it the stately edifice of the Holly Inn, which graced the opposite corner, its white clapboards gleaming in the morning sunlight.

She sipped her coffee and watched a mockingbird dive bomb anyone it felt was a threat to its fledglings, which were nestled in the hedges that lined the walkway that ran beside the deli. Tiring of the game, he landed in the forsythia bushes in front of the deli and entertained Lanie with his repertoire of stolen songs and sounds. Lanie cocked her head, puzzled, as an oddly familiar tapping sound emanated from his sleek gray and white body. She listened for a moment longer, then burst out laughing at his perfect imitation of a putter striking a golf ball. "Get out of here," she said, shooing him away with her paper. Offended, he returned to harassing passing tourists.

The morning air wafting onto the porch was cool, with no hint of the humidity that would descend in the months ahead. The sparkling morning matched Lanie's mood. An overnight storm had rumbled through leaving the grass bejeweled and the streets washed clean. The information Donovan had imparted in her kitchen two nights before made her anxious to talk with Henry Banner. A blaring car horn interrupted her thoughts and caused the mockingbird to retreat momentarily to the safety of a nearby holly.

"Damn Yankees!" muttered the waitress from inside. She slammed the cash register closed. "They don't have any manners!"

Lanie grinned. "That's rich, coming from you Shawn Frances," she yelled through the open door, "seeing how you're a transplant yourself."

"Oops!" Shawn stuck her head out the door, three plates balanced on her forearm and a fourth in her spare hand, and smiled broadly. "You weren't supposed to hear that. Besides, they should have closed the borders after I got here." She winked at Lanie before bustling to deliver the plates to a table of golfers.

"That's what all the damn Yankees say." Lanie tucked a loose strand of blond hair behind her ear and stood up. She shook the crumbs from the waxed paper that had wrapped her biscuit over the porch railing for the mockingbird and slipped a tip under the salt shaker. Leaving the folded paper for the next diner, she strolled across the street to Henry Banner's office.

Barbara Rheiman pressed the telephone receiver tightly to her face and nodded her head as she assured Mr. Peterson *The New York Times* and *The Wall Street Journal* was, indeed, ready and waiting for his daily visit to First Colony's offices. As Mr. Peterson was deaf as a post, this assurance was being delivered at Barbara's maximum volume.

"No trouble at all, Mr. Peterson," she shouted, as she wiggled her fingers at Lanie. "Sorry," she mouthed silently before turning her attention back to the phone. "I *said,* no trouble at all, Mr. Peterson. We're happy to share our *Wall Street Journal.* I'll see you when you get here."

"Sorry," she said aloud as she returned the receiver to the cradle.

Lanie laughed. "I could hear you when I got off the elevator."

"Poor old soul," Barbara sighed. "You'd think he'd at least bring some Krispy Kreme's with him if he's going to spend every waking moment of the rest of his life planted in our reception area. I could do with a couple of glazed doughnuts right now." Her generous mouth parted in a grin. "Not that I *need* them, you understand, but when did that ever stop me." She smoothed her skirt over an equally generous lap and perched her reading glasses on her nose.

She was a stocky, energetic woman with a smile as generous as her nature. She'd been in charge of the Pony Club as long as Lanie could remember, keeping order among both children and ponies with a firm, but gentle, hand. She also led the hill toppers for the hunt club, a thankless job if ever there was one.

"I'm sure it's more for your company than the reading material. You might have a secret admirer on your hands."

Barbara snorted. "Secret? What's so secret about it?" She sighed. "Hell, if he were thirty years younger I might even consider it."

"Is Henry around? "

"Nope. He's taking the day off. Since he announced his retirement, he's been a little more casual about his comings and goings."

"I don't blame him for that. Have they found a replacement yet?"

She shook her head. "Still interviewing and taking their sweet time about it, too. Can't seem to find anyone to suit them." She turned back to her keyboard. "You can find him at home, though. He said he was going to spend the day in his potting shed."

"Thanks, Barbara." She grinned. "Enjoy your visit with Mr. Peterson."

Barbara smiled and shook her head without looking up from her keyboard as Lanie closed the door behind her.

She pulled into the circular drive in front of Henry Banner's house off Connecticut Avenue, turned off the engine, and looked around in delight. Flowers, tall, short, spreading, climbing, filled every available space. The warm, golden stone of the house shone in the soft sunlight, its chimney softened by English ivy.

She walked around the side of the house, following the sandy path through Japanese maples and dogwood, weaving through lush stands of hosta and Siberian iris just beginning to emerge from the richly loamed beds. A waterfall trickled musically down to a small pond. Through the gate she could see a potting shed, its door open to the morning breeze. The back garden was as artful as the front, with the back half devoted to an extensive herb garden. As she approached the potting shed, Henry stepped out, stopping abruptly when he spied her.

"Hi Henry! Sorry to show up unannounced, but I need to talk to you. I hope you don't mind."

"Not at all, not at all, my dear. I thought I heard a car pull in." He was dressed in gardener's pants and stout clogs, his hands full of dried sprigs. Pruning shears peeked out of the pocket of his apron. Pushing his glasses back up his nose with the back of his wrist, he continued, "If you don't mind talking while I work, you're more than welcome. I'm in the middle of mixing up some lotions."

Lanie followed him into the potting shed and looked around, filling her lungs with the smell of dried sage, oregano, basil, and a dozen other herbs and flowers that hung upside down in bunches from the ceiling. A well-worn butcher's block stood in the middle of the room, its wooden surface dominated by a large mortar and pestle. A sizable dip in its center was testament to its many years of service. The shelves of a large Welsh cupboard held rows of small jars and bottles in an array of shapes and colors.

Henry deposited the herbs in the bowl and wiped his hands on his apron.

"What a wonderful place! It's so warm and cozy. And it smells like heaven!"

Henry looked around in satisfaction, basking in the praise. "Yes, it *is* a wonderful place. I spend many hours here working on my concoctions."

"You make lotion? As in hand lotion?"

"Oh yes. It's a skill I learned from my grandmother. I make candles, soaps, creams for the hands and face, all kinds of things."

"Do you sell them?"

"Heavens, no! I give them as holiday and special occasion gifts to friends and a select few of my clients. Some of them suffer terribly from arthritis and the like, you know. I like to think that my potions help ease their aches and pains. It keeps my grandmother's memory alive in a rather meaningful way." He picked up the pestle and began to grind the herbs.

"Are you excited about retiring?" asked Lanie.

"I am indeed, young lady. This old warhorse is ready to hang up his harness and be put out to pasture. I only wish they'd get on with the business of finding my replacement." He looked up from his work. "You should seriously consider throwing your hat in the ring."

"Me?" Lanie said, surprised. "Why do you say that?"

"Because you have a tax and estate planning background, you're an attorney. And you have the people skills. You know as well as I do that the rich are not like you and me." He bent back to his mortar and pestle. "Give it some thought."

"Maybe I will," she replied, surprising herself. She loved her store and the people who frequented it, but, if she were honest with herself, she missed the complicated problem solving of her former profession. She tucked the thought away for another time.

"Now," he said, "how can I help you? I know you didn't come here to talk about my retirement."

Lanie smiled. "Not exactly." She leaned against the butcher block table and picked up a sprig of rosemary, twirling it in her fingers.

"Look, I know that you can't tell me, specifically, what Marge's trust document says, but I'm doing some asking around, trying to figure out who killed her and why. I was hoping you could point me to some people who knew her really well and who might be willing to talk to me about her." She paused, inhaling the scent of the dried rosemary sprig in her hand. "Joy Alexander's sitting in a maximum security prison in Raleigh charged with murdering Marge Cameron, and I believe the police have the wrong person."

"Aren't those sorts of questions best left to the experts?" he replied. "Like Drew?"

"Henry, you and I both know that Drew is a perfectly capable county sheriff, but he's way over his head with this murder. They've essentially taken the investigation away from him."

He nodded. "I see your point, but asking questions, without knowing who you're asking them of, could put you in danger."

"The way she was killed points to a very personal motive. Whoever did this is someone who knew her, and knew her well. Someone who had a very personal reason for wanting her dead. The key to finding that person may lie in her past."

Henry was quiet for a moment, the only sound the crunch of the pestle against the rough stone bowl. After a pause he said, "If you're hell bent on pursuing this, I suppose you could start with Gladys Wrenn. They were life-long friends and very close. If anyone would have the sort of information you're looking for, it would be Gladys. I can't guarantee that she'd be willing to talk with you, but you could try."

"Anyone else?" Lanie pressed.

"There's her former housekeeper, Mary O'Connor, though Mary is a very different kettle of fish from Gladys. Fiercely loyal to Marge and ill as a snake to boot. Plus she's suffered from dementia for some time now. I don't know that she'd even be capable of talking to you."

"It's a start, Henry," Lanie said. "Where would I find these two ladies?"

"A little bit of luck there," he said with a smile. "They're both out at The Meadows, Gladys in the assisted living area and Mary in the Alzheimer's ward."

Lanie straightened a row of small, cobalt blue jars drying upside down on an old towel. "Henry, how did a woman who worked as a housekeeper all her life manage to amass enough money to live at The Meadows?"

"Mary worked for Marge from the time she was a young woman. Nearly fifty years, if I had to guess. She never married and had no family that anyone knew of. When she started having cognitive issues, Marge wanted to make sure she was taken care of in her old age." He looked up at her over the round lenses of his glasses. "She set up a trust for Mary's benefit and funded it with a million dollars, in addition to paying her monthly residence fees." He pointed a finger at her. "You did *not* hear that from me."

"That was good of her," Lanie said wryly, pushing a jar around with her finger.

Henry looked up at her tone. "Marge could be a bitch with a capital B, but she could also be extremely generous when the notion struck her."

Lanie's jar shuffling exposed a gnarled root lying in the center of the table. She peered closely at it, then smiled with delight. "I haven't seen horseradish in a hundred years!" she said, reaching for it. "We used to dig it up and take it home to my mother to make home-made horseradish—"

"Don't touch that!" Henry gasped as he grabbed her arm. "That's not horseradish, it's aconite! Just touching it with your bare hands could be deadly!"

Lanie jerked her arm out of his grasp and rubbed it where his fingers had dug in. "What do you use it for if it's so dangerous?"

"I use it, in extremely small doses, in some of my lotions to ease the pain of arthritis and neuralgia, and it's often effective for sciatica. Its more common name is wolfsbane or monkshood. The ancient Greeks called it "woman killer" because women were supposedly more susceptible to its properties. It's said that on the Isle of Ceos they gave it to old or infirm men who were no longer of any use to the state."

The potting shed became dark as shifting clouds covered the sun, and Lanie shivered in the sudden chill wafting from the stone floor. "Sounds gruesome! So how does it kill you?"

Henry's eyes lit as he warmed to his subject. "It's still widely used in Chinese medicine today, either in the form of an infusion or in lotions. The therapeutic dose is very close to a fatal one, which can cause heart or respiratory failure. It's even been reported to cause the tactile hallucination of having fur or feathers! Unfortunately, as it doesn't affect the brain, the victim remains alert even as the body shuts down. Even applying it to unbroken skin can be fatal, if the lotion contains too much of it."

"That's creepy!"

He shrugged. "There are many common varieties of garden plants that are toxic to man or beast, and a number of them are used in homeopathic therapies. They aren't bad simply because they're poisonous. Goats, for instance, can die from eating azaleas, and wild cherry is poisonous to horses." He pulled on a pair of surgical gloves and removed the tuber from the table, placing it carefully in a drawer and locking it. "So, to finish the lesson, the symptoms of aconite poisoning are numbing and tingling in the fingers and toes that spread to the rest of the body, then intense pain, irregular breathing, and slowing of the heart rate. Death comes from heart failure or asphyxiation." He smiled broadly at her as he pulled off the gloves with a snap and dropped them in the trash. "The moral of the story is to savor monkshood for its beauty in the garden, but keep the kids and pets away. I have neither, so it isn't a concern for me. In fact, I have quite a stand of it by the koi pond."

Something about Henry's smile made Lanie anxious to go. "Well," she said, "I think I've taken up enough of your afternoon. Thanks for letting me drop in. And I promise to keep our conversation about Mary's trust confidential."

"Anytime, my dear. Anytime." Henry turned to the shelves behind him and removed a small, translucent jar. "Please take this as a small gift from me."

Lanie felt a small shiver of apprehension, but she shook it off, telling herself not to be melodramatic. She removed the top, and breathed in the scent of lemongrass. "Thanks, Henry. That's very sweet of you."

"When you run out, just drop by for more! You're always welcome."

She turned to leave.

"And, Lanie," he said. She turned back. "Be careful."

Lanie left him standing in the doorway of the potting shed, hands in his apron pockets, rocking to and fro on his heels.

twelve

Lanie lost no time calling Gladys Wrenn to see if she could schedule an appointment, though she kept the reason as vague as possible. Gladys suggested Lanie stop by her apartment after lunch that afternoon. On her way over, she called Betsy and made plans to get together later that evening and compare notes. "You bring dinner and I'll supply the wine," Lanie offered.

"You're on," said Betsy. "I plan to make Cameron Farms my last stop of the night. I'll talk to Chris and then head your way. I should be there by eight or so."

"See you then."

Lanie pulled up to the gatehouse at The Meadows and gave her name to the security guard, hoping that Gladys Wrenn had remembered to put her name on the visitor's list. The guard waved her through and she parked her truck and entered the spacious foyer of the main building a few minutes early for her appointment. She joined the queue of elderly residents filing into the elevator. Just as the doors were closing, a tiny hand flicked out to stop them. Lanie caught her breath sharply. The doors retracted, and a diminutive woman, mail clutched tightly to the bosom of her 1950s-style housedress, scurried in. "Could you press the third floor for me, dear?" she quavered. Her silver head barely reached Lanie's chest.

"You could lose your fingers doing that," Lanie admonished.

"I haven't yet," she said, as she crowded in next to Lanie, her bright blue eyes twinkling. "I have a guest coming and that elevator takes forever to get back to the lobby. Besides," she whispered, "being in this place with the living dead makes you crave a little risk!" She peered around her stack of mail at the car's other occupants, then winked at Lanie.

Lanie laughed out loud. When they reached the third floor, she held the elevator door for her. They both turned right and began to walk down the broad hallway.

"Who are you going to see, dear?"

"Mrs. Wrenn."

She stopped and looked Lanie up and down. "Are you Lanie Montgomery? You sounded so young on the phone!"

"You're Mrs. Wrenn?"

"I am," she replied. She continued briskly down the hall to her apartment, pushing the door, which was ajar, open with her foot. "Come in, dear, and have a seat. They were serving strawberry shortcake at lunch. It looked so good I picked some up for the both of us. At my age, it's always best to eat dessert whenever you have the opportunity. You never know if you'll make it to dinner!" She cackled as she deposited the dessert and mail on the counter in the small galley kitchen and turned to look at Lanie. "Let's have some tea with our shortcake, shall we? Or would you prefer coffee?" Both hands were clasped over a bosom stained bright red with juice from the strawberries.

"Tea is fine," Lanie said, fighting the urge to giggle. The shortcake had obviously taken a beating on the ride up in the elevator, pressed close to Gladys Wrenn's breast.

"Make yourself at home in the living room and I'll be right there with the tea and cake."

Lanie took a seat on the sofa and glanced around the living room. Every available space was crammed with heavy, antique furniture, and every surface was covered with photographs and knick-knacks. A large gilt-edged mirror hung directly across from the entry to the kitchen, and she watched Gladys Wrenn's reflection as the elderly woman unfolded a step stool, slowly stood on it, and, standing on her tiptoes, reached into the cabinet over the sink. Lanie held her breath, releasing it only when her hostess made it back to the safety of the linoleum floor, teacups and saucers in her gnarled, shaky hands.

"It's so nice of you, dear, to come by and see me," Mrs. Wrenn said as she busied herself with the tea and laid out the flattened shortcake on a tray.

"Can I help you, Mrs. Wrenn?" Lanie asked.

"Oh, thank you dear, but no. I've got it under control." She exited the kitchen, and Lanie watched breathlessly, again, as the tray, laden with cups, saucers, teapot, and cake, made its unsteady way down to the tea table in front of the sofa. Mrs. Wrenn sank onto the soft down of the sofa, feet barely touching the oriental carpet, and poured a cup of tea, which she passed shakily over to Lanie.

"Henry called and told me to expect to hear from you," she said. "He said you were writing an article on Pinehurst and Southern Pines in the early nineteen hundreds. How flattering that you would want to talk to me."

Lanie said a silent prayer of thanks for Henry's paving of the way, though she felt a twinge of guilt at not being completely honest with Gladys Wrenn.

"Actually, Mrs. Wrenn, it's really more to satisfy my personal interest in the time period, particularly as it relates to what Pinehurst and Southern Pines were like."

"Call me Gladys, please dear. Mrs. Wrenn sounds so old!" She smiled and passed Lanie a plate of strawberry shortcake. My driver's license may say I'm ninety, but I still think of myself as twenty-something. It's a big shock to look in the mirror and see reality." She turned her head and looked out the window, blinking back tears.

"Those were different times. I've been thinking about them a lot since Marge was killed." Gladys continued.

Lanie was grateful for the opening. "Did you know Mrs. Cameron well?"

"Oh yes, we were best friends since childhood! We made our debut together. That's where she met her husband, Richard Cameron. He was much older than she, by some twenty years. And very wealthy. When they returned to North Carolina after his diplomatic post was terminated because of the war, we picked up right where we'd left off. My mother used to say that we were soul mates, Marge and me."

She paused to take a breath and a sip of her tea. "I wish you could have known Pinehurst and Southern Pines in those days." Her eyes sparkled with the memories. "Parties at the Carolina and the Highland Pines. Hardly anyone remembers it anymore, but it was elegant in its day. We danced to famous orchestras from New York, fox hunted, played golf and tennis." She sighed and set her cup back in its saucer, the fine bone china ringing. "What elegant, wonderful days they were, my dear. When we were young and beautiful and hadn't a care in the world, and we could still turn men's heads." Her bright blue eyes flashed and Lanie could see the young woman she'd once been shining from them as Gladys cut them coquettishly in her direction. She leaned forward and whispered across the tea table, "Marge was especially popular with the men, you know." She sat up and brought the teacup to her lips again, peering at Lanie over the rim. "I used to warn her she needed to be careful of her reputation, but she'd just toss her head and laugh. She said, 'If they're talking about me, they're giving someone else a rest.'"

"Where was the Highland Pines Inn? I grew up here, but I don't remember ever seeing it," said Lanie, trying to change the subject.

"I'm afraid it burned to the ground dear. January 1957, I believe it was. Anyway it was cold, I remember that." She paused briefly, and then continued the narrative. "I know it was 1957 because my Johnny was getting ready to turn twelve. Marge's little Richard was born the following year. "She was no youngster when she had Richard, thirty-six or thereabouts. He was a surprise to both of them, as you can imagine." She paused. "There was a lot of talk around town that a local writer was more likely his father than Richard Sr."

"Really?"

She nodded. "Oh, yes. If so, Richard treated him like his own, and it was a good thing he came along or Marge would have been all alone when Richard Sr. died. I think little Richard would have been about twelve or thirteen at the time."

Lanie was desperate to get off the subject of Marge's youthful sexual peccadilloes, and on to something more current. "I understand her son died at an early age."

"Yes, the same summer I lost my dear husband, John. July 4, 1979, to be exact. It was a tragedy that Marge never really recovered from." She picked up a forkful of cake and chewed it thoughtfully. "Well," she said, putting down the fork and looking at Lanie, "you don't, do you? You never get over the loss of a child. I tried desperately to see Marge after the accident, called every day and went by but that nasty housekeeper of hers, Mary O'Connor, always put me off. Said Marge wasn't up to seeing anyone." She flashed an indignant look at Lanie. "Wasn't up to seeing her best friend!" She pulled a linen handkerchief from the bosom of her house dress and twisted it in her hands. "I never did understand what Marge saw in her, with those cold eyes and her fundamentalist religious beliefs, pew jumping, speaking in tongues, and the like. She always had her nose stuck in a Bible! I used to tease Marge that Mary must have something really bad on her. She'd just laugh and say, 'Oh Mary's Mary.'"

"So how did young Richard die?" Lanie asked to get her back on track.

"Car accident," Gladys said succinctly. "Went off the road at a high rate of speed not terribly far from the house. He crashed into a bridge and the car burst into flames. By the time the fire trucks got there it was all over. Richard was burned beyond recognition."

"How awful! He couldn't have been very old."

"Twenty-one," Gladys answered solemnly. "She buried him the next day."

"The next day!"

"Oh yes, dear. Marge said she wasn't going to subject herself, or Richard, to a bunch of busybodies lining up at the funeral home to gape at her and gossip behind her back. And she had the pull to get it done. I didn't blame her really. She wanted it done and Marge always got what she wanted. They had a private graveside ceremony at the family cemetery, with just a handful of close friends, and that was that."

"How sad to be left with no one."

Gladys refilled both teacups and sat back against the sofa cushions. "There was a rumor that Richard was involved with the daughter of the gardener and planned to run off with her. The family came back with them from Richard's last posting, you know. The gardener, his wife, and young daughter. I remember the daughter was quite lovely, but being from that island she was very dark skinned, and, of course, spoke with an accent. I put the rumors down to small town gossip, but I stopped by to see Marge one day, and she and young Richard were having a terrible argument. Marge shouting that she forbade him to see her again and threatening to disinherit him if she found out any different, and Richard shouting back that he didn't care what she did, that she could keep her money. Then he stormed out. There must have been some truth to the rumors after all."

"What happened to the young lady?"

"She and her family left town in the middle of the night a few months before Richard died. Just melted away! No one ever heard from them again." Gladys's gaze returned to the window, her expression thoughtful. "That was quite the summer for deaths and disappearances. Marge had a groom that she really liked, if you know what I mean," she said looking back at Lanie. "She said he reminded her of Richard, which I thought a shocking thing to say…" She trailed off, lost in memories of long ago.

"Marge Cameron was having an affair with one of her grooms?"

"I wouldn't dignify it by calling it an affair, but, yes, she was having a fling with him. He was very young, in his early twenties, and terribly good-looking. She said he developed aspirations of moving out of the stable and into the big house. Of course she laughed at him and things got really nasty. He threatened to expose the relationship, so she fired him." She shrugged. "He took off and was never seen again. Frankly, I think it was for the best."

"Gladys, do you have any idea who would want to harm Marge. Anyone in her life currently, or someone from her past?"

"I can't think of a soul, dear! Such an awful way to die! And her ninety-two years old." Gladys's face crumpled. Lanie reached over and picked up her hand. "I'm sorry, Gladys. I didn't mean to distress you." Mrs. Wrenn wiped her tears with the handkerchief she'd stuffed in her sleeve.

"You haven't, dear," she said softly, but Lanie knew she was putting a brave face on it.

"Did she seem different lately? Anxious or worried about anything?"

Gladys sniffed, wiped her nose, and tucked the handkerchief back in her sleeve before replying. "Well, now that you mention it, she was very agitated after Myrtle left."

"Myrtle?"

"Myrtle Simpson, a mutual friend of ours." She wrinkled her nose in disdain. "A silly woman, really. More money than sense, if you know what I mean. From what Marge told me, Myrtle apparently lost a lot of money in a horse deal." She looked at Lanie with disbelief. "What in the world would possess an eighty-something-year-old woman to buy a horse?" Lanie shook her head. "If her husband had still been around that would never have happened, I can promise you that," she said firmly. "Anyway, Marge said Myrtle got conned by some slick talker and she was looking into it for her."

"Was this recently?"

"Oh yes! Myrtle came to visit Marge about three weeks ago and that's when the whole sorry story came out."

"Do you think Myrtle would mind if I gave her a call?"

"I can't see why she would. Let me get her number for you." Gladys got up and went to the secretary, where she rummaged around for a few minutes before returning to the sofa with a satisfied smile. "Found it!" she said. "Myrtle was always more Marge's friend than mine, actually, but we exchanged Christmas cards every year." She leaned across the tea table and handed Lanie a tattered envelope. "I held on to that because she's moved recently and I haven't had a chance to update my address book."

Lanie pulled her checkbook out of her purse and wrote the information on a deposit slip, then handed the envelope back to Gladys. "This is very helpful, Gladys. I'll give her call and see if she'll share the particulars with me."

"Good luck, dear! " She poured herself another cup of tea and settled back for another chat. "Did you know that she had a relationship with Dr. Salisbury, as well?"

"Really!" Dr. Salisbury had been a local psychiatrist who practiced out of his house and also worked at the state mental hospital about thirty miles away. As Lanie recalled, he had been an undistinguished looking man, short and portly and somewhat stooped. Lanie was surprised he would catch the eye of Marge Cameron.

"Oh yes. Marge's appetites were many and varied. In fact, she was carrying on with that groom while she was seeing Doc Salisbury. He must have asked her to marry him every year up until he died. Doc, that is. But Marge wouldn't have it. She liked having him dance to her tune. She loved to juggle men, and the more there were to juggle, the better."

Lanie smiled. "More power to her, I guess. I can't seem to keep one relationship in the air, much less two or more."

"Are you married, dear?"

"No. I don't have the knack for sustaining relationships."

"Well, just make sure you don't end up like that Mary O'Connor," Gladys said, rattling her teacup into its saucer. "If it weren't for Marge, she'd be living out her years in a Medicaid-funded facility and not in the lap of luxury here at The Meadows." She snorted. "I never did understand why Marge was so loyal to her." She leaned toward Lanie and lowered her voice conspiratorially. "Marge paid all her expenses *and* set up a trust to take care of her if something happened to Marge." She straightened up. "Of course, Henry probably shouldn't have told me that, but it's such a small community here, and Henry's been taking care of *my* trust since John died, along with a number of others I know of. Such a dear man! He's always bringing his 'girls,' as he calls us, a little something to brighten our day.

Candied pecans at Christmas and lotions for our old, arthritic joints. I don't know what we'll do without him to lean on. And he always stops in to see Mary, even though she doesn't always recognize him any more."

So much for confidentiality, thought Lanie. She gathered up her purse. "I've taken up enough of your time today, Gladys. I enjoyed meeting you, and hearing about Pinehurst and Southern Pines."

"Come by for a chat next time you're at The Meadows, dear. I have nothing but time."

As Lanie stood in the elevator waiting to be returned to the lobby, she thought over her conversation with Gladys Wrenn, and her interest in Mary O'Connor was piqued. She glanced at her watch. When the elevator reached the lobby she went to the reception desk and asked for Mary O'Connor's room number.

"She's in the Alzheimer's facility," said the elegantly coifed lady behind the desk whose name tag read "Cynthia Josephs, Volunteer." "It's a little confusing to find, so why don't you come with me, I'll show you the way." Lanie followed her through a maze of hallways until they reached the Alzheimer's unit. Ms. Josephs punched a large button to the right of the door and the lock clicked. "Unfortunately, the residents in this unit have a habit of wandering so they have to stay behind locked doors," she said as she pushed the heavy door open. "When you're ready to leave just have one of the staff let you out. Mary's in room 107." She pointed. "Just down on your left."

Lanie thanked her and continued on alone. She stopped outside Mary O'Connor's room. The door was partially open and the sound of a television at full volume assaulted Lanie's ears. She knocked and, when she received no answer, gently pushed the door open.

A wheelchair sat in front of the television, its occupant slumped forward against the restraints that held her captive in the chair. Her chin rested on her chest and arthritis-gnarled hands were clasped around the battered King James Bible that lay in her blanketed lap. The heat in the room was stifling. Lanie could feel sweat begin to trickle down the small of her back and bead on her forehead. Bright afternoon sunshine spilled through the picture window and pooled on the carpet. Over the television was a whiteboard with a large smiley face drawn in red. It proclaimed that today was WEDNESDAY, the month was MARCH and the weather was SUNNY.

Lanie slowly approached the figure in the wheelchair and bent down so she could see her face. The woman's eyes were open, staring unfocused at the floor in front of her. Her gray hair, looking like it hadn't seen shampoo in the recent past, was pulled back tightly from her forehead and gathered in a bun at the base of her neck. Lanie reached out and gently touched her bony wrist. "Miss O'Connor?" she said, over the noise from the television. Rheumy gray eyes, clouded with cataracts, rose slowly to meet hers. She gripped the Bible tighter in one talon-like hand and grabbed Lanie's arm with the other. Her mouth opened, revealing gaps in a row of teeth that looked like broken fence posts. She began a high-pitched keening that made the fine hairs on Lanie's arms stand on end.

"I know you, missy!" Mary O'Connor screeched. "You think you can get away with murder because you have a certain look, don't you!" Her head shook with the strain of holding it up and her body struggled against its restraints. Lanie jerked her arm away and stepped back. "Well I'm here to tell you you're wrong!" Mary O'Connor continued. She beat her fist weakly on the Bible. "He lives! He lives! The proof of it is in this Good Book and you'll pay the price for your sinful, arrogant ways!" She was breathing heavily from the tirade. Spittle pooled at the corners of her mouth and ran down her chin. Her voice dropped to a snarl. "The proof's in this book," she repeated. "He who lives by the sword shall die by the sword."

Horrified, Lanie began to back slowly toward the door. She heard soft footfalls behind her and turned around to find an aide, dressed in yellow scrubs decorated with blue hippopotamuses, standing in the doorway. She beckoned to Lanie, and closed the door firmly behind them as they stepped back into the hall. "Mary givin' you a hard time?" she asked.

"I'm sorry," Lanie stammered. "I didn't intend to upset her. I just wanted to stop in and say hello."

"Don't worry about it, dear. Just goes to prove no good deed goes unpunished." She smiled. "To hear Mary tell it we're all going to hell in a hand basket, so don't take it personal like."

"I think she thought I was someone else. She scared the crap out of me when she started screaming like that." Lanie took a deep breath and let it out slowly.

The woman nodded, tightly permed, gray curls bouncing. "Pro'bly thought you were tryin' to steal her precious Bible. Happens all the time, hon. We have the hardest time givin' her a bath 'cause she won't let go of that thing. Last time we tried to take it, she gave Sherry Persons a nasty bite on the arm." She patted Lanie's arm with a small, warm hand. "Pitches a pure-tee fit! Did the same thing to poor Henry Banner last time he stopped in to see her. Threw his nice little present on the floor and hollered like the devil hisself was after her."

"Has Henry been by to see her recently?"

She nodded again. "Used to come right reglar, but I think even he's given up on the old witch." She smiled to take the sting out of her words. "C'mon hon, let's get you out of here and back into the real world."

Lanie followed her back down the hall to the locked door and waited while she punched in a series of numbers. Thanking her, Lanie slipped through and managed to find her way through the maze of halls back to the parking lot. She unlocked the door and slid into the truck. Despite the heat in the closed vehicle, she shivered.

Lanie looked at the clock. Almost nine o'clock and no sign of Betsy. The bottle of Sauvignon Blanc she'd opened an hour ago was almost empty and her stomach was rumbling. She'd called Betsy's cell phone a half dozen times, but it had gone straight to voice mail. She dialed Myrtle Simpson's telephone number again, this time leaving a message asking her to call regarding Marge Cameron.

Hearing the crunch of tires in the driveway, Snert and Rommel bolted for the back door. Lanie shoved them back with her foot, wineglass in hand, and opened it to find Betsy, arms empty, standing tiredly on the stoop.

"It's about time you got here," she exclaimed. She peered more closely at Betsy. "What's the matter?" she asked, pulling Betsy in the house. "You look like you've seen a ghost!"

"You got another one of those?" Betsy said, gesturing at the wine glass. Her face was drained of color and she looked dazed as she sat down heavily at the kitchen table. Her hand shook as she took the glass from Lanie and downed half of it in a single swallow. "I forgot all about dinner," Betsy mumbled.

"I don't give a damn about dinner! What's wrong? What's happened?"

Betsy shivered violently. "I stopped by Cameron Farms to talk to Chris."

Lanie sat down across from her and picked up her free hand, shocked at its coldness. She chafed it between her own hands trying to impart some warmth. "And?" she prompted.

"And I found him dead in Bubba's stall." She began to sob. Lanie looked at her uncomprehendingly, unable to assimilate the words.

"Dead?"

Betsy nodded. "It was awful, Lanie!" Words began to pour out, as though a dam inside her had given way. "When I drove up his Jag was parked outside the barn, so I went looking for him. The horses were banging around in their stalls, wild-eyed, like there was a grizzly loose in there. I walked down the aisle, and when I got to Bubba's stall he was standing against the back wall, covered in blood and sweat, quivering and snorting. He had welts all over his body, and his right eye was swollen shut." She took a breath. "That eye needs to be looked at by an ophthalmologist."

Betsy gripped Lanie's hand so hard she could almost feel the bones grind together, the pain hard and sharp. "When I opened the stall door, Chris was lying there with his head caved in, lying on top of a dressage whip. I wouldn't have recognized him except for his wedding band." Chris and Angela wore distinctive matching trinity bands with interlocking circles of silver, gold, and platinum. "It looked like Bubba had kicked him to death, and I knew there was no way he was still alive, but I checked for a pulse anyway. And then I called the police." She trailed off, staring vacantly into her empty glass.

Lanie slowly peeled Betsy's fingers from her own and stood up. "Don't move, Bets. I'll be right back." Rommel sat down next to Betsy's chair, and she dug her fingers into the back of his neck. He leaned his body into hers, as if trying to transfer his warmth to her. Snert followed Lanie to the bathroom where she dug around in the linen closet until she unearthed a hot water bottle. Returning to the kitchen she set a pan of water on the stove, and while she waited for it to heat she opened another bottle of wine and refilled Betsy's glass. When the water was hot she poured it into the hot water bottle, wrapped it in a towel, and placed it in Betsy's arms. Betsy hugged it to her chest with one arm, keeping the other hand gripped tightly on Rommel. After a few moments, her teeth stopped chattering and she loosened her grip on Rommel, then took a shuddering breath.

"It was awful, Lanie," she repeated.

"I can't even imagine. It must have been a terrible shock." She rubbed Betsy's arm soothingly with the palm of her hand. "Are you sure he was kicked?"

"I thought that at first." Betsy paused. "But while I was waiting for the police to arrive I had time to think about it. The stalls are too small for Bubba to have kicked him in the head. He wouldn't have been able to get the elevation he'd need." She thought for a moment. "I don't think Bubba killed him, Lanie. I think someone bashed his head in, beat Bubba with the whip, and then put Chris's body in the stall to make it *look* like he kicked him." She put the cooling water bottle on the table and held her glass up for a refill. "When the police got there," she continued, "they finally let me move Bubba to another stall. I flushed the eye out and put some drops in it and told Rick to put some compresses on it. He'll be lucky if he doesn't lose it." She put her arms on the table top and rested her forehead on them wearily. "Then Angela showed up and Drew had a hell of a time keeping her out of the barn. She was hysterical. Screaming and crying and begging to see Chris. They finally got her back to the house, and the EMTs got permission from her doctor to give her a sedative."

"I'm sorry, Betsy," Lanie said, standing up and stroking her hair. "Let's get you to bed. You're exhausted." Lanie led her to the guest bedroom, sat Betsy in a chair, and pulled off her boots. Betsy fell into bed, fully clothed, and Lanie tucked her in with the hot water bottle. Snert jumped up and curled next to her, putting his head on her shoulder. Betsy was asleep before Lanie turned off the light.

Down the hall, Lanie gave Rommel a boost into her high four-poster bed. She needed the big dog's comforting presence. Sleep eluded her, and she lay awake for much of the night while the moon rose and set over the trees, wondering what was happening to her town.

thirteen

It was déjà vu all over again, Lanie thought as she took her seat in the church. The same horse-drawn hearse that had carried his aunt to her final resting place just a week ago now waited outside The Good Shepherd Episcopal Church to take Chris to join her. The same press corps, augmented by crews from as far away as Charlotte, Atlanta, and D.C. milled around across the street, as close as they were allowed to venture.

Angela, still reeling from shock and the sedatives Doc Evans had prescribed, leaned heavily on Bryan as he led her to the front of the church. Betsy was quiet and withdrawn. Chopper, seated across the aisle, looked haggard and worried. As they filed out behind Reverend Tomick, the media pressed forward against the restraining cordon of highway patrolmen and county sheriff's deputies, shouting questions at Drew and Agent Donovan, neither of whom deigned to answer.

Betsy drove to Lanie's farm on Old Mail Road, where they changed clothes. Lanie stood on the back stoop and watched as Betsy led Lanie's retired event horse, Taenzer, out of the barn and mounted. "See you there?" asked Betsy.

Lanie nodded and watched as she rode down the driveway and disappeared around the bend. She closed the door on Rommel and Snert as the crunch of bluestone heralded the arrival of Hugh and Julie Jennings, their beautifully restored carriage pulled by a matching pair of Holsteiners. They rolled to a stop and Lanie climbed into the back seat, dressed in tan riding breeches, a tweed hunt coat, and tall boots. Hugh and Julie were similarly dressed.

They made their way to the Aiken Foundation property, the footfalls of the horses in the sandy, pine-needle-covered trail as muted as the conversation, and made their way toward the cemetery. Chris, like his aunt before him, was to join the select few buried in the cemetery nestled under swaying pines. As they climbed the last hill to the clearing where the gravesites were located, Lanie stared out over the tree tops at the drop zone Fort Bragg used for training maneuvers. From this elevation you could sometimes see the paratroopers, floating like tiny thistles on a stiff breeze.

Hugh deftly maneuvered the carriage into the semi-circle that was beginning to form in front of the open grave. Lanie winced at the raw earth piled to the side of it and turned her attention to the horses and riders appearing through the trees. The only sound was the jingle of bits and the creaking of carriage wheels. Betsy arrived on Taenzer and took her place next to the Jenningses' carriage. Doug Erikson rode up on his favorite gray hunter, resplendent as a cardinal in his hunt jacket. His wife, Giselle, arrived separately in a phaeton driven by their groom. Jennifer rode up from the direction of May Street and stopped next to Betsy. The scent of pine resin wafted over the clearing, stirred by the slight breeze that set the pine needles shimmering and dancing overhead. Lanie smiled at Bud Jackson and his lovely quarter horse mare, Darlin', as they squeezed in on the other side of the Jenningses. Bud doffed his white ten-gallon hat and smiled.

Angela appeared through the trees riding sidesaddle, her long, black riding habit flowing over the tops of her highly polished boots, her face and feelings masked behind a filmy black veil. Chopper, mounted on his big bay hunter, rode beside and slightly behind. He dismounted and stood beside her as the powerful Fresians, straining to pull the heavy hearse through the deep sand, approached the gravesite at a solemn walk, where Reverend Tomick awaited them.

Drew, in his sheriff's uniform, and Donovan, in a double-breasted designer suit, stood behind the curving, semi-circular wall, bracketed by a stone fox and hound, and surveyed the crowd of horses and riders as the reverend delivered his eulogy.

When it was over, he gave the reins of his horse to Bryan and scooped up a handful of the sandy soil piled beside the grave. He gave it to Angela, who kneed her horse forward and tossed the sand onto the coffin as it was lowered into the grave. She backed her horse away and waited quietly while Chopper added a handful for himself.

He was followed by Doug Erikson, and Bryan, who dismounted and added their contribution, then walked their horses to the edge of the clearing, away from the crowd. Bryan put his arm around Doug's shoulders and bent close to him, speaking quietly. Suddenly, Doug shrugged him off, slugged him in the face, then mounted his horse, turned, and trotted off through the woods, acknowledging no one as he left. Giselle sat frozen in the phaeton, her face stony.

Jennifer dismounted and hurried to Bryan's side, dabbing at his bloodied face with a handkerchief as Giselle ordered the groom to drive her home. Drew and Donovan eyed the crowd, gauging reactions. Lanie scrambled out of the carriage and rushed to join Jennifer. Betsy, hearing the whirring of zoom lenses rode Taenzer at a gallop toward a group of news photographers who had arrived, unnoticed, on foot. They scattered in the face of her charge like guinea hens fleeing a hawk and retreated back toward May Street, with Betsy hard on their heels.

"You need to have Doc Evans look at this, Bryan," said Jennifer. "I think your nose might be broken." Bryan, with a little help from Jennifer and Lanie, got slowly to his feet. Jennifer asked what everyone else was thinking, but was too polite to voice: "What did you say to him to make him punch you like that?"

"Nothing," he mumbled, tilting his head back in an attempt to stop the bleeding. "I just said what a terrible thing it was, what happened to Chris, and that I knew he was sorry about not making things right before it was too late." He looked around at the curious crowd. His eyes came to rest on Lanie. "You know, after that altercation they had in your store."

Lanie groaned silently, and wished fervently that Bryan had kept his mouth shut. She watched as Drew spoke into the microphone attached to the shoulder of his uniform and then turned to walk toward May Street and his car. She caught Donovan's eye before he, too, turned and made his way back through the trees in Drew's wake.

The store was quiet when Lanie finally arrived, still trying to process what had happened at Chris's funeral. Rhonda and Dave were unloading the truck and stacking orders in the back room. Both were eager to hear about the incident at the cemetery. News had spread fast and they listened intently as Lanie recounted what had happened.

"That doesn't make any sense," said Rhonda. "Why would Doug hit Bryan?"

"Maybe Doug killed Chris," Dave said, "and tried to make it look like an accident." Lanie's fears at the cemetery were coming to pass: people were already starting to indulge in wild speculation. "Maybe his conscience is getting the best of him and Bryan hit a raw nerve," Dave continued.

"Maybe he's trafficking in drugs," Rhonda said.

"You're both going overboard," said Lanie. "Doug has oodles of money. Why would he take a risk like trafficking in drugs? And besides, how would Marge's death fit in?" She smoothed her eyebrow with a finger. "I can see Doug getting his panties in a wad if he thought he'd been slighted in a horse deal, but I can't see him bludgeoning an old woman to death."

"In my opinion, people who don't have anything to hide don't act like he did this morning," said Dave. "Something's going on."

"You're right, Dave," said Lanie, "something *is* going on. The question is what?"

"I've got to shove off." Dave waved and strode toward the loading dock and his truck. "See you later this week."

"I'm sure he's gone to spread the speculation far and wide," Lanie said to Rhonda. "I don't want any more of that talk in here."

Rhonda ducked her head and disappeared into the back.

The front door opened and Betsy walked in with Rommel and Snert. "They were going crazy at your house so I took pity on them and brought them with me," she said, leaning on the glass counter top.

"Did you catch any photographers?" Lanie asked.

"No, but I did put the fear of God into them." She grimaced. "Ghoulish bastards!" She looked at Lanie. "What'd you find out?"

She briefed her on the aftermath of the confrontation between Doug and Bryan. "I wish Bryan had kept his mouth shut," she said vehemently. "Once this gets around town, everybody's going to be suspecting there's more to the story."

"Do you think he was insinuating Doug had something to do with Chris's death?" asked Betsy when she'd finished.

"Even if that wasn't his intention, it's what people are going to think." Lanie rubbed her eyebrow again, deep in thought. "The two deaths have to be connected, Betsy. Whoever killed Marge also killed Chris. The odds of two members of the same family getting killed by different people are beyond belief. The good news is that Joy's off the hook. She was in jail when Chris was killed, and, if the killings are connected, that means she didn't kill Marge either," Lanie stated.

"You're going to have a hard time convincing Drew and Donovan of that. In fact, you're going to have to hand them the real killer on a silver platter."

"I intend to do just that."

Lanie drove out to her house after work to feed the dogs before heading back into town for a meeting of the group of volunteers who maintained the maze of riding trails that crisscrossed the Aiken Foundation. On the way to Bryan's, she slowed as she approached Cameron Farms. Knowing Angela had no family and would probably be alone in the rambling house, she decided to stop and check on her. As she put on her turn signal, Chopper's truck pulled out of the drive and sped toward town. She sat, undecided, then turned into the driveway and pulled up in front of the house, killing the lights. For a few moments she sat in the truck, listening to the sound of her ticking engine.

She got out and stood at the front door, took a deep breath, and lifted the heavy knocker, letting it fall with a clang. When Angela opened the door, her eyes widened to see Lanie there.

"What do you want?" Angela asked.

"I just wanted to make sure you were okay," Lanie said.

Angela opened the door wider, and reluctantly motioned her in. Lanie followed her to Chris's office where Angela took a seat, leaving Lanie standing awkwardly in the middle of the room. Stale cigarette smoke hung in the air.

"Is there someone here with you?" Lanie asked.

"Like who?" Angela said, her eyes narrowing.

"I don't know," Lanie stammered. "A family member? A friend?"

"I don't want anyone hanging around watching my every move," she retorted.

"Angela, I'm really sorry about Chris. I wish there was something I could do or say…" Lanie trailed off, uncertain how to proceed.

"Oh, let's not mince words, shall we?" Angela said. "It's been a long time since Chris and I lived as husband and wife and everybody knows it." She took a cigarette from the pack on the deed box by her chair and rolled it in her fingers. She smiled ruefully at Lanie's shocked expression. "Did you think I didn't know he was banging every working student that walked on the property? Not to mention all the Grand Prix groupies that trailed after him like love sick puppies." She gazed fixedly at the unlit cigarette. "I gave up trying a long time ago." She stood up and paced restlessly over to the window, unlit cigarette still in her hand.

"He was good to me, in his way," she said reflectively. "I certainly haven't lacked for anything all these years." She stared out the dark window and fell silent.

Lanie felt an unexpected pang of pity for Angela. So beautiful, so wealthy, and now so alone. She'd had everything except a real relationship, and money was a poor substitute for a loving partner. She realized with a start that Angela could now be in line for Marge's fortune. That would go a long way toward assuaging any sense of loss over Chris.

Angela turned slowly from the window. "Drew and that SBI agent were here earlier." Her eyes narrowed. "I thought Bubba killed Chris. Why would the police be snooping around? They should be dragging that vicious nag off to the knackers, not badgering me."

"What did they want?"

"They turned the place upside down, asked endless questions that I didn't know the answers to, took a lot of papers and left." She laughed mirthlessly and gestured at the coffee table in front of her. "All they left me with were the bills."

"Did they say why?" Lanie asked.

Angela shook her head.

Lanie sat down on the sofa and eyed the papers scattered across the polished surface of the table. A color photocopy of a picture of Chris sailing over a jump sat atop the detritus of everyday life—entry forms, a feed bill from Lanie's store, utility and credit card bills. His handsome face was intent on the next jump before his horse had fully left the ground. How typical of Chris, she thought, always looking for the next thrill, the next challenge. Never content with the present. "I don't know how much longer I can Bear it!" was written in the margin at the bottom of the page.

"What does this mean?" Lanie asked, showing it to Angela.

She glanced at it indifferently and shrugged. "Probably a little love note from one of his many admirers," she said bitterly.

"Did he seem worried or concerned about anything in the days before he died?" Lanie asked. "Other than Marge's death, of course."

"Playing amateur detective?" Angela said with a sneer, bending her head to the lighter as she finally lit the cigarette. She sucked in a lungful of smoke and blew it out slowly. "As I told the police, we didn't communicate. In fact we rarely saw each other. We might go for days on end and not speak. If he was worried about anything, I'd be the last one to know it."

"I'm sorry," Lanie replied.

"Don't be."

Lanie stood. "I'll be on my way. If there's anything I can do, please let me know."

Angela blew another lungful of smoke out slowly. Lanie thought she looked strangely relieved, like a dog who was expecting a blow that never materialized. She stubbed the cigarette out in a crystal ashtray sitting on the window ledge, and walked Lanie to the foyer.

Lanie stepped out onto the dark porch, and then turned back. "Angela, I really don't think you should stay in this big house all by yourself. Is there someone I can call to come keep you company?" she asked.

"I'll be fine," Angela said, closing the door.

The sound of laughter greeted Lanie as she entered Bryan's small, cozy house on Indiana Avenue a few minutes after leaving Angela. He was host of this month's Trail Blazer meeting and, from the sound of things, it had turned into an impromptu party. Beautiful oriental carpets covered gleaming heart pine floors. A fire burned brightly in the living room, which was tastefully furnished with a few choice pieces. It was amazing what someone's home revealed about them, Lanie mused. Who would have thought Bryan Dawson would be into chintz and Louis Orr prints. Lanie had two of Orr's original pieces, one of a slave cabin in Anson County and one of the court yard at Christ Church in Raleigh. Bryan had what appeared to be the entire collection, mounted in simple frames and hung on stark white walls.

Bryan was seated in an elegant Martha Washington chair next to the fire, a glass of white wine in his hand, surrounded by a crowd eager to hear the particulars of his run-in with Doug Erikson at the cemetery earlier that day. Jennifer arrived with a tray of heavenly scented gingerbread muffins, dripping with icing and still warm from the oven. Chopper came in right behind her, and joined Hugh and Julie Jennings at the bar. He studiously ignored Lanie as he accepted a glass of wine from Rhonda, who was playing bartender.

Lanie waited for the crowd to disperse before approaching Bryan, who reached for her hand and squeezed it. "My face looks like something Picasso did during his Blue Period, doesn't it?" he said with a grin.

She laughed out loud. "It probably only hurts when you breathe, right?"

Bryan shrugged. "I don't think it was me he was upset with," he said. "He just took it out on me. I don't know what's weighing on his mind, but did you notice he and Giselle showed up separately to the funeral? My guess is that things at Fantasy Farm aren't so fantastic." He took a sip of his wine and pursed his lips. "Or maybe he's regretting not making things right with Chris before it was too late."

Chopper took a seat on the other side of the fireplace. "Wouldn't you love to know what was really behind it, though?" he said, stretching his long jeans-clad legs toward the fire. "Not that that's likely to happen. Doug keeps things pretty close to the vest."

"People don't have to share their every thought and feeling, you know," Lanie said. "They're entitled to their secrets."

"That's rich, coming from you," Chopper retorted. "You've never kept a thought or feeling to yourself in your life!"

"You're keeping a few secrets yourself these days," Lanie shot back. "What were you doing at Angela's tonight? I saw your truck pulling out as I was turning in."

Chopper had the grace to flush. "I was checking on Reinmeister. That eye is looking better, but I'm still concerned about it." He tilted his wine glass at Lanie. "What were *you* doing there? Care to share that secret with everybody?"

"I thought someone should check on her," she snapped, "but you beat me to the punch."

Chopper looked uncomfortable. "I never saw her," he muttered into his wine glass.

Bryan, taking pity on him, came to his rescue. He turned to Lanie. "So, how is Angela holding up?"

"She seemed okay, I guess. She said Drew and the SBI had stopped by. They took a bunch of papers, asked her a lot of questions."

Bryan sat up, interested. "But Chris's death was an accident," he said. "Why would the police be interested in his papers?"

Lanie looked thoughtful. "Good point." She sat down on the ottoman in front of the fireplace and stared at the flames, rolling her empty glass between her hands. "It just doesn't seem possible that Chris is gone, that he'll never ride another horse. There was a picture on the coffee table in his office of him riding a horse over a big fence. In Flight, I think it was."

"I remember that horse," said Chopper.

Bryan nodded slowly and sipped his wine. "So do I. He was very talented, but not very consistent. He would be brilliant one week, and crash right through the fences the next. Chris was very frustrated with him."

"He was a lovely animal," Chopper continued. "I always hoped he would settle down as he got older, but colic got him first. I think the stress of competition was just too much for him. Another brilliant jumper dead from colic."

Jennifer and Betsy walked up together, and Jennifer gave them a bright smile. "Are you guys over here telling secrets? You look very conspiratorial, all huddled together in front of the fire."

"No, no secrets being shared here tonight," replied Bryan. "Just speculating about why the authorities would be interested in Chris's papers. It seems pretty obvious he was being abusive to Bubba, and got his skull crushed for his efforts."

"I don't believe for a minute that Bubba killed Chris," said Betsy. "I think someone *wants* us to believe that, but I'm not buying it. After I had time to process what I'd seen when I found the body, I realized it wasn't physically possible for that horse to cause the kind of damage I observed. I think Chris and Marge's deaths are connected."

Lanie shot Betsy a warning look. "It was a slow day at the store so we had nothing else to do except indulge in some idle speculation. We were just playing 'what if.'" She smiled at Bryan and stood up. "I mean, no one likes to think that Bubba would stomp Chris to death. It would give a whole new meaning to the term 'horse trial.'"

Bryan chuckled. "That it would, my dear."

Jennifer shivered. "I think this whole conversation is gruesome. We need to stop all this talk about Chris's death."

"You're exactly right, Jennifer," said Lanie. "I'm going to sample a few of those gingerbread muffins and maybe even wrap one up to have with my coffee in the morning."

She stopped by the bar and picked up a glass of wine as Bryan called the meeting to order.

After the meeting had adjourned, Lanie walked up to Bryan and kissed him on the check. "I hope you're feeling better soon. Stop by the shop when you feel up to it."

Bryan beamed at her. "I'll certainly do that."

fourteen

Lanie was through with morning barn chores and on her way to the store by four-thirty. It would be another busy Wednesday, and she was anxious to get a new shipment of summer breeches and shirts priced and on the shelves before the onslaught began. As she pulled up in front of the store the vestiges of last night's thunderstorm rumbled away in the distance, headed for Raleigh and points east. Broad Street was cloaked in pre-dawn quiet as Snert and Rommel scrambled from the back seat and bounded around the building in the direction of the loading dock, heedless of her commands to come back.

She dropped her purse in the desk drawer and turned on her computer to check the online orders, oblivious to the fact she'd forgotten about the dogs until Snert's shrill yipping pierced her absorption. She ran to the back and flung the loading dock door open.

"Snert, leave that poor cat alone," she admonished him. The only answer was the sound of a metal trash can crashing to the broken concrete of the alley. Snert reveled in chasing the feral cat that made the alley its home, encouraged by scraps Jennifer left on her back stoop when she closed up shop. Snert's frenzied yipping, along with Rommel's deep basso, continued as Lanie walked cautiously down the dark alley to the back of the bakery.

"Damn it, Snert! Come here!" She cursed as she tripped over the overturned metal garbage can, banging her shin hard and sending the can rolling and clanging. The dogs were at Jennifer's back door, Snert scratching and clawing furiously.

Lanie looked up and saw light on in Jennifer's upstairs apartment. A faint glow leaked through the curtains in the kitchen pantry downstairs. She grabbed Snert by the collar and tried to pull him back to the store, but he squirmed out of his collar and returned to Jennifer's back door, yipping and jumping as though trying to leap high enough to see through the curtained window. Rommel's bark added a deep, urgent counterpoint to the Aussie's frenzied efforts.

"What the hell are you two up to? You're making enough noise to wake the dead." She stepped up on the stoop and wrestled Snert's collar back over his head. She tried to see through the thin curtain, looking for Jennifer. The baker's day typically started about four, but except for the faint glow coming through the curtains, the shop was dark. Curious that Jennifer hadn't responded to all the commotion, Lanie put her hand on the knob and opened the door slowly. She pulled her phone from the pocket of her jeans, selected the flashlight app and shined it around the pantry.

The shelves were neatly stacked with institutional-sized bags of sugar, flour, and cocoa. Gleaming copper pots and pans hung over a butcher-block table piled with mail. A color photocopy of a young Jennifer riding a gray jumper was unfolded on top of the stack. Lanie peered at it briefly before she was distracted by Snert, who was digging at the door from the pantry to the kitchen proper. He finally dislodged the door snake tucked there to keep cold air from seeping in. *That's strange,* Lanie thought. *What's it doing on this side of the door?*

The glow from the kitchen was brighter now and seemed to flicker and dance. As she stood there, smoke began to drift under the door and swirl around her feet. She put her hand on the door. It was cool to the touch so she opened it cautiously. "Jennifer?" she called out as Snert streaked through into the bakery, followed by Rommel. Lanie saw flames licking up the walls behind the Viking range. Jennifer was face down on the tile floor, dressed in the clothes she'd worn at Bryan's the night before. Lanie rolled her over and felt her neck for a pulse. Nothing. "Shit!" Lanie cursed under her breath as she grabbed Jennifer by the arms and began to drag her into the pantry. She dropped Jennifer's limp body to the floor and groped around the butcher-block table for her phone.

She dialed 911, waiting for what seemed like hours for them to answer. "The Cosmos Bakery is on fire," she said when the dispatcher picked up, "and Jennifer's not breathing. Hurry!" She snatched the small braided rug from the pantry floor, ordered Snert and Rommel to stay with Jennifer, and re-entered the kitchen. The fire was fiercer now, spreading to adjacent walls, the smoke thick and acrid as she beat at the flames with the rug, trying to make her way to the stove in search of a fire extinguisher. Her eyes streamed tears and her lungs burned from the smoke. The heat was getting more intense with each passing moment. She finally abandoned the effort, retreated to the pantry, and dragged Jennifer down the back steps into the relative safety of the alley, cringing at the sound of her heels thudding down the concrete steps.

Suddenly the alley was filled with the sound of sirens and the flashing of lights as the fire department and EMTs arrived. While the fire fighters unrolled their hoses and turned them on the bakery, Rhonda's boyfriend, John, knelt next to Jennifer. Another EMT led Lanie to the back of an ambulance, where he placed an oxygen mask over her nose and mouth and began to attend to the burns on her hands and arms—injuries she didn't know she'd suffered.

As she sat there trying to make sense of what was happening, Donovan stuck his head in the back of the ambulance. Despite the EMT's protests she yanked the mask off her face.

"How's Jennifer?" she croaked. Donovan shook his head, whether in ignorance of Jennifer's condition or something worse Lanie couldn't tell. Belatedly, she remembered Snert and Rommel. "My dogs! They're in the bakery!" She struggled to get out of the ambulance, fighting off the EMTs restraining grasp. Donovan caught her as she stumbled and fell, folding her tightly in his arms.

"Your dogs are safe, Lanie," he said soothingly, stroking her hair. "They're in the back seat of my car."

"And Jennifer?" she asked again.

He tipped her head back and gazed down at her for a moment, before shaking his head. "She didn't make it." He released her. "You need to go the emergency room and get those burns looked at." He helped her back into the ambulance, then turned and strode back to the bakery as the EMT closed the door and the ambulance began to bump slowly down the alley.

fifteen

Drew and Donovan sat in Drew's office in the Moore County courthouse complex, the autopsy reports for Marjorie and Christian Cameron spread out on the desk between them. Drew's chair groaned in protest as he leaned back and rubbed his hands over the stubble on his jowly cheeks. His eyes, the lids red and swollen, burned from lack of sleep. "What do you think?" he asked wearily.

"Chris's autopsy report says he died of heart failure several hours before Betsy Anderson found him. The head wounds were all post-mortem. The groom, Rick, says he brought the horses in at five and when he went back for night check at seven-fifteen, everything was quiet. Dr. Anderson says she arrived a little after seven-thirty. That means whoever put that body in the stall had about fifteen minutes to cart it into the barn, smash in his head, and leave before Dr. Anderson showed up." He paused. "Whoever it was knew the routine well enough to be reasonably certain they'd have the place to themselves after the groom left." He rubbed his lower lip thoughtfully. "If Dr. Anderson had shown up a few minutes earlier, she might have walked in on the murderer."

Drew brought his chair back to an upright position with a bang. "Why would the killer beat his head in with a blunt instrument after he was dead!"

"To buy some time by making it appear the horse killed him. Or he's playing games with us." Donovan replied. "Whoever it was had enough nerve to sit with a dead body in his vehicle while Rick put the horses to bed for the night."

"I had a call from Hugh Jennings," Drew said. "He's representing Joy Alexander, and he wants us to release her. He's trying to make the case that she was in jail when Chris was murdered, and if the murders are related, which seems likely, she didn't kill Marge either." Drew looked at Donovan intently. "He has a point."

Donovan shook his head. "I don't believe Chris's murderer is the same person who killed Marge Cameron."

"You're saying I have two murderers running loose in Southern Pines?" He glared across the desk at Donovan. "And how does Jennifer fit into all this?" he asked.

"We won't know until we get the autopsy report. The coroner's preliminary finding is that she didn't die from smoke inhalation. She was dead before Lanie Montgomery stumbled onto the fire. I'm hoping Lanie saw or heard something."

Drew sighed and began to sort the reports back into order. Donovan's cell phone rang and he spoke into it briefly. When he hung up he slipped it into his jacket pocket and met Drew's inquiring gaze.

"Don't tell me somebody else is dead," Drew said.

"That was the medical examiner's office. Chris died from a dose of succinylcholine.'

"Isn't that what they give you before surgery?"

"Yes. It's also used in veterinary medicine."

Drew tapped the reports stacked in front of him with a thick forefinger. "Betsy Anderson's a vet."

"So is Dave Crisafulli," responded Donovan. "They both have access to this drug. The question is, did either of them have a motive to kill Chris Cameron."

"Of the two of them, I'd put my money on Chopper."

"Motive?"

"Hell, I don't know!" said Drew, throwing his hands in the air. "Maybe Chris's suspicions about his wife and Chopper were valid."

Donovan nodded. "It's possible. We've also discovered Dr. Crisafulli left Cornell under a cloud. He was suspected of selling ketamine, though he was never charged due to lack of evidence."

"Selling it for what purpose?"

"Its street name is Vitamin K. It produces a high similar to ecstasy. It was quite popular a few years ago."

"So maybe Chopper and Chris were selling the stuff. Maybe Chopper supplied it and Chris peddled it. He traveled all over the country going to those horse shows. Lord knows they wouldn't be the first drug dealers that had a falling out."

"It's a theory. We need to talk to both Dr. Anderson and Dr. Crisafulli."

"I feel like I'm groping in the dark," Drew said angrily. "Someone, or according to your theory, more than one person, is killing off people right and left. The citizens of Southern Pines are up in arms. My phone's ringing day and night."

"When we find out what connects the victims, we'll find our killer." Donovan stood up. "One of them, anyway. I'm going to talk to Dr. Anderson," he said as he walked out, closing the door softly behind him.

sixteen

Night was falling when Donovan finally tracked Betsy down at Cameron Farms. The fluorescent lights in the barn aisle illuminated the jagged wound on the chestnut mare's shoulder as Betsy and Donovan walked down the brick aisle, Donovan carrying a steel pail of hot water from the vet box on the back of Betsy's truck. He sat on a stack of hay bales and watched as she examined the wound. She began to debride and irrigate it while the tranquilizer she'd injected began to work. Pulling on surgical gloves, she laid out sutures and bandaging, throwing the wrappers on the floor at her feet. The mare's head drooped to her knees as the tranquilizer took effect, her lips loose and eyes half-closed while Betsy made her preparations. Rick held the lead rope in one hand and gently scratched between the mare's ears, murmuring softly to her.

Betsy looked over the mare's back at Donovan as she started stitching, her reading glasses perched on the end of her nose. "So what did you want to talk to me about?"

"Tell me what you know about Dave Crisafulli."

"Chopper?" She tied off a suture and snipped it off. "Are you asking in a professional capacity or a personal one?" When Donovan didn't answer she shrugged and continued. "Chopper's a good vet, one of the best diagnosticians I've ever run across. He was a big star at Cornell before he moved down here." She used scissors to cut off additional ragged flesh from the edge of the wound before she continued. "Do you remember the race horse War Effort?" She glanced up at Donovan.

He shook his head.

"He was highly touted as the next Triple Crown winner. He didn't accomplish that, but he won some pretty big races." She paused. "Then he dropped dead in his stall. Allegedly from colic."

Donovan raised his eyebrows.

"Yeah, well, it happens occasionally. But in this case there were rumors flying around that the owners had War Effort done in for the insurance. That happens, too, probably more than we know. Or can prove."

"Wouldn't he have been more valuable standing at stud?"

She nodded agreement. "He would've. Except that he was gelded as a two-year-old. Geldings have to work for a living."

"Ah."

"Ah, is right. Anyway, Chopper did the necropsy on the horse and had a gut feeling he'd been electrocuted, but he had trouble finding any solid evidence. On the face of it, it looked like a simple colic attack." She paused and scratched her nose with the back of a hand. "The owners were putting pressure on the vet school for him to sign off and release the body for cremation so they could collect on the policy. Several million dollars' worth." Betsy flashed a grin at Donovan's low whistle. "He kept at it though, and eventually found two small burn marks that were initially discounted as damage that occurred when the horse collapsed in his stall. Chop postulated that if someone attached electrodes to the horse in those two spots and lit him up, it would look very much like War Effort had died from colic. As a result of his report, the insurance company denied the claim. Unfortunately, there wasn't sufficient evidence to prove the owners were involved so they never got charged."

"If he was on the fast track at Cornell what made him give all that up and move to Southern Pines?"

"The rumor I heard was that it involved drugs, and that's been the end of many an academic career in veterinary medicine. Even if you're not guilty, the rumors cling to you like stink on a skunk, and they're just as hard to scrub off." She gazed thoughtfully at Donovan. "Of course it could have been the owners of War Effort that started the rumors, or even Chopper's ex-girlfriend. She was a fourth-year vet student and didn't take too kindly to being dumped. Hell hath no fury and all that."

"Using drugs or selling drugs?"

Betsy shrugged. "I couldn't say. Could have been either I guess, or even both. Vets have access to a lot of drugs whose street value is a lot greater than their medical value. "

"Like ketamine?"

"Exactly."

"Could you overdose on it?"

"Not easily. It takes a pretty big dose to kill you, administered intravenously and pretty rapidly. If it were self-administered you'd probably pass out before you could inject yourself with a lethal dose."

"Any other drugs come to mind?"

Betsy gazed at him reflectively. "Why don't you quit beating around the bush and tell me what it is you want to know?"

"You said yourself that vets have access to a lot of drugs," he replied.

"And your point would be what?"

"What about succinylcholine?"

"Hardly a recreational drug, but if I were going to kill someone it would be my choice."

He gave her a sharp look. "Why is that?"

"Because it's easy to administer, it kills you quickly, and the best part is, unless you're a pretty sophisticated medical examiner or you have reason to suspect it was used, you probably wouldn't think to look for it." She concentrated on tying off a suture. "Even if you are sophisticated enough to think of it, it's hard to detect because it breaks down so quickly. Horrible way to go, though."

"Why?"

"Because it doesn't make you unconscious. It just immobilizes you. You'd be fully aware right up until you experienced cardiac arrest, but you wouldn't be able to communicate."

"You seem to know a lot about the subject."

"I majored in chemistry," she replied with a smile. "And I was a big fan of true crime books in my youth."

"Where were you on the night Marge Cameron was murdered?"

Betsy looked up in surprise. "You think *I* killed Marge Cameron?" She bent back to her task, a smile on her face. "Well, there have been a couple of times I'd have *liked* to kill her, but I didn't." She studied the wound for a moment before continuing. "To answer your question, I was delivering a foal out at Broad Creek Farm that night."

"And on the day Chris was killed?"

"I was at the vet school with a colicky horse up until I left for Southern Pines. I went straight to Cameron Farms."

"For what purpose?"

"To talk to Chris."

"Regarding?"

Betsy hesitated. "Lanie and I are trying to help Joy. We thought we'd start by asking a few questions. I took Chris and Lanie took Angela."

Donovan frowned. "The person who committed these murders won't hesitate to kill again. I'd suggest you leave the questioning to the SBI."

He stood and walked down the aisle, peering into the stalls and reading the name plates, occasionally stroking a velvety nose pressed to the bars. "Why doesn't Lanie ride anymore?" Donovan asked, his back to Betsy. "Didn't you say she was a top amateur rider?"

"Yep," Betsy said. "She was the best. Almost certainly headed for the Olympic eventing team."

"What happened?" He walked back and resumed his seat on the hay bale, resting his elbows on his knees.

Betsy sighed. "Well, she was riding a client's big slab-sided ex-racehorse over the advanced course at Morven Park. It had poured rain all day and they were one of the last horses to go, so the ground was pretty churned up, and slicker than owl shit." Betsy grimaced, then continued. "Anyway, they approached this down-hill jump made of two elements, one a fairly straightforward log and the second a pair of logs suspended between two trees. The horse left out a stride at the first jump and hung a leg, but he somehow managed to scramble over. They weren't so lucky on the second. He slipped in the bad footing and slid under the jump, with Lanie still on him, and got his back leg wedged at the stifle. God knows how he managed to do that, but he did."

"How'd they get them out?"

"Eventing cross-country jumps are solid obstacles, meaning they don't fall down when you hit them. They had to dismantle it so they could bring in a front end loader to raise it enough to allow them to rotate the horse, free his stifle, and slide him out."

"Did he survive it?"

Betsy looked at Donovan as though he'd sprouted three heads. "Oh, hell no. They euthanized him on course."

"And Lanie?"

"Well, now…" Betsy shoved her hair back from her face with the back of one gloved hand. "That's another story." She peered at the wound and dabbed it with a folded gauze pad.

"It was a relief to everybody when she finally passed out and quit screaming," she said softly. "I don't know which was worse, the horse screaming or Lanie screaming. She broke her back, pelvis, both femurs, ruptured her spleen—and that was just the major stuff. When the medevac crew took her out of there in the helicopter, I figured the next time I saw her would be at the funeral."

"Does that kind of thing happen often?"

"No, but it's the kind of accident that gives eventing a bad name, and those animal rights idiots that want to ban it something to rant about!" Betsy glared at him over the back of the horse. "Here's what's really happened," she said pointing a bloody finger at him. "Over the years eventing has become a popular sport, and like anything else that goes from being practiced by a select few to thousands of amateurs, and I mean amateurs in the worst sense, you got trouble. You got people that can't ride, on horses that aren't suited for eventing, either by talent or temperament, galloping headlong at solid jumps. It's a recipe for disaster. Most of the riders aren't safe and the horses aren't safe. Anybody that has a horse thinks they can event, and they probably can at lower levels like novice or training." Betsy tied off another suture.

"How long did it take her to recover?"

"You sure do ask a lot of questions. Especially for someone who doesn't seem to take to her all that much."

Donovan eyed her steadily. "Occupational hazard."

"To paraphrase the immortal Etta James, Lanie's life from that point on was one special occasion after another. She was married to this jerk who fancied himself a polo player. He was living off her and looking to ride the gravy train to the top. Anyway, when the doctors said she'd probably never walk again he took off with some dressage queen with a big trust fund. Last I heard they were living in Florida. My fervent hope is that karma will catch up with him, and he'll get his head taken off with a polo mallet." Betsy paused while she tied off the last suture and patted the chestnut gently on the neck. "Stay the hell out of fences you big dumb ass," she said to the horse as Rick led the mare back to her stall. She emptied the bloody water in the pail down the aisle's center drain and dropped the bloody gauze and bandages in.

She sighed. "Anyway, the horses all had to go, of course, and the farm, too. Owners have to have somebody to train and ride their horses, and when they left, Lanie couldn't pay the bills. All in all, she spent over a year in the hospital and rehab. Fortunately, the doctors were wrong about her not being able to walk again, mostly because she just refused to accept that prognosis and proceeded to prove them wrong." Betsy looked thoughtfully at Donovan.

"It broke her heart, though. She lost everything. She's never ridden again." Betsy threw the forceps into the empty steel bucket. "Every time she tries to get on a horse she breaks out in a sweat. Can't get past the fear of it."

"How long ago was this?"

"Going on twelve or thirteen years, I guess. She borrowed the money to go to law school and then went to work for a firm in New York. I left New Bolton to set up practice here, so I lost touch with her for a while. She gave up the law practice five or six years ago and moved back to Southern Pines."

"Sounds like she deserves to catch a break."

Betsy pulled her surgical gloves off with a snap and added them to the bucket. "What she *deserves* is someone who doesn't play silly games."

"Are you saying that's what Chopper is doing?"

She shrugged. "Chopper's an infant. Like most men I know." She began to gather up the soiled gauze pads and wrappers.

"Were he and Chris close?"

"I don't know if you'd call them close. Southern Pines is a small community, and the horsey crowd is an even smaller subset. It's not unusual that their paths crossed both professionally and socially. They both belong to the hunt club. Chopper's expertise is in artificial insemination so he did a lot of work at Cameron Farms." She shrugged. "Not best friends, maybe, but friendly."

"The other night Chris seemed convinced Chopper was being overly attentive to his wife."

"Chopper's a flirt,'" said Betsy dismissively. "It's as natural as breathing to him. I wouldn't put too much stock in Chris's drunken ramblings at the Black and White Ball." Betsy narrowed her eyes. "Why are you asking so many questions about Chris and Chopper?"

"The coroner's report said Chris's head wounds were all post mortem," Donovan responded, watching Betsy closely. "He was dead, and had his head caved in, before he was put in that stall." Betsy stared at him. "It was a short time between the final barn check and when you turned up," he continued. "The killer may have still been there when you arrived. Or wasn't long gone. "

Betsy sat down heavily on a tack trunk across the aisle from Donovan.

"That's exactly what I told Lanie. It just didn't make sense that Bubba killed him. But, whoever killed Chris is a nervy bastard." She looked steadily at Donovan. "Chop may be a lot of things, but he's not a murderer."

"He has access to succinylcholine, and he'd know how to give it and how much it would take to kill someone."

Betsy was incredulous. "What possible motive would Chopper have to kill Chris?"

Donovan shrugged. "Maybe the rumors were more than just rumors. He and Chris could have been partners in the illegal sale of ketamine and had a falling out. Or, maybe Chopper really did put the move on Angela and Chris decided to take up the discussion where they left off the other night. If so, he could have come out on the wrong side of that discussion."

"Maybe," said Betsy doubtfully.

seventeen

Lanie sat propped against the pillows in her hospital bed while a nurse busied herself adjusting the saline drip flowing into her arm. The hospital was Thursday evening quiet. Betsy was seated in a hard plastic chair next to the bed, an open box of chocolates in her lap, examining the lid in an attempt to locate the caramel-filled pieces. "Why can't they come up with an easier system?" she asked, peering at the chocolates nestled in their brown paper cups. "You think you're getting a caramel until you pop it in your mouth and find out it's raspberry, or some such crap."

"Beggars can't be choosers," Lanie replied.

"Of course they can. Who told you that?" Betsy finally settled on a chocolate and chewed it with slow, deliberate enjoyment.

"Aren't those supposed to be for me?" Lanie said testily.

"Somebody's got cabin fever," Betsy said, her attention on the chocolates. "When are they letting you out of here?"

"Damned if I know. I'm waiting for the doctor to show up." She shifted uncomfortably, her hands, lightly bandaged, ached slightly. The door opened and Lanie sat up expectantly. Bryan walked in with a bouquet of yellow tulips and a brightly colored balloon. Lanie slumped back against the pillows, disappointed.

"That's fine greeting!" Bryan said with a grin.

"I was hoping you were the doctor. I'm ready to get out of here."

"I bet you are," he replied, leaning over to give her a kiss on the cheek. "We make a fine pair don't we?"

Lanie looked at his blackened eyes and swollen nose and laughed.

"How are you feeling?" he asked, setting the tulips on the table by her bed. He sat down in the remaining chair, uncertain what to do with the balloon. Betsy took it from him and tied it to the IV stand.

Lanie flexed her fingers. "My hands hurt a little, but nothing I can't live with."

"I'm sure they're more concerned about smoke inhalation damage than they are about your hands. As long as your lung function's okay they'll cut you loose," Betsy commented.

The nurse exited as Rhonda walked in, followed by Doug Erikson. "We've been so worried about you!" Rhonda exclaimed. She rushed to Lanie's bedside. "Everybody's talking about what happened to Jennifer. I just can't believe we've had another murder in this town."

"Murder?" Lanie said. "Who says it was murder?"

Rhonda looked around nervously. Bryan was gazing at her with interest, his eyes bright with curiosity. Doug Erikson looked pained. He walked to the window and sat on the narrow ledge, hands in the pockets of his jacket, staring fixedly at the linoleum floor between his feet.

"Well, no one officially," Rhonda stammered, "but John thinks she was dead before you found her."

"John needs to keep his opinions to himself," Betsy said sharply. "We don't need any more rumors flying around."

"Well *something* sure as hell's going on," Rhonda said hotly. "First Marge, then Chris, and now Jennifer!" She looked at Lanie. "You were there, Lanie. What do you think?"

"Yeah, Lanie, tell us what happened," Bryan said.

They all listened intently as Lanie recounted Snert's odd behavior and finding Jennifer's body in her burning kitchen.

It seemed to her that it took longer to tell it than the actual happenings.

"Maybe Snert heard the murderer," Rhonda said excitedly. "If you'd been a few minutes earlier you might have run smack into him."

Lanie thought about the crashing of the garbage can, which she'd attributed to Snert's attempts to corner the cat. She and Betsy exchanged a look.

"That's entirely possible," Betsy said with concern. "Donovan told me that Chris was dead before he was put in Bubba's stall and that I could easily have interrupted the killer. Maybe the same thing happened with Jennifer. Whoever killed her set the fire to cover it up, or to mislead the police. They didn't count on you being at the store so early." She popped another chocolate in her mouth and chewed reflectively. "Whoever it is has nerves of steel, I'll give them that."

"Did you see or hear anything suspicious?" asked Bryan.

Lanie shook her head. "Just the garbage can, and I thought Snert did that chasing the cat." She rubbed her sore hands absently, lost in thought. "I did notice the door snake was on the wrong side of the door," she continued softly. "I remember at the time thinking it was odd, but then I found Jennifer's body and I forgot about everything but getting her out of there."

"Jennifer couldn't have put it there," said Bryan, sitting up on the edge of his chair in excitement. "The killer had to have done it! Think, Lanie! Maybe you saw something and didn't realize the significance at the time!"

Something was nagging at her, but it remained elusive. Doug sighed heavily and pushed himself to his feet. He looked exhausted, Lanie thought, his handsome face drawn, dark smudges under his eyes. "I need to get on with my errands," he said tiredly. "I just wanted to stop in and make sure you were okay."

"Thanks, Doug," Lanie replied. "You taking Giselle to Raleigh for some shopping?"

His face turned stony. "No. Just a trip to the post office," he said abruptly.

The image that had been eluding her clicked into place. "That's it," she cried. "That's what I was trying to remember. The mail."

Doug looked confused, and a little wary. "Glad I could be of help," he said as he walked toward the door. "I hope you feel better soon, Lanie."

"Stop by the shop when you can."

He nodded and pulled the door closed behind him.

Lanie sat up, excited. "When I was in the pantry I saw a stack of mail on the table. There was a picture of Jennifer jumping a gray horse over a fence! Doug's comment made me think of it."

Bryan laughed. "That's your clue?" His blue eyes sparkled in amusement. "Some detective you are."

"Taken by itself it might not seem significant. But the other night at Angela's I saw a similar picture of Chris on the coffee table. Maybe the murderer sent them as some kind of warning!" Lanie took in their expressions, ranging from disbelief to amusement. "We've been trying to figure out how the murders were connected. Well, maybe the common thread is horses." A thought flashed across her face.

"What?" demanded Betsy.

"Remember when I went to see Gladys Wrenn? She told me Marge was looking into some kind of horse scam involving a friend." She had everyone's attention. "Maybe it had to do with horses. It could be the theme that ties all these deaths together."

Bryan scoffed. "That's a pretty big leap. Every competitor in the world of show jumping has hundreds of pictures of themselves taking fences."

"You're right Bryan, but I have a feeling there's something to my theory." She flung the covers back and started to get up.

"Whoa," said Betsy. "Don't yank that IV out."

"Well get rid of it," Lanie said impatiently. "I want to see those pictures again."

"You can't just walk out of here. They haven't discharged you yet."

"They'll figure it out." Lanie pointed to the needle in her arm. "Get rid of this thing," she repeated.

"Don't get your panties in a wad," Betsy said, head bent over the IV needle. "Give me a second will you." She rummaged in the bedside table for gauze and tape before removing the needle. Folding a gauze pad, she placed it on Lanie's arm, secured it with tape and hung the tubing on the IV stand. Lanie grabbed her dirty, smoke-smelling clothes from the closet with awkward hands and disappeared into the bathroom. A few minutes later she emerged and threw the hospital gown on the rumpled bed.

"Let's go," she said to Betsy. "I need a ride to the store."

The sun was setting when Betsy drove Lanie away from the hospital.

"Drive me to Angela's," Lanie said.

"I will not. You need to go home and straight to bed. And I'll spend the night again. You don't need to be alone."

Lanie gave her a dirty look. "It won't take but a minute, and I want to get it before she throws that picture away."

Betsy set her mouth grimly, but she turned the truck and trailer toward Connecticut Avenue. She pulled up to the front of Angela's house and waited while Lanie went to the front door and knocked. Lanie emerged in a few minutes, with the photo-copy in her hand.

"That was easy," Lanie said. "She didn't even ask me why I wanted it." She glanced over at Betsy. "Let's go by the store, and then we'll call it a night." She didn't find it necessary to mention that she wanted to go by the bakery and retrieve the photo in Jennifer's mail.

Betsy pulled up in front of the shop and killed the engine. The streets were empty of tourists and golf widows, waiting for the nightlife crowd to descend.

"There's something I think I should tell you," Betsy said. "Donovan really grilled me about Chopper last night."

"Why?" asked Lanie, startled.

Betsy shifted in her seat. "I didn't want to say anything at the hospital, but Donovan told me Chris died from a dose of succinylcholine. I was right about Bubba not being the cause of his death." She paused before continuing. "And he knows about the rumors that Chopper was selling ketamine when he was at Cornell."

"That's all they were. Rumors."

Betsy nodded. "That's what I said, too. But you have to admit it doesn't look good. He and Chris get into it at the Black and White, and next thing you know Chris turns up dead from a drug readily accessible to vets."

"Betsy Anderson! Are you saying you think Chop's a murderer?"

"I'm saying from the police's perspective he's got to be at the top of their list."

"But, what possible motive would he have? And what about Marge? And Jennifer? Do you think he killed them, too?"

"Right now, Donovan appears to be thinking along the lines of Chop and Chris having a drug dealer spat."

"Is that what you think?"

"Hell, I don't know! All I know is all of a sudden I'm looking at people I've known for years in a different light. A serial killer didn't put in at Southern Pines on the way to Aiken just to knock off a few town folk for the fun of it. It's someone local, someone we interact with on a daily basis. And that's the part that *really* scares me."

"Chop may be an immature jerk but he's not a murderer," Lanie insisted.

"You're preaching to the choir," Betsy said. She changed the subject. "Donovan also asked a lot of questions about you."

"No doubt he thinks I'm Chop's accomplice in knocking off our friends."

"Actually, I think he's just interested in you."

Lanie gaped at her. "He thinks *I* killed Chris?"

Betsy sighed. "No, I mean he's interested in you on a *personal* level."

Lanie snorted. "Not likely," she replied. "I'm sure the Ice Queen is all he can handle."

Betsy's brows knit in puzzlement. "The Ice Queen?"

"That woman he was with at the Black and White."

"I didn't notice." Betsy drummed her fingers on the steering wheel, then shrugged. "I'm just telling you what I think," she finally said.

Unbidden, the events of the previous morning rose up as Lanie recalled the feeling of safety she'd had when Donovan folded her in his arms in the alley outside Jennifer's bakery. The comforting feel of his hand stroking her hair, the sound of his heartbeat as she buried her head against his broad chest. She felt heat rising into her face and was glad of the darkness in the cab.

"Betsy, I'm convinced these murders are connected and I'm convinced the pictures are important somehow."

"So you said."

"So I'm going to prove it," Lanie said, getting out of the truck and slamming the door. She ran up the steps and let herself in the door. Striding to her office, she began opening and shutting drawers in the desk, rummaging through them rapidly until she found what she was looking for.

"Ah ha!" she said triumphantly, dangling a key on a piece of ribbon.

Betsy had followed her to the office, leaning against the door jamb as she searched. "What the hell is that?" she asked.

"A key to Jennifer's. We gave each other keys to our businesses just in case we ever had need for them."

A wary look flitted across Betsy's face. "And what do you plan to do with it?"

"I'm going to Jennifer's and get that picture so I can compare it with the one Angela has." She slipped around Betsy and headed for the back door.

"You can't do that," Betsy exclaimed, grabbing her by the sleeve. "That's breaking and entering. Or disturbing a crime scene. Or something equally bad."

"How can it be breaking and entering? I have a key!" Lanie broke away, grabbed a flashlight from the storage room, stepped out onto the loading dock, and raced down the stairs.

"You are going to get yourself arrested." Betsy hissed, joining her in the pitch-black alley. "Have you lost your mind?" she asked as Lanie strode away. "Her place is covered in crime scene tape. If you get caught they'll put you *under* the Moore County jail."

"They have to catch me first," she said, walking up the steps to Jennifer's back door and peering at the yellow tape, the bright light from the flashlight lens dimmed by her fingers.

"Jesus, Mary, and Joseph," Betsy muttered. "Wait up. You can't go in there by yourself. It's dangerous."

Lanie grinned at her. "What is it you always say? 'On the plains of hesitation lie the bones of countless thousands?' I'm done hesitating. I'm going to find out what's going on and who's killing our friends."

"Yeah, well, I talk too much."

"All I want to do is get that picture and we'll be out of there. I promise."

"Right," Betsy said looking around nervously. "Let's just get it over with."

Lanie gently peeled the tape off and inserted the key, but was unable to turn it because of the bandages on her hands. She turned to Betsy. "I need you to turn this key. I can't do it."

"Even better," said Betsy, turning and heading down the stairs. "We shouldn't be doing this anyway."

"Come on, Betsy! I need your help."

Betsy reluctantly rejoined her and turned the key in the lock. Lanie eased the door open, and Betsy slipped in behind her and closed and locked it. Lanie's flashlight played across the table where she'd seen the stack of mail early Saturday morning. The stack of mail was gone.

"It's gone," Betsy said with relief. "Let's forget this."

"Maybe they just moved it," Lanie whispered, opening the door to the bakery. "I can't imagine they'd want it. It looked like junk mail, for the most part."

Water from the fire hoses still puddled on the floor, and they stepped through it cautiously, shining the flashlight over the counters and display cases.

"Lanie," hissed Betsy from behind her, "this is stupid. The picture's gone. Let's go!"

The sound of laughter and footsteps floated in from the sidewalk outside the bakery. They froze as a group of revelers passed the large plate glass windows of the bakery, headed for one of the local bars. Lanie shut off the flashlight and crouched behind the display case. "Shit, shit, shit," said Betsy as she crab walked over to join Lanie.

"Shhhh…"

The group passed on and Lanie slowly stood up, her legs aching and her heart pounding.

"That could have been the police coming to arrest our asses," Betsy pointed out, but Lanie was already creeping up the stairs to Jennifer's apartment, staying close to the wall, testing each step before committing her full weight to it. Betsy reluctantly followed.

They emerged from the staircase into a small foyer that opened into a living room. To the right was a small galley kitchen. A doorway to the left revealed Jennifer's bedroom and a small bath. Though the fire damage had been confined to the bakery downstairs, the acrid smell of smoke permeated the small space.

"I'll take the bedroom, you start in the kitchen," Lanie whispered. "Maybe you can find another flashlight somewhere." She stepped into the bedroom and looked around. The bed was neatly made, a nightgown folded and placed on the pillow. Jennifer's reading glasses rested atop a paperback book face down on the nightstand. Lanie scanned the top of the dresser, opened and closed the drawers, checked the bathroom and even the seat of the small chintz covered chair in the corner. The closet held Jennifer's clothes, sorted by color, hanging in neat rows on either side, but no papers, and no mail.

She returned to the living room to find Betsy going through the drawers of an antique secretary. She looked up as Lanie entered.

"Good," said Lanie. "You found a flash light."

"Yep. Everybody has a junk drawer." She stood up from the chair in front of the secretary and turned off the flash light.

"There's nothing in here but the usual stuff people squirrel away," she said with a sigh. "The police must have taken everything else." She gently closed the glass doors on the secretary's bookcase. "Did you find anything?"

"No."

"My grandmother had a secretary just like this when we were kids," Betsy said. "We weren't supposed to touch it but, of course, every time we went to visit we'd poke around in it when Nana wasn't looking." She ran her finger over the mahogany dividers in the glass. "She was a champion baker, used to win all kinds of blue ribbons at the state fair. She was paranoid somebody was going to steal her recipes, so she'd hide them." She stopped abruptly, then bent down and reached under the fold out desktop. There was a soft click and Betsy lifted the desktop to reveal a small drawer. She turned the flash light back on and its soft glow illuminated nothing but an empty red leatherbound ledger, the sole occupant of the felt-lined space. "Damn, I thought we'd find something," Betsy whispered, plainly disappointed.

"It was worth a shot," said Lanie. "Come on, let's get out of here.

They retreated back down the stairs and through the kitchen to the storage room, where Lanie shone the flashlight around the shelves one last time. The light illuminated a line of cookbooks on a shelf behind Betsy's back. Lanie scanned the titles on the spines, then stopped as her flashlight located a small book, tucked between two larger ones.

"What's that?" she asked softly.

Betsy turned around, examining the shelf. "What are you talking about?"

"That little red book between the two cookbooks."

"What do you care? You can't cook."

"Just check it out, would you? We're running out of time."

Betsy sighed and pulled the small volume off the shelf, flipping open the cover. She read for a moment and then looked up at Lanie. "It sure as hell isn't a cookbook, but I can't see well enough to determine what it is."

"Bring it and let's get out of here!" Lanie hissed. "We can look at it back at the store."

Betsy tucked the ledger inside the waistband of her jeans

They exited onto the back stoop, where Lanie carefully replaced the tape. As they were tiptoeing down the stairs the feral cat darted between Betsy's feet and she fell into the metal garbage cans, sending them clanging and rolling into the alley.

"Damn!" said Betsy. "I think I twisted my ankle."

Lanie pulled her to her feet and they hobbled down the alley to the feed store loading dock. Once inside, Betsy slid to the floor, her shoulders heaving with laughter. "So much for stealth," she gasped.

Lanie started giggling and soon they were both sitting on the floor, guffawing. "I wish you could have seen yourself," Lanie said, wiping tears from her face. "You could have wakened the dead."

"I'm surprised Barney Fife didn't come down on us like ducks on a June bug," Betsy said.

"Probably asleep somewhere." Lanie scrambled to her feet.

"Help me up," Betsy grumbled. "Since we risked our lives to find this stupid thing I want to read it." She stood up and pulled the ledger from inside her jeans. "Our luck, it's probably my grandmother's long lost recipe book."

"You check that out while I take a look at the picture."

Betsy shrugged. "I'm going to get my reading glasses," she said, hobbling toward the front door.

When she returned, Lanie was sitting at her desk absorbed in the photograph Angela had given her. Betsy sat down across from her and began to read the ledger. After several minutes she looked up.

"This is really odd," she said, slipping her fingers between the pages to mark her place. "It looks like a list of horses' names, with three columns with different amounts of money next to each name. They're all dated and they go back several years."

"Prize money?" Lanie ventured. "Maybe she had to split it with owners or backers or something."

Betsy shrugged. "Could be." She returned to studying the pages. Suddenly she sat up straight in her chair. "Here's something interesting. Episodic's listed here."

"Who's that?" Lanie asked, not looking up from her study.

"Remember that list you found in Joy's day planner? His name was on that list."

"What about the others?"

"I don't know. I can't remember the other names on the list. I wish you still had it so I could cross check against the names in this ledger."

Lanie sat up, excited. "I think I do still have it. I stuck it in my jeans pocket, or under the truck visor, and forgot all about it. I'll find it when I get home."

Betsy sighed and set the ledger on the desk. "Anything interesting in the picture?"

"No," said Lanie, rubbing her eyes, "nothing jumps out at me, no pun intended. I'll call Drew in the morning and see if he'll let me have a copy of the one Jennifer received."

"I'm so tired I could sleep for a month," Betsy said yawning.

"Me too. Take me home."

Across town, Chopper Crisafulli finished the notes he was writing on the surgery he'd performed earlier that afternoon and walked out into the barn area to check on his patient, a year-old Dutch Warmblood, who'd had a benign tumor on his optic nerve. The strong smell of DMSO, the potent anti-inflammatory he'd given his young patient, assaulted his nostrils as he passed the stalls, their occupants quiet in the late-night hour. He opened the stall door and checked the bandages that covered the eye and adjusted the drip of DMSO leading from the bag hanging overhead before turning off the lights. The colt had an excellent chance of regaining full sight, an optimal outcome for the owner, who'd spent thousands on the youngster as a jumper prospect.

He stopped at the sink in the barn aisle and washed his hands slowly and thoroughly. The surgery had taken longer than he'd anticipated, but he'd welcomed the reprieve from thinking about Chris's death, and what it meant for him.

He walked out the back door of the clinic, locking it behind him, and got in his truck. He drove slowly to the Sanderson Farm, where he was renting the guest cottage until he could decide what he wanted to do about permanent lodgings.

As he pulled in the driveway, he saw the glow of a lit cigarette winking like a firefly from the front steps of the guest cottage. He cut the engine, got out, and walked over to sit beside Angela.

"Everything okay?" he asked.

She took a long pull on her cigarette before replying. "Yes. I just wanted to see you. I'm worried Chop."

He didn't respond immediately. She ground the cigarette out on the brick steps and clasped her hands in her lap, twisting her long, slender fingers, absent her wedding band.

He propped his elbows on his knees and rubbed his face wearily. "Me too. That SBI agent and Drew came by the clinic earlier. They grilled me about Chris. Where I was, what I was doing the night he died." He sighed.

"Did you tell them where you were?"

"No. I danced around it as best I could, but I'm not sure they bought it. They'll be back."

"I've been thinking about Chris a lot." Her voice wavered. "About how neither one of us ever had to grow up. How totally irresponsible we were. We did a lot of damage to ourselves and our relationship. And to other people."

He picked up her hand and squeezed it, before releasing it. "You can't unbake a pie, as my grandmother used to say. All you can do is learn from it and move forward."

She glanced at him. "I can't run away from how I feel about you, Chop. I came to apologize for the position my—*our*—actions have put you in." She stood up. "That's all I wanted to say." She slung her purse over her shoulder and stepped off the porch.

"Wait," Chop said. "Don't go, Angela." He walked to her and put a hand on her arm. "I don't think either of us knew what we wanted. Lanie's a great person, and I really care for her…" He stopped, uncertain how to proceed, unused to expressing his emotions, and ever mindful that talking with Angela was like walking through a minefield. You never knew when she'd go off, especially on the subject of Lanie. "Bottom line is we're just not well matched, Lanie and me." He stumbled to a stop.

Angela waited for him to continue. When he didn't, she spoke. "I was just a kid when I married Chris," she said. "I thought marriage was about having a big house and wads of money and hot sex." She took a deep breath. "How was I to know it's about having someone to share your dreams with, having someone who 'gets' who you are, and loves you for it, warts and all."

Chopper nodded miserably.

"Chop, do you still love Lanie?" she asked, standing perfectly still, barely breathing.

"I'm tired of the secrecy," he equivocated.

She put her hand on his sleeve. "We don't have to be a secret anymore," she said softly.

Doug Erikson stood in the alley behind the bakery, hands in his coat pockets, looking up at the dark windows in Jennifer's apartment. Earlier, he'd watched from the shadows as Betsy and Lanie had gone in, and then out again, wondering what they were looking for and if they'd found it. Water from the fire hoses still pooled on the broken concrete and dripped from the eaves, and the acrid smell of smoke hung thick in the air. He knew he'd been there long enough. There was nothing he could do.

He turned and walked slowly up the alley to New Hampshire, where he turned left and walked across Broad Street to the local pub where his truck was parked. Noisy laughter spilled out the open door of the bar as he climbed in and pulled the door shut behind him. Baby scrambled over the console, worming her way into his lap. He wrapped his arms tightly around her as she licked away the salty tears that streamed down his face.

Drew and Donovan knocked at Chopper's door at four o'clock that Friday morning and took him to the Moore County jail in Carthage. On the short ride up Highway 15-501 he gazed out the window at the familiar landscape sliding by in the dark, trying to keep his mind off the interrogation he knew was imminent. His mind skittered crazily as he went over and over his story, like a tongue exploring a sore tooth. How much should he tell them? Would they believe him? He wondered if she would be there for him. He also wondered how early in the morning he could call Hugh Jennings at home.

eighteen

Lanie slouched in her office chair, her feet on the desk and the photograph in her lap, sipping on her fourth cup of coffee. Snert and Rommel were at the front of the store with Rhonda, greeting customers as they entered, vying for attention and lint-covered treats from their pockets. Losing interest, Rommel padded into the office and pushed his head under Lanie's arm, jostling her coffee cup.

"Knock it off, you big lunk," she said crossly. "Can't you see I'm busy?"

In response, he wedged his head between her knees, knocking her feet off the desk and bringing the chair down with a thump. He laid his head in her lap, the mahogany spots over his brown eyes cocked and attentive. Lanie set her coffee cup on the desk and absently ran her thumb up his broad muzzle and between his eyes, lost in thought. She'd called Drew's office the moment she got to the store, but was told he was tied up and wouldn't be available for some time. She'd left a message for him to call her, but it was now after lunch and he hadn't returned her call. She needed that picture from Jennifer's.

She picked up the phone and called Betsy, but it went straight to voice mail. Frustrated, she hung up without leaving a message and returned to the photo. For what seemed like the one-hundredth time she scanned the crowd of people in the background. Spectators and exhibitors lined the fence, their faces intent on Chris and his mount, In Flight. A woman in a bright spring dress, a large straw hat obscuring her face, stood next to a stocky man in tan breeches and boots. Aviator glasses shaded his face, and his red hair was haloed by the sun behind him. Next to him, a young girl was caught by the camera in the act of scraping the toe of her riding boot in the sand, her face a study in boredom. Coppery tendrils of hair escaped from under her riding helmet. Her hands were jammed in the pockets of her jacket. Lanie read the inscription at the bottom of the page again: *I don't know how much longer I can Bear it.* She wondered why the 'b' was capitalized. Sighing, she tossed the photo on her desk and scrubbed at her tired eyes with the heels of her hands. Angela was probably right: some conquest of Chris's being cute. She looked up as Rhonda stuck her head in the door.

"Can you cover for me while I grab some lunch?" Rhonda asked.

Lanie glanced at the clock—almost one o'clock. "I'm sorry, Rhonda. You should have interrupted me."

"No problem," Rhonda said, flashing a quick smile. "We had a bit of a rush, but it's quiet again so I thought I'd slip out for a few minutes. Can I bring you something back?"

Lanie shook her head. "I'm not hungry." She waved Rhonda out. "Take your time."

Rhonda wiggled her fingers and left. Out front, Snert, curled in his dog bed by the loveseat, opened one eye as Lanie and Rommel approached before dropping back to sleep. Rommel jumped on the loveseat and curled up, his eyes following Lanie as she stocked shelves.

They all looked up as the bell over the front door tinkled. Doug Erikson strode in, followed by Baby. She trailed behind him reluctantly, as though trying to distance herself from him. Doug's expression was stormy, his cheeks red and mottled with anger.

"Hey Doug," said Lanie. "Is everything okay?"

He stopped in front of her and shoved his face close to hers. "No. Everything is *not* okay," he growled. "That red-neck boob of a sheriff has had me down at the jail, insinuating I had something to do with Chris Cameron's death!" Baby slunk behind a rack of hunt jackets, ears flat, and pressed her body to the floor. Snert sat up and bared his teeth. A growl rumbled from Rommel's throat.

Lanie backed slowly away from Doug, bumping up against a rack of saddles. "I'm sure it was just a formality. You and Chris *did* have a disagreement in my store last week."

"They didn't have to drag me down to Carthage in a police car!"

"If you didn't have anything to do with Chris's death, then I'm sure you have nothing to worry about." She took another step back.

"Once word gets around that they've had me in for questioning, everybody in town will think I did!" He followed her, eyes blazing.

"I don't know if you had anything to do with Chris's death, but I know you're scaring me," she said, unable to retreat any further.

His hand shot out and gripped her forearm, his blunt fingers digging in hard. "I guess you think I killed Marge as well," he snarled. "And why not throw in Jennifer while we're at it. I'm just a homicidal maniac, huh?" He shook her hard. "You need to get your nose out of this murder investigation, young lady. Quit snooping around, or you're going to wind up getting hurt!"

Suddenly he screamed and grabbed the back of his thigh. Rommel had silently left the loveseat and moved quickly, but stealthily, across the floor to sink his teeth into Doug's leg. Snert was standing rigidly on his toes between Doug and the front door, snarling. Lanie could hear Baby whimpering from her hiding place beneath the coat rack. She stepped around Doug and grabbed Snert by the collar with one hand and Rommel with the other.

"I think you need to leave, Doug," she said, her voice shaking, "before I call the police."

His gaze shifted between Lanie and the dogs. "Go ahead and call them," he said, suddenly deflated. "It doesn't matter any more. Nothing matters any more."

He turned and limped toward the door, his khaki pants ripped and bloody above the back of his knee. He turned around, and Lanie flinched.

"Scared?" he sneered. He pointed a finger at her. "You need to be scared. I meant what I said about you keeping your nose out of this." He whistled for Baby, who crawled from under the coat rack and slunk to his side, her tail tucked tightly between her legs.

"Great," Doug muttered as he flung open the door, "even my dog's scared of me." He paused and turned back to look at Lanie, his face crumpling as tears streamed from his eyes. "You need to reconsider your decision about Chopper," he said. "He really loves you, you know. And love's too hard to come by to just throw it away with both hands like the two of you are doing."

Lanie stared at him in astonishment.

"I mean it, Lanie. Don't wait until it's too late." He left, closing the door behind him.

Lanie stood rigidly in the middle of the floor, straining to hear the sound of Doug's truck pulling away, afraid he might be coming back. Her hands, still gripped tightly on the dogs' collars, ached from the strain of holding them back. She slowly became aware that her phone was ringing and walked stiffly to the counter to pick it up. It slipped from her bandaged fingers and clattered on the glass countertop.

"Damn it!" she said, finally securing it. "Hello?"

"I'm calling for Lanie Montgomery?" said a quavering voice.

"Yes," Lanie responded cautiously.

"Are you okay dear? You sound out of breath."

"Who is this?" Lanie asked.

"Myrtle Simpson," the voice quavered again. "You left a message for me to call."

"Oh yes, Mrs. Simpson. Thanks for calling me back." She sank down on the loveseat, suddenly tired. "Gladys Wrenn gave me your number. She said Marge was looking into something for you, and I wondered if you'd be willing to talk to me about that."

"Did she find him?" Myrtle's voice brightened with hope.

"Find who?" Lanie asked, confused.

"The man who sold me that worthless horse!" the small voice said impatiently. "Isn't that why you're calling? Marge was asking around for me."

Lanie rubbed her forehead, trying to stave off the headache she felt coming on. "Mrs. Simpson, maybe we should start from the beginning."

After several minutes of prodding and cajoling, Lanie finally wrenched the story from Myrtle Simpson. A story of unscrupulous people taking advantage of an elderly, lonely, and, most importantly, wealthy widow, enticing her to invest in the glamorous world of horses and then bilking her out of her money.

"It seemed like such a safe thing, dear," said Myrtle Simpson at the end of her tale. "After all, Marge's nephew, Christian, introduced us."

"Introduced you to whom?" Lanie asked.

"The man selling the horse, and another lady who invested with me," she responded, as if Lanie was a particularly stupid child. "The first horse we bought got sick and died, but he was insured so we got our money back," she continued. "That sometimes happens you know. They're really very delicate creatures, to be so large."

"When did you discover it was a confidence game?"

"It was Marge who figured it out. She was so knowledgeable about horses." Lanie gritted her teeth, willing her to get on with the story. "She came to Middleburg to visit me and watch my horse perform, but he had an off day and didn't do well. I was so disappointed, you know?"

"I do," Lanie said encouragingly.

"So afterwards we went to the barn area to meet my friend, Bobby, the one who sold us the horse? But he never showed up. I was disappointed about that, too, but he was such a busy man, always on the go."

I bet he was, Lanie thought.

"But we did get to see the horse. His name was Passing Through, and such a pretty thing. Marge actually went into his stall, if you can believe that, at her age, and looked him over. She told me he wasn't suited to jumping or much of anything else. Something about being over at the knee or bowed tendons, whatever they are. She asked me what I paid for him and when I told her, she looked very disapproving and started asking me all kinds of questions I couldn't answer. She said he wasn't worth selling for dog food, that I'd been scammed. She was quite determined to look into it." Her voice trailed off and Lanie was afraid she'd lost the connection.

"When was this, Myrtle?"

"Oh, just in the last few weeks, actually. Not long before she died."

"And Chris introduced you to these people? Did Marge know that?"

There were several seconds of silence on the other end of the phone. "Well," Myrtle said, "I wouldn't say he actually *introduced* us. It was more that they used him as a *reference*, if you see what I mean. They said Chris and Marge had purchased horses from them."

"And what about your co-investor. What did she think of all this?"

"I haven't been able to get up with her, dear. And the bills are mounting up. She owes me for veterinary care and boarding. I've tried to call her, but her phone is out of service. Don't you think that's odd?"

"I think Marge was right, Myrtle. I think you had the misfortune to run across a bunch of con artists who took advantage of you."

"So what do I do now?"

"I think you should see about donating the horse to a therapeutic riding program, if he's quiet enough for that, and consider yourself lucky to be done with it."

"Oh dear," Myrtle replied. "I've become so fond of him. It gave me such purpose, going to the shows."

"That's what they count on, Myrtle," said Lanie. "I'll check with my friend Betsy. She's an equine vet. Maybe she knows someone who'd like a pasture ornament."

"Would you dear? I'd be so grateful. I wouldn't want anything bad to happen to him, you know."

Lanie sighed. "You're a nice lady, Myrtle. I'm sorry this happened to you. I'll see what I can do."

Lanie turned off her phone, and sat, lost in thought. Maybe Marge was killed because of her investigation into her friend's horse troubles. The timing was too coincidental for the events not to be connected. But who was the mysterious Bobby? And who was the woman who'd invested, along with Myrtle, in a worthless horse? Was she an innocent victim as well, or a part of the scam? And how did Chris tie into all of this, if at all? She sighed in frustration. All she had were more questions and there wasn't enough information to answer any of them. She needed to do some more digging.

The tinkling of the bell over the door interrupted her musings, and Bryan came in, with Rhonda right behind him slurping nosily on a cherry Icee.

Bryan removed his cap and rubbed his shaved head briskly. "I just got stung on the head by a wasp. Hurts like a bastard," he said with a sheepish grin. "You look pensive," he said, putting the cap back on his head and sitting down beside her. "What's up?" The bruising around his eyes was shading into green and yellow, and most of the swelling was gone.

"A lot, actually." Lanie said. She related the confrontation with Doug, leaving out his comments about Chopper, and her conversation with Myrtle Simpson.

"Maybe Doug is Bobby," Rhonda said, pointing her Icee cup at Lanie excitedly. "Maybe Marge figured it out and he killed her to keep her from turning him in."

"Why would a man as wealthy as Doug be involved in a scam like that?" Bryan asked.

"Why would Kirk Jackson, who's father was worth half a billion dollars, have horses killed for the insurance money?" Lanie asked. "The rich are not like you and me, for sure."

Rhonda's jaw dropped. "He did that?"

"I'd forgotten about that," Bryan said in agreement. "He did some jail time."

The bell tinkled again as Betsy entered. "What's up guys?" she asked as she bent down to ruffle Snert's ears. She cupped Rommel's face in her hands and planted a kiss between his eyes. "I'm headed out to the horse park. They're having a cross-country schooling day and I volunteered to be on site in case somebody does something stupid, like fall off. Anyone care to go with me?"

Lanie shook her head. "Thanks, Betsy, but I think I'll pass. I've had enough excitement for one day." For the second time she related the encounter with Doug and her conversation with Myrtle.

"Do you think Fred Harris could shed some light on this?" she asked Betsy. "If there's a horse scam going around, surely he'd know about it."

Betsy pursed her lips, considering her question. "It'd be worth asking him. He might have a line or two on people running that kind of thing."

"I think I'll give him a call," Lanie said, standing up slowly.

Betsy whistled. "You know what this means, don't you? It means Joy might have a get-out-of-jail-free card," she said. "At the very least, it points out a different motive for Marge's death." She scratched the side of her nose. "Of course we still don't have a clue who this Bobby person is." She looked at Lanie. "Did you share this with Drew? Or better yet, Donovan?"

"Not yet. I have a call in to Drew about the photograph. I'll tell him when he calls me back."

Betsy dug a couple of dog treats out of her pocket, made Snert and Rommel sit and balanced a treat on each of their noses. "Let's see who can last the longest."

"That's mean," said Rhonda.

"You're right," Betsy responded with a grin. She snapped her fingers and the treats disappeared with a collective snap.

"Okay, if nobody wants to go with me, I'd better get on the road. Let me know what Drew has to say," Betsy said to Lanie.

"You'll be the first."

After she'd left, Bryan turned to Lanie. "In all the excitement I forgot about what I came here to tell you. I heard they questioned Chopper early this morning."

Lanie stared at him, speechless. "Why?" she finally managed to ask.

"For questioning in Chris's murder. He's been at the jail in Carthage since they picked him up."

"Who told you this?"

He shrugged eloquently. "News gets around fast in a small town."

Rhonda and Lanie exchanged glances. Rhonda came out from behind the counter and put her arm around Lanie's shoulder. "I'm sure it's just a formality," she said soothingly. "Chopper's not a murderer. We all know that."

Lanie worried the information about Chopper's arrest like Snert gnawing a bone as she brought the horses in and fed them. Her restlessness propelled her to clean all the tack in the barn after she'd scrubbed out the water buckets and skipped the stalls spotlessly clean. It was dark by the time she dragged herself to the house, her steps heavy, and fell into bed exhausted.

The shrilling of the phone beside her bed woke her from a fitful sleep. She squinted bleary-eyed at the clock on her nightstand—one o'clock on a Saturday morning. "This had better be good," she mumbled crossly as she reached for the phone.

""Hello?" she muttered.

"Lanie? It's me." Betsy's voice was tight and clipped. "I need your help. I got called to the vet school in Raleigh for a colic case. I've got to take this horse into surgery right away. They're inducing him now."

"Okay," said Lanie quizzically.

"The problem is that I've got Bubba standing on my trailer out in the vet school parking lot. That idiot Elisabeth fell off of him at the schooling trial and went to the hospital for some x-rays." Betsy paused for breath. "Anyway, I didn't have time to stop at Cameron Farms to drop him off, and I couldn't leave him at the schooling grounds, so I stuck him on my trailer and brought him with me. I thought I had this horse stabilized and headed for home, but just past Tramway they called and said he was going downhill so I had to haul ass back to Raleigh." Betsy's voice faded as she put her hand over the receiver. "Okay, I'll be right there! Lanie? I gotta go. Look, can you drive up here and get him? You could leave your truck for me in the parking lot and take my truck and trailer. My keys are on the seat. Otherwise, he'll be standing out there all night."

"Sure, no problem," Lanie said, throwing back the covers. "I'll be there as soon as I can. I'll leave my keys on top of the driver's side tire."

"Thanks. Talk to you tomorrow." Betsy was gone.

Lanie drew on a pair of jeans and a turtleneck, laced up her paddock boots, and headed north to Raleigh. A little over an hour later she was speeding down the inner beltline, peering anxiously out the windshield for signs indicating the exit for the vet school. She took the Hillsborough Street exit, turned right, and followed the signs down the deserted street to the vet school campus. She turned right again and made her way slowly along the curving road. As she approached the large animal hospital, the electronic gate slowly rolled open to admit her into the parking lot. Several truck and trailer combinations, ramps down, were scattered about, their owners and occupants having made the dreaded middle of the night trek for treatment. Seeing Betsy's truck and trailer at the far end of the lot, Lanie parked and walked over. Behind her, she could hear another rig pull in and stop, diesel engine idling while an injured or sick horse was unloaded.

She peered in through the slats of Betsy's stock trailer and saw Bubba standing in the far corner, head high, eyeing her calmly, but warily. Lanie cursed under her breath. He was still saddled and bridled, legs encased in protective cross-country boots, standing loose in the trailer. "Betsy *knows* better than to put a horse in the trailer like this!" she said out loud, "You could have hurt yourself!" As if in agreement with her, Bubba snorted loudly, shaking his head, causing the reins to loop down dangerously close to his front legs.

Lanie opened the tack storage door on the side of the trailer and selected a halter. Slipping into the trailer with Bubba, she pulled it over his bridle, looped the reins through securely, and tied the lead rope to one of the slats. She patted him soothingly on his sleek mahogany brown neck. "Okay, Bub," she murmured, "I'll get you home as soon as I can and give you a nice long bath, get the cross-country mud off you." She removed the protective boots, probing the tendons for any sign of swelling or heat. Nothing. Betsy had been lucky, *really* lucky. After checking each leg, she rummaged in the tack compartment of the trailer until she located a blanket. She tossed it over his back, saddle and all, and secured it, so that he wouldn't get chilled in the open trailer on the ride home.

She turned right out of the large animal hospital parking lot and headed back for the I-40 extension, which would take her to the beltline. A mile down Blue Ridge Road she realized the trailer was pulling sluggishly. A flat tire. She pounded her fist on the steering wheel. "Damn it!" She eased off the accelerator, and the truck began to slow. She passed the entrance to the highway looking for a place to pull off. A short distance up the road, on her right, the parking lot of the North Carolina Museum of Art came into view, its entrance flags snapping in the stiff breeze. She slowly pulled into the lot and parked under a light. Nearby signs announced the entrance to the museum and the Reedy Creek greenway. She hopped out and surveyed the damage, confirming she had a flat tire. Sorting through Betsy's tack compartment again, she found a tire jack and a spare tire buried under heaps of old, unwashed horse blankets, lead lines, fly masks, and sweaty saddle pads.

She debated leaving Bubba on the trailer, but decided that the tire changing operation might cause him to skitter around and hurt himself, so she unloaded him and tied him to the chain link fence surrounding the construction site for the museum's new addition. As she knelt to loosen the lug nuts, a car eased into the parking lot and stopped with its headlights pointed at her. She shielded her eyes, squinting in the light from the car's halogen lamps, hoping museum security had come to her rescue. On the other side of the trailer, she could hear Bubba moving restlessly, the chain link fence humming slightly with his movement. The car continued to idle, and Lanie began to feel uneasy. "Maybe they can't see me very well Bub," she said out loud. "I might be making them as nervous as they're making me." She stepped out of the shadow of the truck and waved her arms.

The car began to slowly roll toward her, then suddenly accelerated, the engine roaring in the silence of the parking lot as it hurtled toward them. She ran for the bed of the pickup and threw herself over the tailgate just as the car sideswiped the trailer and then traveled down the side of Betsy's truck, sending sparks from the screeching metal and the trailer slamming into the fence. The truck rocked on its wheels. Lanie peered over the side rails and saw the car looping around to make a second pass. Bubba was thrashing at the lead rope securing him to the fence, rearing in panic, his iron-shod hooves slipping on the asphalt surface of the lot. Miraculously, he didn't appear to be hurt. Lanie leapt from the truck bed and yanked hard on the safety tie of the lead rope, freeing him from his struggles.

The thought of getting on a horse caused her stomach to knot up. Sweat broke out on her forehead, and she could feel it running down her ribcage, but she had to get herself and Bubba out of danger. The squeal of tires as the car came around again goaded her into action. She ripped off the blanket, dropping it to the asphalt, grabbed a fistful of mane, and flung herself into the saddle. She booted Bubba forward to the greenway entrance. She could hear the car accelerating behind her as she took the path away from the museum at a gallop, Bubba picking up speed with every stride. The car picked up speed as it raced down the greenway after them. They came to an open field and Lanie kicked Bubba on, angling through the field on her right as they galloped beneath three giant horseshoe-shaped sculptures. She looked over her shoulder in fear, confirming the car was gaining on them.

They crossed the field, took a sharp right, and hurtled down the hill, Bubba slipping and sliding until the cross-country studs in his shoes dug in. The car was going too fast to make the turn, and skidded around to the left, tires protesting as the driver slammed on the brakes. Lanie and Bubba galloped on through the dark, the greenway trail becoming more visible as their eyesight adjusted. Lanie's breath whistled through her constricted throat as she clung to Bubba's mane and tried to stay balanced, tried not to think about how easily he could slip and fall. She could hear the car continuing its chase. There was no way they could continue to outrun it on the greenway, she thought, and there was no safe way to get off the path. They'd have to go on and wait for the right opportunity.

Bubba settled into a rhythmic, ground-covering gallop as they raced down a steep hill, over a wooden bridge, and followed a steep, climbing S curve. At the top of the hill Lanie pulled him up sharply. Behind them, she could hear metal scraping as their pursuer tried unsuccessfully to negotiate the tight turns and the car slammed into the stone retaining wall. Its engine stalled. As Bubba tossed his head in impatience, she heard it start up again. She wheeled Bubba around, continuing their flight through the dark.

As they neared the top of the hill, the expanse of the pedestrian bridge spanning the Raleigh beltline loomed in front of them, its blue Art Deco lights casting an eerie glow. Footlights along either side glowed like an airplane aisle. Several feet wide, its graceful span crossed six lanes of traffic, the chain-link sides soaring well above her head. She glanced behind her and saw the headlights of the car through the trees. Before she could change her mind, she turned Bubba toward the bridge and kicked him into a gallop. "Please God, don't let him panic," she prayed under her breath.

As they sped across, Lanie could see the headlights of early morning commuters on the beltline below. As they raced toward the other side, their pursuer stopped at the entrance to the bridge, then continued after them. Lanie chanced a quick glance over her shoulder. When she turned backed she was horrified to see a five-foot chain-link gate closing off their escape at the other end. She tried to slow Bubba, but he took the bit in his teeth and galloped on, closing the distance to the gate alarmingly fast. As he got closer, Lanie closed her eyes, took a tighter grip on his mane, and gave him the reins, telling herself a jump was just a canter with a hump in the middle as she felt him gather beneath her. She said a silent prayer that she wouldn't fall off—and then they were over. Lanie laughed as they flew past the sign at the end of the bridge stating that access to Meredith College's grounds were prohibited after dark and that the gate would reopen in the morning. "That'll be too late for us, won't it Bubba?" she exulted, throwing her arms around the galloping horse's neck and giving him a tight squeeze. Behind her, there was no sound of their pursuer, but she didn't want to take any chances.

Bubba slowed to a walk, with Lanie bent low to his neck, as they passed through the tunnel under Wade Avenue, the sound of his shoes reverberating off the concrete sides and roof of the underpass. They picked up a canter when they exited and climbed the hill. To their left, Lanie could see the goals on the Meredith soccer fields, ghostly spider webs in the moonlight. She brought him down to a trot and steered him onto the soccer field, pulling up behind a stand of pines and scrub trees that separated them from the greenway. She looked behind, but still saw no sign of a pursuer. Steam rose up from Bubba's sweaty neck and flanks in the cool air.

Lanie knew that, as the crow flew, they weren't far from the vet school. She could continue across Meredith's campus to Hillsborough Street and make her way back, but the thought that their pursuer might still be out there gave her pause. She walked Bubba in a wide circle to keep him from stiffening while she considered their options. Her cell phone was back in Betsy's truck, nestled safely in her purse. She'd have to see if she could find a Meredith security guard and a phone. She kicked her feet out of the stirrups, slid out of the saddle, and crumpled to the ground, her wobbly legs refusing to hold her up. Her hands ached from the burns and the unfamiliar task of gripping the reins. She knelt beside him for several minutes, the reins clutched in her left hand, then grabbed the stirrup and pulled herself to a standing position. Slowly, she began to walk Bubba toward the main entrance of the college. Through the trees to their right a few cars passed on Hillsborough Street, and Lanie could see the lighted sign of a Waffle House. It was still open and a rowdy celebration was going on in the parking lot. She walked up to the guardhouse, but finding it empty, returned to the main campus entrance and turned right. She led Bubba across the street at a trot and down to the Waffle House where the crowd of students in the parking lot gaped at her as she and the horse walked up.

"Does anybody have a cell phone I could use?" she asked.

"Where the hell are you?" Betsy barked when she answered her cell phone. "We're worried sick about you!"

"At the Waffle House on Hillsborough, across from Meredith. Bub's with me and we're fine." At the familiar sound of Betsy's voice, tears filled her eyes and she struggled not to break down. "Your truck's in the museum parking lot and I'm afraid it's damaged."

"I know that already. What the hell are you doing at the Waffle House? Never mind. Don't move. I'll be right there."

"Don't worry, I won't," Lanie said to a dead phone. She returned the phone to its owner and sat down on the curb to wait.

"Hey lady, your horse is bleeding." The cell phone's owner pointed to one of Bubba's rear legs. "I'm a third-year vet student. Want me to take a look at it?" he asked eagerly.

Lanie got wearily to her feet and examined the leg. It looked superficial, but she would be glad when Betsy got there to verify that.

"Thanks, but I've got a vet on the way," she replied. Fifteen minutes later, Betsy's truck and trailer pulled into the small lot. The students scattered as Betsy stepped out.

"What happened?" she asked, slamming the truck door and walking to where Lanie and the tired horse were standing. "Did he get away from you? He looks like he just came off the cross-country course!" She peered at Bubba's leg. "And his leg's bleeding, for Chrissakes!"

"We might as well have been on a cross-country course." Lanie explained about the flat tire and the terrifying chase down the greenway.

"Did you get a look at the car?"

"No, it was in the shadows. And then when he tried to run us down all I could think about was getting away. The last I saw of him was on the pedestrian bridge."

Betsy stripped Bubba of his saddle and bridle, eased a halter over his head, and covered him with a sweat sheet, followed by a thick blanket. She eyed Lanie from across his back. "I'm really proud of you," she said quietly as she adjusted the belly straps on the blanket. "I know how hard it must have been for you to get on a horse."

Lanie, shoulders slumped with exhaustion, fought the urge to burst into tears. "I didn't have any choice. I just hope he isn't seriously hurt."

"It looks minor, but I'll take him back to the vet school and take a closer look." She grinned. "Come on, hop in."

In the vet school parking lot Lanie stepped down from Betsy's truck to find Donovan propped against the door of his car, arms crossed, a scowl on his face.

"What's he doing here?" she asked Betsy.

"I called him when the art museum security guard found my truck and trailer in the parking lot, missing a horse and a driver," she replied.

"We need to talk," Donovan said brusquely.

"It'll have to wait," said Lanie. "Right now I just want to get home."

He walked around to the passenger side of his car and yanked the door open. "Get in."

Lanie bristled. "No thanks, I have a ride." She turned to walk away.

"That wasn't an invitation, Ms. Montgomery, it was a directive."

Lanie walked back to where he stood. "I need to get my truck back to Southern Pines, and I don't take direction from you."

Betsy whistled tunelessly as she unloaded Bubba from the trailer and led him toward the entrance to the large-animal hospital, studiously ignoring the confrontation.

"I've taken care of that," he said, looking toward the door to the hospital reception area.

Lanie turned to see the blond woman from the Black and White Ball striding gracefully across the parking lot. She approached Donovan and gave him a smile and a kiss on the cheek. "I'm glad to see that everyone's all right," she said warmly. She turned to Lanie and held out her hand. "I'm Faye Donovan." Lanie shook it reluctantly as Faye continued. "Sounds like you've had quite a night."

"You could say that," Lanie replied ungraciously. She was exhausted, and wanted to be on her way back to Southern Pines and her bed.

Donovan pulled Lanie's keys from his front pocket and handed them to Faye. "We'll be right behind you," he said. "Drive safely." He watched her walk to Lanie's truck and drive slowly out the gate. When her taillights disappeared around the curve he turned back to Lanie. "Let's go, Ms. Montgomery," he said. "We have a lot to discuss. Your purse is in the passenger floorboard."

She heaved an exasperated sigh and slid into the passenger seat, slamming the door. They drove in silence while Donovan negotiated the light outer beltline traffic and headed south. Lanie wrapped her arms around herself and fought to keep her teeth from chattering. The adrenaline had fled, leaving her drained and cold. Donovan glanced at her and turned the heat all the way up.

They rode in silence for several minutes before he spoke again. "Tell me what happened."

Lanie recounted the phone call from Betsy, the terrifying incident in the art museum parking lot and the harrowing chase down the greenway.

"Did you see anyone suspicious in the vet school parking lot?" he asked.

Lanie shook her head. "No. Just a couple of empty trailers. There may have been a car or two. I can't remember."

"Anything else out of the ordinary happen yesterday?"

She hesitated. "Doug Erikson was in the shop in the afternoon. He was upset because Drew had questioned him about Chris's murder."

"Define upset."

"Well, angry really. Threatening. Rommel bit him in the back of the thigh.

"He threatened you?"

Her brow creased in confusion. "I don't know what's going on with Doug lately. He's always had a short fuse, but for the last month or two he's been more cranky than usual." She shrugged. "Maybe something in his personal life is weighing on him. Anyway, he said to stay out of the murder investigation or I'd get hurt."

"Good advice." He gave her a searching look. "Too bad you didn't follow it." He looked back at the road, drumming his fingers lightly on the steering wheel, lost in thought. "Anyone follow you from Southern Pines?" he asked.

She looked at him, surprised. She reviewed her drive up U.S. 1, then shook her head. ""No. I'm sure I would have noticed someone else on the road at that hour."

She chewed on a ragged fingernail, not wanting to admit the extent of her continued involvement in the case after Donovan had warned her to stay out of it, but the terror she'd felt as the car rushed at her in the parking lot still made her heart pound.

"I spoke to a friend of Marge Cameron's yesterday," she began hesitantly. She told him about the conversation with Myrtle Simpson, and her idea about consulting Fred Harris about any recent horse scams, the words spilling out faster and faster. "I think Marge's death, and maybe even Chris's, are tied to this horse scam."

"What did the insurance guy have to say?"

"I haven't had a chance to call him yet."

"You should have told me about this as soon as you found out. Or, at the very least, talked to the sheriff. Whoever this person is, they weren't just trying to scare you or send you a warning, Lanie." He looked at her steadily before turning his attention back to the black ribbon of highway. "They obviously think you're getting too close. And they *will* hurt you. Or kill you."

She turned to face him. "When I was in Jennifer's pantry the other morning there was a picture she'd received in the mail on the butcher block, a picture of her riding a jumper over a fence. Chris received a similar picture before he died. Don't you think it's significant that the two people who received them are both dead?"

"Did you hear what I just said?" he asked sharply.

"I left a message with Drew asking if he would give me a copy of Jennifer's picture."

He sighed. "Who else knows about these pictures? And about your conversation with Mrs. Simpson?"

"Well, Betsy of course. She was there at the hospital and so were Bryan and Rhonda and Doug Erikson. And I told Rhonda and Bryan and Betsy about the incident with Doug and my conversation with Myrtle Simpson. They were all in the shop just after it happened."

Donovan drove in silence for a few minutes. "I think the pictures are coincidental," he finally replied. "We got the autopsy results on Jennifer. She died from an injection of succinylcholine. I think it's likely the murderer has a medical background."

Lanie digested the information in silence. "So the same person killed both Chris and Jennifer. But, that doesn't mean they didn't send the pictures as a warning," she replied. "And, what about the information Myrtle Simpson gave me about Marge poking around in what was apparently a scheme. That's plenty of motive to kill her. Myrtle told me that this Bobby person used Chris's name as a reference. Maybe Marge was getting close to figuring it out and they killed her. Maybe Chris was more than a reference."

Mrs. Cameron's death doesn't fit the pattern." He glanced at Lanie. "I still think there's a medical connection. Or a veterinary one."

Lanie stared at him in stunned silence. "You think *Betsy* is behind this?" He shrugged. "She called you in the middle of the night to come rescue the horse. She knew you would be alone." He shot her a quick glance. "Don't you think it's a little coincidental that her truck and trailer had been sitting in the vet school parking lot for hours, and didn't develop a flat tire until you were leaving?"

Lanie stared at him. "No way." she said emphatically. "I know Betsy as well as I know myself. She wouldn't harm a fly.

Much less kill someone. Especially me. We've been friends since college."

Donovan dropped it. "How about your ex-boyfriend? Either one of them would have had access to the drug, and the knowledge to administer it," he continued.

"So would any number of doctors and nurses at the hospital."

"There are also the rumors about Dr. Crisafulli being involved in the illegal sale of ketamine."

"And rumor is all they were," said Lanie hotly, "spread by a neurotic vet school student who wanted to make him pay for ending their relationship."

"Maybe."

Donovan turned left on Young's Road and they rode the rest of the way to Lanie's farm in silence. He pulled into her driveway and parked. "I repeat, Lanie, you've touched a nerve with someone," he said. "You need to be careful." He reached into the driver's side map pocket, brought out a folded paper, and handed it to her. His brown eyes held her gaze. "I shouldn't do this, but you have to promise me you won't go haring off on your own if you find anything you think is significant."

Lanie unfolded it to find the picture of Jennifer she'd requested from Drew.

"You should also know we let Dr. Crisafulli go." He paused. "He had what appears to be an iron-clad alibi." He looked out the driver-side window at the barn before turning back to her.

"I told you it couldn't have been Chopper," she said with satisfaction.

"Angela Cameron came into the sheriff's office and gave a statement. She and the good doctor were together the night Chris Cameron was killed."

Lanie ran her fingernails over the folds of the photocopies, creasing them over and over again. She refused to meet

Donovan's gaze. "The wife of the deceased, who's having an affair with one of the prime suspects, is hardly an iron-clad alibi," she finally replied. She felt a flash of anger that Chopper had lied to her. Again.

"True. He's not off the hook entirely. We're still working on his alibi for the night Jennifer died, but Mrs. Cameron said they spent the night of Chris's death at the Umstead in Cary, and offered the receipts to prove it. The room service staff vouched for their presence. It doesn't mean he couldn't have left, killed Chris, and returned without anyone seeing him, but we've let him go for now." He turned in his seat and faced Lanie. "I'm sorry," he said quietly.

"I don't need your pity," she said angrily, pushing the door open and getting out, slamming the door behind her. She started toward the house, then abruptly turned back. As she leaned down to the window it slid silently down. Donovan looked at her curiously.

"Tell the Ice Queen I'm sorry to have interrupted her evening," she said.

Donovan looked out the windshield as Faye got out of Lanie's truck and walked toward them. He smiled. "She's used to it."

nineteen

The Crepe Place was crowded with the Sunday brunch crowd and early lunch patrons. The cheerful buzz of conversation swirled around Lanie as she sat down on the small bench just inside the door, waiting for a table and for Betsy to arrive. Her eyes felt gritty from lack of sleep, her movements lethargic and leaden. She'd sat at her kitchen table after Donovan dropped her off, unable to sleep. The parking lot scare and the subsequent chase down the Raleigh greenway kept repeating over and over in her head, along with the bomb Donovan had dropped about Chopper and Angela.

She wondered if part of Angela's attraction was money. If she'd left Chris, she'd have walked away with a substantial divorce settlement, but now that Chris was dead she could be a very wealthy woman indeed. And Donovan had said that Chopper wasn't cleared of suspicion in Chris's death, despite Angela's alibi.

Betsy's voice startled her from her reverie. "You look like you've been dragged through a knot hole backwards," she said as she plunked down next to Lanie. "Did you get a lecture on the way home last night? Mr. SBI was pacing like a tiger in a sideshow cage until you called. I definitely think his concern was a wee bit more than a professional one."

"Really? I wonder what Mrs. Donovan would think about that?"

Betsy's eyebrows rose in surprise. "What Mrs. Donovan?"

"The one that drove my truck back to Southern Pines last night."

"You think?"

A harried waitress arrived to show them to a table, giving Lanie an excuse not to answer. She was tired of thinking. The waitress seated them at a table in one of the windows fronting Broad Street, set down two glasses of ice water, and took their drink order.

Lanie scowled at the menu. "I love this place, but they really need to get a beer and wine license. I mean, what's the point in having brunch if you can't order a mimosa or a glass of wine?"

"We could've gone to the Ironwood," Betsy replied evenly, eyeing her choices. She peered at Lanie over the top of her menu. "Are we a little out of sorts this morning?"

"No. We're tired, hungry, and frustrated."

"Hey," Betsy said, lowering her menu. "I didn't mean to upset you."

"You didn't." She took a deep breath and told Betsy about Chopper's alibi. After a moment's hesitation, she also told her about Donovan's suspicions that Betsy was behind the flat tire and the terrifying pursuit. "I told him that was ridiculous, that you weren't capable of setting me up like that."

When she'd finished, Betsy jammed her reading glasses on and returned to the menu. "Chopper's lower than a snake's ass in a wheel rut," she said firmly. "Just goes to prove my momma was right. It takes a hell of a man to be better than no man at all."

Lanie laughed.

"I'm serious," Betsy continued. "Consider it confirmation that your decision to end the relationship was the right one. A Roomba would have been more loving and at least it would have vacuumed your floors." She waved her hand dismissively.

"He and Angela deserve each other. Move on and be glad you didn't waste any more time on him."

Lanie sighed deeply. "You're right." She kept her eyes on the melting ice in her glass.

Betsy relented. "I'm sure he loved you, Lanie, as much as he could ever love anyone other than himself. He just doesn't have the capacity to give you what you want." She drained her tea and set it back down on the table. "Though, as far as I'm concerned, if you did anything short of bludgeoning him to death with a fire ax, he got off light. Go find yourself a man who celebrates and appreciates who you are." She sat back in her chair. "Like Donovan."

Lanie's mouth dropped open. "Donovan!" she said in disbelief. "Are you mad? He practically accused you of the murders and trying to kill me!" She scraped at some dried crepe on the tabletop with her fingernail. "Besides, I told you he's married."

Betsy smiled. "I'm flattered he thinks I'm capable of such deviousness," she said. She gave her friend an appraising look. "Hell, if I looked like you I'd have five men dangling on a string at all times." She sat forward, her face earnest. "And why not Donovan? He's good looking, doesn't need you to support him, and he obviously likes you." She grinned. "What was that line Dolly Parton said in that movie? That best way to get over one man is to get under another one? You need to take that to heart."

Lanie looked around to make sure they weren't being overheard, then turned back. "Did you not hear what I said?" she hissed. "He's married!"

Betsy hid a smile behind her menu. "That last bit wasn't in reference to anyone in particular."

Lanie hoped the waitress didn't notice her flaming face when she returned to take their order. She opted for her favorite, the egg bowl. Betsy decided on the Pedro, wrapped in a savory crepe. Their order complete, Lanie pulled the two photos from her purse and passed them across the table.

"Take a look at these. Each is a picture of Jennifer and Chris riding a horse over a jump. Both of them have a handwritten note at the bottom. Chris's says, 'I don't know how much longer I can Bear it!' Jennifer's says, 'It's your cross to Bear.' They're in the same script, and the 'b' in bear is capitalized in both. I think they were sent as a warning."

"Marge didn't get one."

"That we know of," Lanie reminded her. "Do you see any other commonalities in these pictures? I've looked at them until I'm cross-eyed, but nothing else really jumps out at me."

"No wonder you're cranky this morning," Betsy responded as she studied the pictures. "That red-headed guy's in both pictures, but the same trainers, competitors, farriers, you name it, travel the Grand Prix circuit, so I doubt that's significant. We just don't have enough information." She pointed at Chris's horse. "I'd bet you a hundred dollars, though, that that's a Desperado baby. See that little dime-sized spot on his belly?" She turned the photo so Lanie could see it. "Almost every one of his foals have it. In the exact same place." She set the photo down and picked up the other. "Genetics was one of my favorite courses in vet school."

Lanie sat forward. "Does Jennifer's horse have it?"

"Not that I can see, but then again, he's a gray so it would be hard to tell."

Lanie sat back in her chair, discouraged. "Have you made any progress on the ledger?"

"Not really. Did you remember to bring that list of horses you found in Joy's day planner?"

Smiling, Lanie drew it out of her purse. "I found it in the pocket of a dirty pair of jeans. Good thing I didn't wash it."

Betsy tucked it in her shirt pocket. "Speaking of Joy, have you heard from her?"

Lanie waited for the waitress to deposit their food before she answered. "I talked to her earlier this week and gave her an update on how Bubba's doing and how the investigation's going. She's hoping Hugh can get her out on bail."

"Let's hope so," Betsy said before turning her attention to her food.

As they were finishing the last of their eggs and crepes Lanie heard her phone buzzing from the depths of her purse. She pulled it out and looked at the display. A local number, but not one she recognized.

"Hello," she said cautiously.

"Hello, dear. It's Gladys Wrenn. I hope I haven't caught you at a bad time." Her thin voice warbled up in an anxious question at the end.

"Not at all, Gladys. How did you get my cell phone number?"

"I'm not in my dotage, you know," she said with a touch of asperity. "I called your store and wormed it out of your employee."

Lanie laughed. "I applaud your detective work! How can I help you?"

"Well, you remember my telling you about my friend Myrtle? The one who got mixed up with that nasty bunch of horse thieves?"

"Yes. In fact, I spoke to her just a few days ago."

"She's in town, dear, visiting friends. In fact she's coming by to see me in a few minutes. I thought you might like to speak with her in person."

Lanie sat up in her chair and flapped her free hand at Betsy, who was engrossed in the desert menu. "I would love to!" Lanie said. "When will she be there?"

"In about fifteen minutes. Shall I run downstairs and see if there's any strawberry shortcake left over from lunch?"

"No thanks, Gladys. I'm trying to watch my weight," Lanie said with a smile.

"Pish! You're too skinny to be worrying about any such thing. So we'll see you in a few?"

"I'll head your way just as soon as I can get my check."

She hung up and smiled broadly at Betsy. "That was Gladys Wrenn. Myrtle Simpson's in town for a visit."

Betsy picked up the photos and passed them across the table. "Good. Have her take a look at these. Maybe she'll recognize someone."

"We should be so lucky."

Lanie took Broad Street to Midland Road and turned north on Route 24-27, which divided the Pine Needles golf course. A few miles up the road she turned east on Camp Easter Road and sped the short distance to The Meadows. She didn't know that Myrtle would have any more information than she'd imparted on the phone, but it was worth the short trip to find out.

Gladys Wrenn greeted her at the front door of her apartment and introduced her to Myrtle Simpson, a tall, slim woman in her late seventies or early eighties. Her gray hair was cut in a youthful bob and beautiful rings graced her elegant hands. Reading glasses hung from a chain around her neck and rested on her St. John's knit top.

"So nice to meet you," she said to Lanie. "I hope we two old ladies haven't imposed on your afternoon, but I was hopeful you might have unearthed some information."

"I'm really not any further along than I was when we last spoke, but I do have a couple of photos I'd like you to look at." Lanie took a seat in the chintz chair Gladys offered and waited for them to settle on the sofa before pulling the photos from her purse and passing them to Myrtle.

"Both of these pictures were taken a number of years ago, but I'd appreciate it if you'd look them over and see if you recognize anyone. Both Chris and a friend of mine, Jennifer, received them in the mail just before they were killed, and I think there's got to be some significance in the fact they both received them."

"Of course." Myrtle slipped her glasses on and studied the first photo. The color drained slowly from her face and she pointed with a shaking finger at the photo in her hand.

"That's him!" she said. "He's much younger in this picture, of course, but that's definitely him!"

Lanie moved over to perch next to Myrtle on the sofa. "Show me!"

Myrtle pointed at the red-haired man on the rail. "His hair's not red anymore and he's a little heavier, but I'm sure that's Bobby." She handed the picture to Lanie and turned her attention to the second one. "And here he is again," she said excitedly, "standing next to that woman and child."

Lanie leaned over to see where Myrtle was pointing. "Are you positive?"

"Yes! Yes, that's definitely him. Do you know him?"

Lanie shook her head. "I'm afraid I don't recognize him. I rode eventers, not show jumpers, and I'm not familiar with who the players were on the Grand Prix circuit back then. But I know people who were that I can ask. Can you remember at which show you last saw him?"

Myrtle slowly took off her glasses and let them drop to the bosom of her knit top, a look of bewilderment on her face.

"Didn't I say, dear, when we spoke last time? I saw him right here in Southern Pines. At Marge's."

"At Cameron Farms?" Lanie asked, incredulous.

"Yes. It was the last day of my visit and I was up in my room packing to go to the airport. I looked out my window and saw him walking into the barn. He had on one of those hoodie things, but I recognized him. People can change the way they look, but they can't change their body language, don't you agree?" Lanie nodded in agreement. "I nearly broke my neck racing down the stairs to tell Marge, I can tell you that," Myrtle continued. "She really needs to spend the money to put in an elevator." She came to a halt and her fine, pale skin flushed. "Oh, dear. I'm so sorry. It's just hard to believe that she's dead."

"I understand," Lanie said, anxious to hear the rest of the story. "What did Marge do when you told her you'd seen him?"

"She forbade me to say a word to anyone about it. She wanted to do some digging before we brought the hammer down on his weasely head." She flushed again, but this time with anger. "Marge said he wasn't going anywhere and once we had our ducks in a row we'd go to the authorities." She looked suddenly horrified. "Do you think *he* killed Marge?" she asked. "She was so precipitous. Maybe she confronted him and he killed her to keep her from going to the police."

"I honestly don't know," said Lanie, "but I'm going to find out." She directed Myrtle's attention back to the photos. "Does anyone else look familiar?"

Buoyed by her earlier success, Myrtle scanned the crowd of spectators and competitors. After several minutes she looked up. "I can't swear to it because I can't see her face clearly, but this woman looks familiar." She laid a perfectly manicured forefinger on a woman in a bright floral dress and straw hat. "There's something about her that reminds me of my co-investor." She looked sad as realization dawned on her. "It appears I was duped all around, doesn't it? Was she a shill do you think?" She turned and looked at Lanie. "I was a foolish old woman, wasn't I? I thought—never mind what I thought," she said firmly, straightening her shoulders. "Just let me know how I can help."

"You've been a big help, Myrtle. I need to do some nosing around, but I promise I'll let you know what I find out." Lanie patted her on the arm. "I need to go make some phone calls. I'll be in touch."

Gladys rose and walked her to the door. "Thank you for coming, dear. Someone needs to look after us silly old women." She smiled ruefully.

Lanie gave her a hug. "You're not silly old women. Myrtle just made the mistake of putting her trust where it wasn't warranted. The world is full of people who'll take advantage of people's trust, and it isn't just the elderly who succumb to them."

"That's very generous, dear." She hesitated, struck by a thought. "Did you get a chance to talk to Mary O'Connor?" she asked. "I heard that she took a turn for the worse this past week so you'd better not wait too long." She shook her gray head. "It seems like everyone I've known is going. Not that Mary was a friend, you understand, but she was a part of my past, of Marge's past, and with her passing, another connection with it will be lost." She peered up at Lanie, her blue eyes rimmed with tears. "Getting old is *not* for sissies!"

Lanie smiled. "You're too young at heart to be old." She leaned over and gave Gladys a kiss on her papery cheek.

Gladys's face brightened and she smiled as she gently closed the door behind Lanie.

Lanie waited for the elevator, her mind racing. Who was the man Myrtle had seen from her window? Not Chris, certainly, but possibly someone associated with him? Perhaps Chris was involved in the scam involving horses. If not directly, then by identifying potential victims, using his name to dispel any distrust. And what better victim pool than elderly ladies, with loads of money and a need to be needed, to be important to someone or something. The man had to be someone who frequented Cameron Farms and was known to Marge.

When the elevator announced its arrival with a soft ping, she stepped in automatically, lost in thought. When the doors opened on the ground floor her steps turned in the direction of the Alzheimer's unit. Her last visit to Mary O'Connor hadn't worked out so well, she thought, but if Mary's condition was deteriorating she ought to give it one more try before it was too late.

After a few wrong turns, she found herself in front of the locked door to the Alzheimer's wing. She pushed the button and walked in, taking in the sight of the ward's denizens, strapped in their wheelchairs and lined against the wall. A volunteer was chatting with one of the nurses, her therapy dog, an appealing tri-colored Pembroke Welsh Corgi, at her side. One of the women strapped in a wheelchair was straining to reach the dog, her fingers outstretched, her face a study of frustration. It broke Lanie's heart to watch her struggle.

"Trying to get out?"

Lanie started and turned around. She hadn't heard the aide come in behind her.

"No, just coming to visit someone."

"The code to get out is seven eight three nine."

"Thanks," Lanie replied. She waited for the aide to turn the corner ahead of her before proceeding toward Mary's room.

The volunteer and the nurse were still engrossed in their conversation, the Corgi, now loose, trailing his lead behind him as he sniffed the polished floor for crumbs. Lanie scooped him up and walked with him in her arms to the woman strapped in the wheelchair. Lanie held the dog where she could reach him and was rewarded with a bright smile. The Corgi stoically endured the clumsy stroking of his head and threw in a lick to boot. Lanie gently set him back on his feet and fondled his ears. "Thanks, little one. You just made someone's day."

She walked the short distance to Mary O'Connor's room and paused at the door, wondering what she hoped to accomplish. She took a deep breath and pushed the door open. There was no noise from the television today, only the ragged, irregular sound of Mary's labored breathing. The heat was stifling, even though the shrunken form on the bed was blanketed.

She walked to Mary's side and looked down at her, certain she would not be conversing with anyone this side of eternity. Mary clutched the worn Bible in one hand and as Lanie stood there she slowly opened her eyes and smiled. "He lives!" she whispered triumphantly. She weakly lifted her fingers and Lanie reached down and clasped them in her own. The smile faded from Mary's face and she closed her eyes as her labored breathing slowed, then stopped. Her hand released its grasp.

The sound of the Bible hitting the floor on the other side of the bed made Lanie jump. She gently placed Mary's hand on the blanket and walked around the bed to pick up the fallen Bible and several pages that had escaped its confines. She glanced at the papers and was surprised to find one of them was a birth certificate. She read more closely. At first the information it contained didn't register: a male child, born June 15, 1979. Father: Caucasian. Mother: Hispanic. Child's name: Richard Cameron Alvarez. Signed by the father, Richard Cameron.

Lanie sank slowly into the chair by Mary's bed, trying to assimilate what she'd just read. The child was born a few weeks before Richard Cameron died in a fiery crash. But what had happened to the baby? A baby that was now potentially in line for an enormous fortune. A direct lineal descendant, if still alive, would trump Chris's position as heir. Did Marge know about this child? And how did Mary come by this document? She looked at the body on the bed. Too many questions, and now the only person who could, at least theoretically, have answered them, was gone.

She turned her attention to the other piece of paper and scanned it. When she was done, she collapsed back into the chair, her hand over her mouth, afraid she was going to be sick. She jumped from the chair and bolted into the hallway, deserted now of all but the patients suspended in their chairs, slumbering in the late afternoon stillness. Looking around wildly, she spotted a nurse at the station at the end of the hall, a phone pressed to her ear. Lanie took off at a run, Bible and documents clutched tightly in her hand.

"Mary O'Connor is dead," she said breathlessly to the startled nurse. "I was visiting her and she passed away while I was there."

The nurse hung up and headed purposefully down the hall, silent in her crepe-soled shoes.

"Are you okay? You look like you've seen a ghost!"

Lanie spun around. Faye Donovan was standing behind her, two ginger ales in her hands and a look of concern on her face.

"It's Lanie, isn't it?" she asked. "I'm Faye Donovan. We met the other night." She shifted one of the soda cans to her other hand and gently grasped Lanie's arm. "Do you need to sit down? You look like you might faint."

Lanie shook off her hand. "I need to talk to your husband. Now!"

"My husband?"

"Yes, your husband. Agent Donovan."

"Michael's not my husband. He's my brother. We're visiting our mother." She stepped back. "I'll go get him," she said, turning away.

Lanie paced restlessly in front of the nursing station. A few minutes later, Donovan emerged from a room down the hall and strode toward her.

"What the hell is going on?" he demanded.

Lanie rushed to him and grabbed his arm. "Mary O'Connor died. I found a birth certificate in her Bible and something worse, much worse." She stumbled over the words as they poured out, knowing she sounded disjointed.

"Who's Mary O'Connor?"

"Marge Cameron's housekeeper."

Donovan turned her around and led her to an empty conference room. He pushed her firmly into a chair and closed the door, then took a seat across from her.

"Okay," he said quietly. "Take a deep breath and start from the beginning."

Lanie pushed the birth certificate across the table. "I found this in Mary O'Connor's Bible," she said more calmly. "Richard Cameron, Marge's only son, had a child, a boy. The mother was a young Hispanic girl, the daughter of Marge's gardener and maid."

Donovan kept his steady gaze on her face, ignoring, for the moment, the birth certificate. "So?"

"So," Lanie said impatiently, "he signed the birth certificate acknowledging paternity of the child. At that time, under North Carolina law, a child could only inherit from its father if the father acknowledged paternity. One way of doing that was for him to sign the birth certificate."

Lanie slid the remaining document across to him. "I also found this in Mary's Bible. It's a copy of an admission record to Cherry Hill Hospital." She paused to gather her thoughts. "It details the admission of a young man to the hospital on the night of July 4, 1979." She pointed at the admission record. "According to that, he was arrested in Fayetteville that night for threatening to kill several people in a bar on Hay Street. He had no identification on him and, purportedly, couldn't provide his name or address. He was extremely agitated and violent, so they involuntarily committed him."

"I'm not following you," Donovan responded.

She stood and leaned her hands on the table. "I think that young man was Richard Cameron. I think he told his mother about the baby, and that he was going to marry the mother of his child. That's not something Marge Cameron would tolerate. She couldn't, and wouldn't, let her son marry an uneducated servant. I think she had him committed to the state mental hospital. He's alive, Donovan, or he was. When I visited Mary O'Connor the first time, she kept pounding on her Bible and yelling, 'He lives!' I thought she was referring to Jesus, but I was wrong. She was referring to Richard Cameron, and she had the proof in that Bible all these years. That explains why Marge established a trust fund for her and paid her expenses here, to buy her silence."

"Mrs. Cameron couldn't have gotten away with that," Donovan reasoned. "All Richard had to do was tell them who he was and walk out." He shoved the paper back at her. "And, If Richard Cameron was locked away in the state mental hospital, who was in the car?"

"She could have done it if she'd had some help," Lanie insisted. She pointed to the signature at the bottom of the admission sheet. "It's signed by Dr. Salisbury." She related Barbara

Rheiman's story about Doc Salisbury's obsession with Marge Cameron, and his position at Cherry Hill. "With Salisbury's collusion she could have had him committed as punishment for defying her, and to shut him up. Think about it! The more he protested, the more he dug his own grave. They would have pumped him full of Thorazine and locked him up."

"Even if this wild conjecture was remotely true," he said, "it still doesn't explain the body in the car. One that's now buried in the Cameron family cemetery, I might add."

She sat back down in the chair and rubbed her tired eyes with the heels of her hands. "That's the worst part," she finally said. She told him of Gladys's tale of the handsome young stable hand, his affair with Marge, and his disappearance.

"Gladys said he thought he was going to move into the big house and be set for life. Instead, he mysteriously disappeared and was never seen again." She sighed wearily. "I bet if you exhumed that body from Richard Cameron's grave you'd find the DNA doesn't match. Marge had the poor son of a bitch killed, or killed him herself, and had him put in Richard's car and then set it on fire." She shuddered. "And I'll also bet you the real Richard Cameron has spent the last forty-some years rotting away in a mental institution." She fell silent, trying to gauge his reaction.

Donovan finally sat forward and leaned his forearms on the table. "She couldn't have done any of this without the complicity of a lot of people, including the sheriff. There's no way she could have pulled it off by herself. The chance of that happening, and of all parties keeping silent about it all these years, isn't worth mentioning."

Lanie shrugged. "Money talks. More importantly, money keeps other people from talking. It would just have been a matter of striking the right price with the sheriff, Dr. Salisbury, and apparently Mary O'Connor." She leaned back in the hard chair and closed her eyes. "Sheriff Blackwood died of a heart attack not too long after Richard's supposed death. You might want to consider two exhumation orders."

Donovan picked up the birth certificate and the admission record, folded them in half and tapped them on the table top, his eyes fixed on Lanie's face.

"If all this is true, then who killed Marge?" he asked.

"You're the detective. You figure it out." She stood up wearily. "I'm going home and take a long, hot shower. I feel dirty after reading that." She turned and walked to the door, then turned back.

"It still doesn't explain who killed Chris and Jennifer. Or why," she pointed out.

He stared at the tabletop, nodded slowly, and then met her eyes.

"I'll be in touch," he said.

twenty

Lanie sat in her truck, drained and exhausted, unable to turn the key. She couldn't get the horror of what she'd discovered out of her mind. Despite Donovan's skepticism, she was certain the events had gone down the way she'd outlined them. She found she didn't care who killed Marge Cameron; she'd deserved it for the enormity of her betrayal of her son, and others. Was Richard Cameron still alive? Was he still trapped in the nightmare of the state mental institution, his only crimes those of his defiance of his mother and his refusal to disavow his son?

She started the truck wanting only to get home to the comfort of her dog. Dogs, she corrected. "Damn Betsy Anderson," she muttered under her breath. The thought of giving up Rommel had become unthinkable. The over-sized, deaf lunk had managed to worm his way into her affections in a very short time.

On the drive down Young's Road she decided she didn't want to spend the night alone in her house. She needed the warmth and comfort of friends and a glass of wine. Betsy will just have to put up with the three of us, she decided. Feeling better already, she pulled into her driveway and parked, whistling for the dogs as she stepped out of the truck.

They hurtled around the corner of the house, Snert leaping and yapping in excitement. Rommel, in his usual self-contained way, insisted on pressing as close to Lanie as he could get. She knelt and threw her arms around them, squeezing tight, thinking about the woman in the nursing home and hoping fervently she never got to that place, strapped in a wheelchair, unable to touch her beloved dogs.

She opened the back door to the truck and Rommel and Snert flew in and curled up on the back seat, ready for a ride to wherever she was going.

"Be right back, guys," she said, closing the truck door. "I just need to pack a few things and then we'll make an unannounced visit to Aunt Betsy." She left them in the truck and walked into the house and down the hall to her bedroom. "She better have her refrigerator stocked with cold wine," she muttered as she gathered up toothbrush and toothpaste, a hairbrush and a change of clothes. Betsy would have to supply a tee shirt for sleeping. Lanie was anxious to be on the road.

She stuffed the few things in a small bag and returned to the kitchen, where she stopped to fix a vodka and water for the road. It's only three miles, she thought. Surely I won't get stopped by the police in that short distance. On reflection, she nixed the water and poured straight vodka into a plastic cup. She heard the screen door slam and looked up. Bryan was coming through the kitchen door, a pizza box in one hand and a six pack of Red Stripe in the other.

"I stopped at Mellow Mushroom and picked up a Mega Veggie hoping you'd share it with me," he said cheerfully.

"Damn!" she said, hating to disappoint him. But the sun had gone down in the short time she'd been home and she wanted to get on the road to Betsy's. "Mega Veggie's my favorite. Any other time I'd be thrilled to join you, but I've had the day from hell so I'm going to surprise Betsy with a spur-of-the-moment girls' night in. I was just leaving."

He shrugged. "No problem! More for me! I should have called before I dropped by. We'll do it some other time."

He set the pizza box on the counter and twisted the top off a beer. The smell of the pizza made Lanie's stomach rumble with a reminder that she hadn't eaten since the egg bowl at The Crepe Place. It seemed like a thousand years ago.

"Take a sec and tell me about your day from hell while I finish this beer," he said with a smile. "Troubles shared and all that." He waggled his reddish blond eyebrows comically.

Lanie couldn't help but smile. "Oh Lord," she said, sitting down at the kitchen table, "I don't even know where to start."

She began with her trip to The Meadows and Myrtle's identification of the man in the photos. "Though, I'm no further along than I was in solving the mystery," she admitted. "We don't know who it was that Myrtle saw from her window. And we don't know how, or even if, it's connected to Chris and Jennifer's murders." She took a sip of her vodka and continued. "I'm going to have to show the pictures to people who travel the Grand Prix circuit, see if anyone recognizes him. Surely *someone* will, don't you think?"

"Bound to," Bryan replied, one elbow propped on his arm and swinging his Red Stripe bottle from side to side. "Someone will know who he is." He gave her a sympathetic smile. "You *have* had a bad day."

"That's not the half of it," she said, and she launched into the saga of Mary O'Connor's death, her discovery, and how it all came together suddenly.

"I'm sure Donovan thinks I'm deranged," she said when she'd finished, "but my gut tells me I'm right." It's the only explanation that makes sense."

Bryan whistled. "That's incredible. Who would have thought you'd turn out to be such a great detective?"

"Not," she said with a laugh. "Anyway, after the day I've had I really don't relish being by myself tonight."

"Can't blame you for that."

Lanie's phone rang. She turned away, reaching for her purse, fumbling around in the bottom of it until she located it. "How do these damn things always manage to end up at the bottom?" She pulled it out, looked at the name on the display, and hit the "accept" button. "Speaking of Betsy," she said, turning back to Bryan. He was holding a nine millimeter inches from her face. She heard the hammer cock as Betsy's excited voice assaulted her ear.

"I figured it out!" Betsy yelled gleefully. "I figured out what the entries in Jennifer's ledger mean. The horses on that list you found at Joy's are all here."

"Betsy," Lanie said in an attempt to stem the flow, keeping her eyes on Bryan and the gun.

"I think the money represents insurance pay offs on horses that they killed. In Flight's in there, and so are a dozen others whose names I recognize. The initials at the top of the columns stand for Bryan, Jennifer, and Chris."

"Betsy," Lanie said again, "I have to go. I'm late for dinner at my Aunt Barbara's. You know she expects me for dinner every Sunday. I'll call you later." She disconnected and clutched the phone to her chest.

"Best decision you've made all day," Bryan said quietly. He waved the gun toward the back door. "Let's go. You drive." Lanie's phone began to ring insistently.

"Leave that on the table and let's go," he said impatiently. "You aren't going to need it."

She walked out her back door on rubbery legs and headed for Bryan's truck. He grabbed her arm and jerked her toward her own vehicle.

"We'll take yours." He opened the passenger door and waved her in. "Crawl over. I'll be right behind you."

She crawled awkwardly over the console as Bryan got in behind her and shut the door. Her hand shook as she turned the key, bringing the engine roaring to life.

"Where are we going?" she asked, afraid to look at him.

"Cameron Farms. The scene of the crime." He smiled, and stuck the gun in her side. "Don't do anything stupid."

She pulled out of the drive and made her way to Young's Road, where she turned toward Cameron Farms. As they picked up speed she heard a growl from the back seat.

"What the hell is that?" Bryan looked over his shoulder into the back seat.

"It's just Snert and Rommel," she responded. "I was taking them with me to Betsy's."

"Pull over and let them out," he demanded, raising the gun to the side of her head. Biting her lip, she took her foot off of the pedal and the truck began to slow. She hated letting them out on the side of the road, but she was afraid Bryan would kill them if she didn't. She pulled off on the shoulder and put the truck in park.

"Same thing in reverse," Bryan said, getting out and motioning for Lanie to follow him. When she was standing on the shoulder beside him he motioned again with the gun. "Open the door and let them out. Then get back in."

She complied, tears stinging her eyes. She prayed Rommel would stick close to Snert and that they'd make their way safely back home. Rommel's deafness would mean a horrible death for him if they wandered into the path of a car. As they pulled away, she could see them chasing after her in the glow of her tail lights. A small sob escaped her lips.

"Oh, quit whining," he said. "If they're still out there when I come back I'll put them out of their misery." His teeth bared in a grin. "If a car doesn't get them first."

They drove in silence for a mile or so. "It was you, wasn't it, that Myrtle saw?" she asked finally. "And when Marge confronted you, you killed her."

"No, you stupid little bitch, I didn't kill Marge," he snarled. He leaned across the console. "Why did you have to stick your nose in where it didn't belong?" He was so close Lanie could feel spittle hit the side of her cheek. "Shut up and drive! And take the back entrance to the farm. We don't want to disturb Queen Angie's beauty sleep."

They bumped down the rutted road to the barn and topped the hill at the back gate, which was standing open. Bryan's teeth flashed a grin in the darkness of the cab. "As you can see, I plan ahead. Just in case you were considering making a break for it."

Within a few minutes, they arrived at the front entrance to the darkened barn, and he directed her to park and get out. He grabbed her by the back of her shirt and shoved her into the barn. She stumbled, almost falling to her knees in the aisle. The startled horses banged around in their stalls. A rising moon filtered down through the sky-lights and gleamed off the barrel of his gun, still aimed at her head.

"Since it's obvious you're going to kill me, why don't you tell me what your deal was with Chris?" Lanie asked.

He frowned. "He and Jennifer and I had a good thing going until Chris got greedy. He'd identify some old hag with a ton of money and no brains, and charm them into investing in a worthless dog-food candidate. Jennifer pretended to be an investor, too, and she'd write a check for her half of the cost of the horse so they wouldn't be suspicious. Then we'd just tear up Jennifer's check and split the shill's money. If one of the old biddies got suspicious because their nag wasn't performing up to snuff, we'd kill the horse for the insurance money." He laughed. "And then we'd turn around and sell them another worthless horse. Anybody that stupid deserves to be relieved of their money."

"And Jennifer?"

"She made the fatal mistake of falling for one of our marks, Doug Erickson. When it came time to do the deed on Doug's horse, she got cold feet. Stupid bitch threatened to tell him."

"Doug was going to kill his horse for the insurance money?" Lanie was confused.

"No, stupid. *Giselle* was. She gave him that horse as a gift, but kept the papers and insurance in her name." He shifted restlessly. "That one was going to be a bit messy though. The horse had a history of colic so we couldn't light him up like usual." He smiled nastily. "He was going to suffer an unfortunate accident, with the help of a crowbar. Amazing how fragile their legs are, isn't it?"

Lanie felt sick to her stomach.

"Enough gabbing," he said. "I can't afford for your meddling to ruin a good thing. But don't worry, it won't hurt. I promise."

A figure stepped out of the shadows of the wash stall and approached them. "Let her go, Bryan. There's been enough killing. Of people and of horses." Rick walked forward into the fall of moonlight from the skylight overhead.

"That's interesting coming from you, Rick." Bryan giggled. "I saw you running out of the house the night Marge was killed. I'm guessing you murdered her, though I still haven't figured out why." He flashed a smile. "I must say it was a fitting end though."

"No need for anyone but me to know why," Rick replied quietly. "It was a private matter between her and me." He reached his hand out for the gun. "Let Lanie go," he repeated, "and let's put a stop to this before someone else gets hurt."

Bryan slowly dropped the gun to his side, then swung it back up and fired, point blank, at Rick. He crumpled to the brick floor and was still. Lanie gasped and clapped her hands over her mouth, her eyes wide with shock.

"Where were we?" Bryan asked, turning back to Lanie. "Oh yes! It's time to put a stop to your meddling. I can't have you following up on your little amateurish inquiries so I'm afraid we'll have to bid each other adieu."

"It's too late, Bryan. Or Bobby. Or whatever your name is," Lanie said softly. "Betsy and I found Jennifer's journal detailing the horses you killed and the moneys you collected. Betsy figured out the scheme. Myrtle Simpson won't let this drop either. You can't kill us all."

"Maybe not," he said, "but we'll start with you and see where we end up."

"I've figured everything out except why you would send Chris and Jennifer those pictures? Why would you call attention to yourself like that?" Lanie asked in an attempt to keep him talking.

"*I* didn't send those pictures. But when I find out who did they'll wish they hadn't. It put those two idiots into a panic, and because of that, you have to die."

"I don't think so, Dad," said a quiet voice from behind Lanie. Elisabeth stepped up to stand beside her, a revolver in her shaking hands.

"*I* sent those pictures. I wanted each of you to know that I knew what you did, and that you were going to pay for it."

"Elisabeth?" said Bryan, his face a study of confusion and disbelief.

She took a few steps closer, her hands steadier on the gun. "Did you think I didn't know that you killed Bear for the insurance money?" she cried angrily, her voice breaking. "That horse was the only sane thing in my life and you killed him! You broke his leg with a crowbar! I've hated you ever since."

She took in a deep, steadying breath. "I vowed you'd pay for it, and now you will."

Bryan took a step toward her, his gun now pointed at Elisabeth. "Give me the gun before someone gets hurt," he said.

"No," she screamed, her fingers tightening on the grip. "You're going to die like Bear did. Suffering. Screaming."

His face hardened and Lanie watched, breathless, as his finger tightened on the trigger. "No," she cried out, shoving Elisabeth to the floor. Everything seemed to happen in slow motion as Bryan swung the barrel of the gun toward Lanie. From out of the darkness, a black streak bolted past her and leapt for Bryan's chest. The sound of the gun going off was deafening. Rommel's weight and momentum carried him forward into Bryan, slamming him onto the brick floor with a sickening thud that Lanie felt, more than heard. The big dog collapsed on top on him, his blood pooling with Bryan's, spreading in an ever-widening circle around them.

Lanie rushed forward to kneel beside Rommel as sirens and flashing lights signaled the arrival of help. The barn filled with sheriff's deputies, first responders, and SBI agents. Betsy barreled through the barn door and fell to her knees beside Lanie. Together they pulled the big dog's body clear, and Betsy ripped off her flannel shirt, wadded it into a ball and pressed it to his chest, applying pressure to the jagged wound.

"Hold this," she said to Lanie, standing up and running toward the entrance to the barn. "I need to grab some stuff from my truck."

Lanie held the shirt tight to the wound and prayed as it became saturated with blood. Betsy returned with pressure bandages and wrapped them around the shirt, her brow creased in concentration. Paper wrappings flew as she opened a sterile package with an IV needle, picked up Rommel's front leg and inserted it.

Donovan strode down the aisle toward them and Betsy waved him over. "I need someone to help me get this dog to my clinic or he's not going to make it," she said urgently.

Donovan motioned for two Southern Pines police officers to help Betsy place Rommel on a litter and carry it to her truck. Then he knelt down next to Lanie.

"Are you alright?" he asked.

She nodded slowly, then burst into tears. "Rommel saved my life," she sobbed, clinging to Donovan's neck.

"I know he did,' he said gently, holding her close. "We'll just have to hope that he pulls through."

He stood up, took her by the arm and helped her to her feet. "Come on," he said gently, "I'll have someone take you home. We can take your statement later."

As they made their slow way down the aisle the EMTs were lifting Rick onto a stretcher. Lanie paused, and he turned his head to look at her, his skin white and papery. She walked over to the gurney and grasped his hand. He squeezed it tightly in his own.

"You *are* Richard Cameron, aren't you?" she asked gently.

He nodded weakly and spoke. She leaned over, her ear close to his mouth. "I didn't hear you," she said.

"Find my son," he whispered.

twenty-one

The moon was setting as Betsy and Donovan carefully slid Rommel's litter from the back of Betsy's truck and carried him toward Lanie's kitchen door, Betsy holding the bag of saline solution above her head and Donovan carrying the IV pole in his free hand. Lanie grabbed Snert by the collar and held the screen door open for them. Their slow progress and measured steps made her think of a funeral procession.

Betsy hung the fluid bag on the pole and adjusted the drip. Putting the stethoscope in her ears she knelt on the kitchen floor beside Rommel and checked his lungs and heart rate. She pulled the stethoscope down around her neck and pointed at Donovan.

"Get a pot of water heating. Enough to fill five or six two-liter bottles." Her gaze shifted to Lanie. "Do you have any two-liter soda bottles?" Lanie nodded. "Empty them and have them ready to fill." As Lanie headed to the pantry Betsy called after her, "And get some towels to wrap them in."

Donovan opened and closed cabinets, searching until he found a stockpot. He filled it with water and set it on the gas stove, turning the flame on high. "So what's this for?" he asked, drying his hands on a kitchen towel.

"We need to keep him warm," Betsy replied.

"Couldn't we wrap him in blankets?"

"We could, but it'd be about as useless as tits on a boar hog. His core temperature has dropped, and his ability to generate his own body heat is compromised so we need to help him," she explained patiently. "Hot water bottles will do that. Blankets won't."

Lanie returned to the kitchen with an armload of towels and handed them to Betsy. She took six bottles of Coke from the pantry and poured the contents down the sink, then rummaged in drawers until she found a funnel. When the water was almost boiling Donovan lifted the pot from the stove and carefully filled the bottles. Lanie replaced the caps and handed the hot bottles to Betsy, who rolled them in towels and tucked them around Rommel. Then she sat on the floor and lifted his head into her lap, stroking his ears. His shallow breathing filled the suddenly quiet kitchen, the white bandages binding his chest rising and falling almost imperceptibly.

Donovan pulled a chair from the table and firmly pushed Lanie into it. He disappeared into the dining room and returned with a bottle of Woodford Reserve bourbon, poured some into a glass and set it in front of her. He raised the bottle, and an eyebrow, at Betsy, who shook her head. He poured himself a drink, turned a chair to face Betsy and sat down, crossed his arms on the chair back and took a sip of bourbon.

"Now what?" he asked.

"Now we wait," Betsy responded, "and hope he has the will and the strength to pull through." She looked up at Donovan. "I know you think I'm crazy for bringing him here, instead of taking care of him at the clinic, but I didn't want him to die in a strange place."

Donovan nodded. "What are his chances?"

She shrugged. "He's lost a lot of blood. Miraculously, the bullet missed all the major stuff. We'll just have to wait and see." She scrubbed her tired face with both hands before dropping them back down to the dog's head, absently running his ear through her fingers. Snert rose from his place at Lanie's feet and sniffed Rommel. Then he squeezed himself between the wall and Rommel's back and stretched out, his head propped on Rommel's bandaged shoulder.

Lanie stirred in her chair. "Did Rick make it?" she asked, staring into her glass. Betsy looked up expectantly.

Donovan shook his head. "He died on the operating table." He gave her an appraising look. "But not before confirming that he was Richard Cameron, and that he killed his mother in a fit of rage for having him locked up in a mental institution for the last several decades. He knew, of course, about the argument Joy and his mother had, and he knew that Joy was hiding in the ice house, so after he murdered his mother he put the weapon in the ice house to throw suspicion on Joy." He gazed into his glass of bourbon, then lifted his head. His dark brown eyes locked on Lanie's face. "On the night he supposedly died, he and his mother had a raging argument. He told her he was leaving forever, that he planned to marry the mother of his son and he didn't give a damn what she did with her money. As he turned to leave, Mrs. Cameron hit him in the head and knocked him cold. Mary O'Connor called Dr. Salisbury and the sheriff, and between them they concocted a plan to have him committed to Cherry Hill." His gaze dropped, and he rattled the ice in his empty glass. He sighed and looked up again, his eyes traveling between Lanie and Betsy. "We faxed his picture to the state hospital. They confirmed he was their escapee."

"Jeez Louise," said Betsy. "How could Marge go on living her life, knowing her son was locked up in the looney bin? What kind of person does that to her own flesh and blood?"

Donovan shrugged. "A complete and total narcissist."

Lanie shivered. "Bryan just gunned him down," she said, reliving the shooting. "And he would have shot Elisabeth and me, too, if Rommel hadn't attacked him. He would have killed his own daughter!"

"He turned out to be a nasty piece of business," Betsy agreed. "How's he doing?" she asked Donovan.

"The doctors said he should pull through. Once he's recovered sufficiently he'll be moved to Central Prison in Raleigh. Elisabeth was able to provide some additional information that led to co-conspirators in the insurance fraud, as did your friend, Fred Harris. The FBI is in the process of rounding them up. Apparently Elisabeth's father had quite a racket going killing horses." He shot a look at Lanie before continuing. "If you wanted to collect the insurance on your horse, you'd contact Bryan. He'd make it look like they died of natural causes by electrocuting them. Apparently it makes it look like they died of colic. He killed Elisabeth's horse for the insurance as well, but because the horse had a history of colic he couldn't use his method of choice. So, they broke the horse's leg with a crowbar and claimed he slipped off the ramp while they were trying to load him in a transport van."

It was Betsy's turn to shiver. "How could anyone break a horse's leg with a crowbar? Or electrocute them?"

Neither Donovan nor Lanie had an answer for her.

"At least the killings are over with," Betsy said.

Donovan looked pained. "I need to let you know that Doug Erikson died in a murder-suicide earlier today," he said.

Lanie and Betsy gaped at him.

"Doug killed Giselle and then killed himself?" Betsy finally managed to ask.

Donovan shook his head and swirled the amber bourbon in his glass, studying it intently before he responded. "We found him in his truck, parked behind his barn with his cell phone in his lap. It looked like he was going through Jennifer's text messages." He raised his eyes and looked from one to the other. "He shot his dog and then turned the gun on himself. He left a note saying that Baby and Jennifer were the only two people who loved him for himself. He couldn't live without the one and couldn't leave the other behind."

"Well, at least he got the part about Baby being people right," Betsy said, standing and brushing off the seat of her jeans. She checked Rommel's drip and then sat at the table. "With that news, I think I'll change my mind about that drink."

Donovan reached behind him for the bourbon bottle and a glass, and handed them across the table. Betsy poured two fingers worth and chugged it.

"At least the poor bastard didn't find out his wife was going to have his horse killed and his girlfriend was involved in the plot."

"There is that," Donovan reflected. He turned to Lanie. "What did Rick say to you as you were leaving?"

Lanie set her empty glass on the table and rested her head in her hands. "He asked me to find his son."

Betsy looked bewildered. "Someone want to clue me in?"

Donovan told her of Lanie's discovery at Mary O'Connor's death bed. "I admit I thought Lanie was crazy," he said, shooting a glance at Lanie, "but she turned out to be right. He confirmed to Lanie that he was Richard Cameron. Her statement, and the supporting documents, should be enough to get an exhumation order to confirm it's not Richard Cameron's body in that grave."

"So if his son is alive somewhere and we can locate him, what does that mean for Marge's estate?" Betsy asked Lanie.

"*If* the documents say her estate goes to her lineal descendents and *if* we can find a living child, or even grandchild at this point, of Richard Cameron's, then the assets will pass to the more direct descendents."

Betsy threw back her head and roared with laughter. "I don't mean to be ugly, but—I'd love to be there when they break *that* news to Angela!"

Lanie smiled briefly. "I want to know how you knew where to find me," she said to Betsy.

"I didn't. But when you said you were late for dinner with your Aunt Barbara, I knew there was something bad wrong. She's been dead for fifteen years."

Lanie smiled, happy that Betsy had picked up on her non sequitur.

"So I jumped in my truck," Betsy continued, "called Donovan, and headed to your house. I passed you just as you turned off Young's Road toward the back entrance to the farm. I would have been there sooner, but, as I was turning around to follow you, Snert came out of the bushes, so I had to stop and throw him in the truck. The rest is history."

"Yes, it certainly is," Lanie replied sadly. She suddenly remembered her manners. "Thanks for helping," she said to Donovan.

He nodded.

Snert stood and began to lick gently at Rommel's face and ears. The big dog stirred restlessly in his sleep and moaned. Undaunted, Snert continued the damp assault on his face, pausing occasionally to gauge its effect. Rommel moaned again and slowly opened his eyes.

"Hey! Look at that!" Betsy cried. "He's awake!"

Donovan and Lanie smiled broadly.

"Looks like you might luck out, Lanie. As soon as he's recovered I can start looking for a permanent home for him." She smiled slyly and winked at Donovan.

Lanie glared at her. "He has a home," she said firmly.

Donovan poured them all a shot of bourbon and raised his glass.

"I'll drink to that!"

twenty-two

A soft breeze caressed her hair and wafted the national flags of the horse trial competitors as Lanie parked, hung the exhibitor's pass on the rearview mirror and locked her rental car. The grassy grounds of the horse park sparkled in the morning sun as she made her way through the barn area and across lush damp grass to the cross-country course. She wanted to stake out a good viewing spot at the water complex, one of the most popular spots, to watch Joy and Bubba. Assuming he makes it that far, she thought with a smile. North America's only four-star horse trial was just that—a trial for both horse and rider.

She shifted the strap of her lawn chair to a more comfortable position as she considered which way to go. She fell in behind a small group of competitors walking the course. They were close enough that she could hear their serious, but excited, discussion as they approached each obstacle: striding, pace, changes of footing and light. It brought back memories, most of them good ones, of her own days galloping a cross-country course. She said a silent prayer that all horses and riders competing on this glorious spring day would have a safe cross-country round.

The area around the water complex was already beginning to fill with spectators when she arrived. She selected a sunny spot well clear of the galloping lane and settled down to wait for the first horse on course to come through. Slipping on her sunglasses, she closed her eyes and tilted her face to the sun.

The metallic noises of another spectator setting up a lawn chair beside her woke her from her reverie.

"If I'd known I was going on a ten-mile trek I'd have worn my hiking boots."

She opened her eyes in surprise, then smiled and removed her sunglasses. "How'd you find me?" she asked.

"I'll have you know that I'm not the lead homicide investigator for the state of North Carolina because of my good looks," Donovan responded. "I followed you from the barn area."

Lanie sat up and removed her sunglasses, turning to face him.

"What brings you all this way?" she asked. "And where did you get a pass to the barn area?" she asked suspiciously.

He grinned. "Betsy gave me her tickets." He studied the water complex. "I've been to a lot of trials, but never a horse trial. I thought I'd check it out. So, what are the charges, and when do they pick the jury?"

"We *do* have a jury," she replied, slipping her sunglasses back on. "They're called the ground jury. Among other things, they're responsible for settling any problems. Like riding that endangers the safety of the rider, their horse, or the spectators. Speaking of which, you need to be prepared to pick up your stuff and run if one of the horses comes out of the water in the wrong direction."

"Hmm," he said. "I thought the competitors were supposed to *ride* this course. How come everyone I saw was on foot?"

Lanie explained the importance of walking the course. In the background, the announcer declared the first horse was on course and safely over the first fence, heading for fence two.

"Why's the water so popular with spectators," he asked, eyeing the big crowd. "Aren't there lots of other jumps to congregate by?"

"It's the most entertaining. Lots of riders come off at the water, so, as long as no one's inured, it can be pretty comical."

They fell silent as the first horse approached, breezed through the series of jumps into the water, and out the other side. Over the next few minutes, Lanie gave Donovan a primer on eventing: the significance of the flags, the penalties for being too fast or too slow, the optional routes around difficult elements that were easier but ate up time.

"I had no idea it was so complicated," Donovan remarked. "Or so dangerous."

When the loud speaker announced, *"Joy Alexander and Reinmeister are now on course and clear at the first fence,"* Lanie sat up in excitement. "They'll be here in no time."

Minutes later, she and Donovan stood up so they could watch as Joy and Bubba approached through the trees and galloped toward the water complex. Bubba lifted effortlessly over the first element, put in a perfect one-stride and jumped the second log, dropping several feet down into the water with a splash. He splashed through the water at a canter and exited over a large water trough without a second look at the squeaking water wheel that noisily dumped a continuous stream of water into the trough. The crowd hooted and clapped as Joy patted his neck, checked her watch, and galloped on to the next jump.

"That was nicely done!" Lanie said. "Picture perfect!"

"What now?"

Lanie folded up her chair and slung it over her shoulder. "Now we walk down to the finish line to meet Joy and Bubba and get a debrief of the ride. We can come back later if you'd like to watch some other riders go."

"Wait." As she stopped, Donovan reached into his pocket. "I have something for you." He held out his hand and slowly opened his fingers. A round gold disc glittered in the sun.

Lanie picked it up and read the inscription:

ROMMEL

I AM A DEAF DOG
I BELONG TO LANIE MONTGOMERY

Her cell phone number was inscribed at the bottom.

"Betsy suggested I call the Dalmatian rescue club in Raleigh because Dalmatians have a high incidence of deafness." He paused. "I was going to have the jeweler put 'I am deaf' under Rommel's name, but the rescue people said someone might mistakenly think the owner was deaf. They said it was better to be specific."

Lanie blinked back tears, and closed her hand tightly around the dog tag.

"You know," she said quietly, "I think I kind of like you."

He smiled. "That's a good place to start."

**Follow Lanie Montgomery's
latest adventures in**

Deadly Deception

preview of chapter one

He cut the engine and let the Boston Whaler's momentum carry it to the dock as he tossed the fenders over the starboard side. The boat bumped gently against the dock, and he threw the stern line over the cleat before scrambling to the bow to secure it as well. As it rocked to a halt, he hit a button to light the face of his watch and checked the time. The operation had taken longer than he anticipated. If he was going to make it to the beach in time for low tide he would have to hurry.

He left the key in the ignition where he'd found it, knelt on the dock, and began to replace the cover. The owner would never know he'd borrowed it, and probably wouldn't miss the cushion lost in the Atlantic. *Serves them right*, he thought as he snapped the last button into place and stood up. He glanced up at the dark house that overlooked the creek and surrounding salt marsh. The long days spent in reconnaissance had paid off. The house was isolated and rarely used, the owner careless. He gave a grateful salute before striding down the dock toward shore.

Behind him he heard a sharp whistle and whirled around, his heart pounding in his chest. His eyes strained to see in the starlit quiet of the marsh. Off the end of the dock he saw a spray of water as the dolphin rose and whistled again. He cursed under his breath, wondering if it was the same one that had followed him out into the ocean.

He'd first noticed the dolphin as he exited Bald Head Creek and turned left into the Cape Fear River. A silent, ghostly escort off to his right, it continued to follow as he crossed over the sandbar, submerged now at high tide, and entered the waters of the Atlantic. When he reached his destination, it had hung around the drifting boat while he struggled to get his awkward cargo up and over the side.

He slowly released his breath. *What difference does it make,* he thought. *It can't tell anyone.* Turning, he walked down the dock, across the lawn, and into the tangle of live oaks and yaupons shrouded in ghostly strands of Spanish moss.

Eric Evans stepped out of the Island Bound Cafe, cup of coffee in hand, and strolled down to the dock, anxious to see her before he retrieved his bike for the short ride down Federal Road to the Bald Head Conservancy. It was the perfect job, he told himself again, allowing him to do research on his beloved sea turtles, as well as give seminars and guided tours to the volunteers and tourists. If only it paid enough to cover his living expenses, he thought, and the exorbitant alimony the court had ordered him to pay his ex-wife. That obligation was the reason he'd agreed to the dead-of-night drop-offs into the ocean of he-knew-not-what. He felt like a spy in a John LeCarré novel — meetings in the depths of the maritime forest, clandestine exchanges of cash. He sighed. It was becoming too risky; the fear of getting caught was keeping him up at night. He knew he needed to extricate himself, but he didn't know how.

Determined to put it out of his mind for the moment, he set his coffee on the dock and jumped down onto the metal grate he'd installed about a foot below the marina water level. He scanned the horizon. Water lapped gently just above his knees, flirting with the hem of his khaki shorts. The normally calm harbor had a slight chop to it this morning, testament to Abby, the first named hurricane of the season still languishing in the Caribbean. With wind speeds hovering at just seventy-six miles per hour, the storm was barely spinning fast enough to deserve the category, but preliminary forecasts predicted she could be a threat to the Southeastern coast, and Bald Head, in the near future. He turned and picked up the Styrofoam cup of coffee, blowing gently on its surface before taking a sip.

She was late this morning, and he felt a pang, worried she'd decided to leave. He knew he should let her go, break off the re-lationship once and for all. But the sheer joy of seeing her, being the beneficiary of her carefree, happy nature made it impossible to do what he knew in his heart was the right thing for both of them. For whatever reason, she'd chosen him, and he intended to enjoy it as long as it lasted.

His reverie was broken by the sound of footsteps coming down the dock. He turned to see a man strolling in his direc-tion with a small tow-headed child scraping her fingers on the marina wall as she trailed reluctantly behind, keeping as far away from the water as she could get. The man was short and heavily built, with a faded Pittsburg Pirates tee-shirt stretched over a prodigious beer belly, a matching baseball cap shading his eyes from the already-fierce sun. A bottle of Miller beer, beaded with condensation, dangled from the fingers of his right hand.

"Looks like it's going to be another hot one," he said, stop-ping behind Eric.

"Bald Head can be pretty hot, even in June," Eric replied, turning to smile at the child as she caught up to her father. "Hi, my name's Eric," he said to her. "What's your name?"

"Justine," her father answered for her. "Justine the fraidy cat. My name's Randy." He gave his daughter an impatient glance. "Me and the wife been here all week, and haven't been able to get her to put a foot in the water. She's afraid some fish will nibble on her. We're going home tomorrow."

Justine flinched at the accusing tone of his voice and ducked her head as she scraped the toe of her sandal on the weathered wood of the dock. Eric turned around and crossed his arms on the dock, giving her a reassuring smile.

"I used to be afraid of things in the water when I was your age," Eric said to Justine. "It's kind of scary when you can't see what's down there, isn't it?"

She looked up at him from under the fringe of blond hair that fell across her eyes, then quickly down again.

"But the ocean's full of fascinating creatures, and not many of them want to harm you," he continued. "If you stick around for a minute you can meet one of them. Would you like to do that?" He smiled encouragingly. "I promise you'll love it."

Justine peered up at him, and a flicker of longing flashed across her face before she glanced up at her father and retreated back behind the corn-silk hair.

Eric heard a splash of water behind him and turned to see a broad round head pop up in the marina a few feet from where he stood. Warm water struck his face as she ducked and sprayed water from the blowhole in the top of her head. Justine squealed and ducked behind her father, clutching tightly at his legs.

"Justine, this is Soka," said Eric, keeping his eye on the dolphin. "Soka, can you say 'good morning' to Justine?" He signaled with his right hand, and the dolphin rose partially from the water, chattering noisily, before gliding over to Eric and rolling onto her back for a belly rub. He laughed, and pulled a whistle from under his tee shirt. "No rewards until you've earned them, lazy girl."

He glanced back at Justine and grinned. "Soka is a bottle-nosed dolphin, a young one. I've been teaching her a few tricks. Would you like to see them?"

Justine peered around her father's stout legs, her eyes wide. She nodded slowly.

"Okay, here we go!" said Eric, raising the whistle to his lips. He blew a few short blasts, and Soka rose from the water, her sleek gray body glistening in the morning sunlight. She balanced on her tail and took several leaps backward before flipping over and disappearing beneath the water. She surfaced again, dipped her rounded nose in the water, and splashed it at him, dousing Eric, Justine, and her father.

"Hey!" he protested, wiping his face dry with his shirt. "That wasn't nice."

Behind him, he heard Justine giggle. He turned and gave her a mock frown, shaking his forefinger at her.

"Don't encourage her to be bad!" he said.

Justine giggled again. "She splashed me!"

"That she did," he said, nodding solemnly. "So, her punishment will be that she has to give you a present to make up for it."

He turned back to the dolphin, bobbing in the water, and blew on the whistle. "Soka, go get Justine a present." He waved his hand, and the dolphin rose from the water, flipped backward, and disappeared.

"That was really something," Randy said, waving the beer bottle in the direction Soka had disappeared. "How'd you get her to do that?"

"I spent a couple of years working with the dolphins at a resort in the Bahamas."

After several minutes, Justine cautiously ventured out from behind her father. She crouched down on the dock beside Eric.

"Where did she go?" she whispered. Standing up, she peered intently around the marina.

"To find you something pretty as an apology for getting you wet. You might want to step back a few feet, because when she comes back with it she's going to drop it on the dock about where you're standing. I don't want you to get any wetter than you are." He and Justine shared a smile before she scrambled back toward her father.

Moments later, the dolphin rose from the water next to Eric and deposited a barnacle encrusted object on the dock before subsiding back into the water. She chattered away, proud of her accomplishment.

He turned and peered at the oyster shell, then turned back to Soka. "Justine doesn't want a filthy oyster shell!" he said, waving his hand. "Go find her a real present." He blew on the whistle, and Soka disappeared, slipping rapidly under the water, headed for the marina entrance and the Cape Fear River. Water lapped gently at Eric's knees as they waited for her to return.

She was gone so long Eric was afraid the ferry would arrive from Southport before she got back. He scanned the water anxiously, and was rewarded with the sight of her fin slicing along, headed fast in their direction.

"There she is!" Justine said, pointing.

"Sure enough," Eric replied. "Step back."

Justine retreated a few more steps and waited as Soka rose from the water, depositing her gift with a clatter, before disappearing back toward the river.

Eric peered at it in puzzlement. It looked like a heavy metal band wrapped around a doughy substance, like a small jellyfish or squid. He poked it gingerly with his finger, rolling it over. It was a ring, with a large greenish-yellow stone, the surface of which was carved with a heraldic crest. His gaze returned to the substance it was wrapped around, and he gasped.

"What is it?" asked Randy. He leaned over to get a closer look. "It almost looks like a finger!"

Eric snatched the baseball cap off of Randy's head, and covered the bloated object with it. He nodded at Justine. "Get her out of here."

Her screams faded away down the dock as the Bald Head Island ferry made its first dock of the morning. Eric reached into his pocket for his telephone and called the police.

CPSIA information can be obtained at www.ICGtesting.com
Printed in the USA
BVOW11s0118200814

363468BV00007B/29/P